More than 50,000 pieces of artwork
are stolen each year worldwide.

The black market for stolen art is
valued at between $6 and $8 billion
dollars annually.

Source: artworkarchive.com

Also by Alfred M. Struthers:

THE THIRD FLOOR MYSTERY SERIES
The Case of Secrets
The Phantom Vale
The Curse of Halim
The Demon Tide
The Stone Ghost
The Grim Fugue

PICTURE BOOKS
(illustrated by Cathy Provoda)
Did You Hear That?
Pepperoni Macaroni

The Watchman's Keep

A Third Floor Mystery

By Alfred M. Struthers

Third
Floor
Books

First paperback edition November 2022

Book design by Third Floor Books

ISBN: 979-8-9870736-0-5
Published by Third Floor Books, LLC
thirdfloorbooksllc.com

For Mike Rousseau,
My brother from a different mother,
the rhythm king, and above all else,
an unwavering beacon of light

"It's not overanalyzing. It's a beat, you play it. Let it go."
David Garabaldi

Prologue

September 19, 2007
Hammond Books, Cambridge, MA

The first inkling that something was wrong hit him shortly after lunchtime. Henry Hammond was on the sales floor stocking the new arrivals endcap when he rushed to the bathroom and vomited. In the hour that followed, a surge of abdominal pain gripped his body, growing worse by the minute. He went to his desk in the back office and sat down as a wave of numbness slowly paralyzed his extremities.

His good friend and trusted bookstore employee, Jameson, was cleaning and pricing a stack of used books at the front counter when he heard something hit the floor with a heavy thud. He scanned the shop, trying to find the source of the noise, then went to the office where he found Henry lying on the floor.

Henry grunted incoherently as Jameson gently propped him up against the side of the desk.

"What happened?" Jameson asked, taking inventory of his good friend's condition. His eyes were half open and he was sweating profusely.

"Hospital," Henry said, speaking barely above a whisper.

Jameson helped him to his feet and walked him outside to his car. After going back to lock the bookstore, he made the short drive to Mt. Auburn Hospital, less than five minutes away.

"What are your symptoms?" Jameson asked, as he darted through traffic.

Henry tried to speak but could only manage single words. Even at that, each syllable tore at his stomach muscles like a hooked blade. "Stomach…" he said.

"Your stomach," Jameson repeated. "What else?"

"Headache…" Henry whispered, sweat drenching his face. That's when the convulsions started.

Jameson drove faster. Looking at Henry, and hearing his symptoms, he knew this wasn't some seasonal bug. Henry had ingested something toxic. The question was: did it happen by accident, or was it the work of some demented soul? As he sped through traffic, he recounted every customer who had come into the shop that day, trying to recall if any one of them acted in a suspicious manner or said anything that would indicate foul intent. Other than the usual customers, friends and acquaintances, and the usual delivery drivers, no one stood out.

Henry's body convulsed again.

"Hang on," Jameson told him. "We're almost there."

"You…have to…tell him," Henry said, clutching his stomach with both hands as he spoke.

"What are you talking about?" Jameson said. "Tell who?"

Henry's body convulsed again. "Nathan," he said, wincing. "Must…explain…everything."

Jameson knew full well that Henry was referring to the old bookcase in the back office of the bookstore. In keeping with tradition, as Henry had told him, it would be passed on to another member of the family, just as it had been passed to Henry by his father. But Nathan Cole, Henry's grandson, was only six years old. He was much too young to comprehend the bookcase's mysterious past, or the important role it had played in the Hammond family since it was smuggled into America in the mid 1800s.

Henry buckled over in the seat, resting one hand on the dashboard to try and steady himself. "You must…warn him…" he said.

"Yes, yes, of course," Jameson said. "But that won't be necessary, my friend. Once we get you to the hospital, the doctors will have you patched up in no time."

Henry didn't respond.

He had passed out, his body slumped sideways against the door.

At the hospital, Jameson flagged down two emergency room attendants who put Henry in a wheelchair. Just before they rushed him inside, he grabbed Jameson's forearm. "Tell him…" he managed to say.

Twenty minutes later, Jameson was sitting in the waiting room when Henry's daughter, Elizabeth, came rushing in with her husband David.

"How is he?" Elizabeth asked, panic in her voice.

"They've admitted him," Jameson explained, solemnly.

"Do they know what it is?"

"No," Jameson replied. "If they do, they haven't said."

Before Elizabeth could ask for more information, a young doctor stepped into the waiting room, holding a narrow plastic binder in one hand. He walked over to Jameson and said, "Are you the one who brought in Mr. Hammond?"

"Yes," Jameson replied. He motioned with his hand and said, "This is his daughter, Elizabeth Cole, and her husband, David."

"What can you tell us?" Elizabeth asked.

"He's in considerable pain," the doctor said. As he spoke he opened the binder and reviewed his notes. "He's had severe muscle cramping and convulsions, and he's been vomiting blood."

Elizabeth's expression grew darker.

"Does your father have a history of gastrointestinal problems?" the doctor asked.

"No," Elizabeth answered.

"Ulcers?"

"No."

"Any liver issues?"

"None."

The doctor closed the binder and said, "I've ordered a CBC, a tox screen, and a liver panel. Once we get those results back, we'll know how to proceed."

"Can we see him?" Elizabeth asked.

"Yes, but I have to ask you to keep it brief. He's groggy, and with the pain he's experiencing, talking will only aggravate his condition."

"You go," Jameson said to Elizabeth and David. "I'll wait here."

The doctor led them to Henry's room, opened the door and then stepped aside to let them enter. "Remember," he said, "keep it short."

Henry was lying in the bed with both hands clamped on his stomach, his shirt soaked with perspiration.

"Dad, what happened?" Elizabeth asked, rushing over to his side.

He shook his head, indicating that he didn't have the strength to explain what he believed to be the cause of his current condition, then gestured with his fingers for her to come closer.

She leaned down until her ear was inches from his mouth.

"Bookcase," he said, in a ghastly whisper.

"Bookcase?" she repeated. "What bookcase? The one in your office?"

He nodded once, fighting through the pain.

"What about it?" she asked.

"Hide it…" he said, grimacing as he spoke.

"Hide it? But…why?"

He took hold of her hand. "Promise me," he said.

Elizabeth looked back at David, confused. *What's he talking about?*

David glared at her. *Say it!*

"Okay, Dad," she said. "I promise, we'll hide it."

There was a knock on the door and then it swung open. The doctor stepped inside, accompanied by a nurse. When he cleared his throat, signaling that it was time for them to leave, David took Elizabeth by the arm and gently eased her away from the bed. "Come on, let's go," he said. "Let the staff do their job."

"We'll be right outside," Elizabeth said over her shoulder as David guided her toward the door.

They filed back out into the hallway and stopped several feet from the door. "Hide the bookcase?" Elizabeth said. "What was that all about?"

"I have no idea," David replied. "But your father must have a good reason for asking. So…we do as he says. We hide it."

"Where?" Elizabeth asked.

"In the last place anybody would look for it."

"And where might that be?"

"In the furthest corner of the attic," David said. "Buried behind all those piles of junk."

"And then what?" Elizabeth asked.

"And then, nothing. We leave it there until we figure out what to do with it."

From the intercom overhead came an urgent voice. "Code Blue! Room six."

Seconds later, a code team came racing down the hallway and pushed through the door to Henry's room. Elizabeth made a move to follow them when David grabbed her arm. "No! Don't go in there," he said, holding her back.

As the door was closing, she looked through the opening and saw her father on the bed, writhing in pain as a seizure rocked his body.

It was the last time she would see her father alive.

A sight that would haunt her for the rest of her days.

1

Ginette

Nathan Cole never saw it coming.

He sprinted out of the house and down the front porch steps, running across the lawn toward the mailbox like he'd done countless times before. As he stood at the box, pulling out a thick stack of junk mail, a black Mercedes sedan with tinted windows glided to a stop five feet behind him. The passenger-side window slid down and a .30 caliber suppressor appeared.

Pfft…pfft…pfft.

Three shots.

One second apart.

Center mass.

Nathan's body rippled from the impact and he collapsed on the pavement, blood pooling at his side. The passenger-side window rose and the Mercedes drove away just as quietly as it had appeared.

"Hey...you still with me?"

Jameson felt a hand gripping his shoulder, gently shaking his body. His body flinched and his eyes snapped open as the nightmare image of Nathan's lifeless and bloodied body faded from his mind. "My apologies," he told Brunner.

Ever since landing in Zurich four days earlier, the grueling hours that followed were finally taking their toll. Long, seemingly endless days. Late nights that bled into early mornings. Anticipation at every turn. Chasing an invisible target, only to encounter one dead end after another. With each passing day, he'd been nodding off more and more, haunted by the same terrifying nightmare.

Working with Mats Brunner, an *Oberleutnant* with Task Force TIGRIS, the specialized tactical arm of Switzerland's Federal Criminal Police, they had used telecommunications surveillance and a platoon of well-placed informants in a nationwide manhunt for Ginette Dampierre, overlord of the Covin, the criminal network Jameson had pursued for the better part of his adult life. After the recent arrest of her younger brother Edouard, Ginette had become Jameson's prime concern, and the source of his terrifying dreams.

"For a moment there you had me worried," Brunner said.

"I'm fine. Just tired, that's all," Jameson replied, turning away from the glare of oncoming headlights.

They had arrived in Lucerne late that afternoon. Now, with the moon hanging high in the night sky, they were sitting in an unmarked car directly across the street from the Hotel Dübendorf. The occupant of the penthouse suite, according to the hotel records, was Lina Burri, a 28-year-old economics professor from the University of Zurich. Jameson and Brunner believed otherwise. If the tip they'd gotten from a trusted informant was correct, the woman was none other than Ginette Dampierre.

Brunner's radio squawked.

"Preparing to breach."

It was Zaugg, the lead officer.

"Copy," replied Brunner.

In the dimly lit hallway of the top floor, the officers stood on either side of the door. Each was clad in a black combat uniform and helmet, a Heckler & Koch MP5 rifle in their hands. Zaugg motioned to the jittery young night manager who was standing nearby. *Do it.*

With shaking hands, the manager stepped up to the door and fumbled with the key card, nearly dropping it, before stabbing it into the lock's narrow slot. It gave off a sharp click and a tiny green light flashed. He twisted the handle and started to push the door open when he was abruptly shoved aside and the officers stormed the room.

Less than a minute later, Brunner's radio squawked again.

"Premises secure."

"Is the suspect in custody?" Brunner asked.

"Affirmative," replied Zaugg.

Brunner smiled at Jameson, then radioed back. "We're coming up."

When they entered the top-floor penthouse minutes later, they saw two officers standing on either end of a small, pearl-white leather couch. Directly across from it was a horizontal glass-front propane fireplace set into a towering wall of Calcutta marble. Sitting on the couch, terrified by the guns pointed at her, was a middle-aged woman with long side-swept auburn hair, dressed in a pink cotton nightgown and a thick hotel robe.

Jameson approached the woman and studied her facial features. Something wasn't right.

"What wrong?" Brunner asked, seeing the dubious look on Jameson's face.

Jameson yanked the cheap wig off the woman's head, revealing her closely cropped black hair. "This isn't her," he said, flinging the wig on the couch.

"A body double?" Brunner exclaimed. "No!"

Jameson shook his head, disgusted. "We should've anticipated this," he said.

Brunner bent down, coming within inches of the woman's face. "Where is she?" he demanded.

The woman recoiled in fear. "I don't know who you're talking about."

"THE TRUTH!" Brunner shouted. "NOW!"

When she didn't respond, he reached for the 9mm SIG Sauer P226 pistol on his hip.

"No," Jameson said, grabbing Brunner's arm. "That won't be necessary." He sat down on the couch next to the frightened woman and spoke in a soothing voice. "Don't be afraid. You can talk to me," he said. "When was the last time you saw her?"

The woman averted her eyes and spoke in a low voice. "Last night."

"What was that?" Jameson asked.

"Last night," the woman said, louder.

"You saw her last night," Jameson confirmed. "Here?"

The woman still refused to look at him. "She stopped by to pay me the rest of the money."

"That's it? She just paid you the money and then left?"

The woman shook her head. "No, she used the bathroom first, then left."

"Just so I understand. She stopped by, gave you the money, used the bathroom, then left. Is that correct?"

Again, the woman nodded.

"And what did she say to you?" Jameson asked.

"Nothing."

"You're lying!" Brunner barked.

"No, I'm not," the woman insisted. "The only time she spoke was in the bathroom."

"What are you talking about?" Brunner asked.

"While she was in the bathroom, I heard her talking on her phone."

"Did you hear what she was saying?" Jameson asked.

"Only bits and pieces."

Jameson rested his hand on her arm. "Tell me everything you heard," he said calmly.

"She was angry, almost yelling," the woman said. "That's how I was able to hear her."

"Go on," Jameson said.

"She wanted names."

"What names?"

The woman finally looked at him. "She said, 'get me names', and then, 'I'll see you in eight hours'."

Jameson closed his eyes and let out a troubled breath, the disturbing images from his nightmare flickering like a strobe light in his mind.

"What is it?" Brunner asked.

Jameson stood. "I know where she is."

He pulled his phone from his pocket and walked over to the large picture window on the far wall. It stretched from floor to ceiling, offering a stunning view of the *Zürichsee*. The moon's reflection was a jagged spike on the rippled surface of the water, and it held his gaze for several long seconds as he contemplated the terrifying prospect that now faced Nathan Cole, the person who was instrumental in the recent capture of Ginette's younger brother, Edouard.

Keeping his back to the others, Jameson punched a string of numbers into his phone. It was the first of several calls he would make in the next 30 minutes, because if his suspicions were accurate they would need all the bodies they could muster.

And that still might not be enough.

As the call connected he pressed the phone to his ear and stared out at the bleak night, praying it wasn't a harbinger of darker days to follow, and the demise of the boy he had promised his good friend Henry Hammond he would keep safe from all harm.

Sixty minutes earlier, and 3,700 miles away, Ginette Dampierre stepped off Flight 709 at Boston Logan International Airport. She was dressed in an Alexander McQueen single-breasted blazer and Bruno Magli black-leather pumps, a Salvatore Ferragamo handbag hanging from her arm. To anyone who bothered to look, she had the appearance of a successful young business executive. A long blonde wig cascaded gracefully over her shoulders like falling water, and her stylish pair of Luxottica tortoiseshell eyeglasses suggested she was just south of her 36th birthday.

Her actual age was well north of 50.

The wig and fake passport produced the intended result, allowing her to breeze through airport security without a hitch. Had the TSA agents known her true identity, and that for the past two decades she'd been living anonymously in Switzerland, running a centuries-old criminal organization called the Covin, which specialized in high-end art thefts, things would have gone much differently.

She knew the eight-hour flight to Boston posed a considerable risk, given her fugitive status and the fact that authorities were scouring the globe in search of her and her Covin associates. But it was a gamble she had to take. After Edouard's arrest there was much work to be done to salvage their North American operation, a pipeline that generated tens of millions of dollars each year. But first, she had a score to settle.

Someone was going to pay for getting her brother arrested.

Pay for crippling the Covin's business.

And pay for dragging her out of hiding after all these years to clean up the mess.

To do that, she first needed to understand how such a fate could befall her brother. After all these years without so much as a hiccup, how could someone so easily infiltrate the Covin's flawless and seemingly impenetrable network?

Sitting in the back of a Mercedes-Benz S-class Pullman limousine on Commercial Wharf in Boston, she directed her questions at Ray Pantano, a late-30s muscle man for the Covin, recruited years earlier by Edouard.

"How is my brother holding up?" she asked.

"From what my source tells me, he's fine," Pantano replied. "The other inmates are leaving him alone."

"Good," she said. "They do know what will happen to their families if they so much as lay a hand on him, right?"

"Absolutely."

"Did he say who did this to us?"

"He mentioned only one name: Nathan Cole."

"And we're to believe this man…*Nathan Cole*…acted alone?" she asked.

"He didn't say, but I don't see how it's possible."

"Why is that?"

"Because Nathan Cole is only 12 years old."

She leaned forward as if she'd misheard him. "Excuse me?"

"He's 12 years old," Pantano repeated.

"No. That can't be," she shot back, her voice growing louder. "There's no way a 12-year-old boy could've pulled this off."

Pantano nodded slowly. He could hardly believe it himself.

She sat back in the seat, dumbfounded. The situation was even worse than she'd first been led to believe. "You've dealt with this boy, I trust?" she asked.

"Not yet," Pantano said.

"What are you waiting for?" she asked impatiently. "Find him and deal with him."

"Deal with him how?"

"Think!" she exclaimed, the anger in her voice surging. "If he was able to do this to us, how much more damage is he capable of? I, for one, have no interest in finding out. He's a threat to our operation and needs to be neutralized."

"By neutralized, do you mean…?"

Her eyes burned into his and she spoke through clenched teeth. "I want him *eliminated*."

2

Moran

Ray Pantano had grown up in Boston's North End. In that time, he'd put together an impressive criminal resume and was known as a guy who wasn't afraid to get his hands bloody. But upon hearing Ginette's extermination order, he shook his head apprehensively. "I'd think twice about harming the boy," he said.

"What was that?" she fired back.

Pantano raised his hands defensively. "Hear me out."

She took in a deep breath and let it out slowly. It was everything she could do to keep from scratching his eyes out.

"Your brother already tried and failed to get rid of the boy," Pantano explained. "Because of that, he's going to be well insulated."

"So? How is that a problem?"

"All I'm saying is, any action against the kid is going to draw added attention…the kind we don't need right now."

"You let *me* worry about what we need right now," she growled. She let out a frustrated breath and stared out the side window, her mind hard at work calculating their options. Through the limo's tinted glass, the boats moored at the dock nearby were nothing more than rough silhouettes, backlit by the lights of East Boston across the bay. "What I want to know is this," she said, turning from the window. "How did this child, this…*infant*…manage to do this to us?"

Pantano offered a weak shrug. *Beats me.*

As the silence mounted, Ginette's anger boiled hotter. "Did my brother say anything else?" she asked, hoping for some small tidbit that might explain how a mere boy could wreak such havoc.

"He mentioned something about documentation," Pantano said.

"Documentation? What documentation?"

"Couldn't tell you."

She took a deep breath, counted to three to calm herself, then slowly exhaled. "Tell me what he said…exactly," she said.

"He said it was hidden inside a second bookcase," Pantano said. "Whatever that means."

Her expression grew tense. "A second bookcase?"

Pantano nodded.

"You're sure that's what he said?"

"That's what my source told me."

"And this source, he used those exact words?"

"Yeah," Pantano replied with a shrug. "What about it?"

Her jaw fell open and she stared at him, awestruck. Growing up she'd heard the stories: tales about the damaging information compiled over 150 years earlier by an apothecary named Nicholas Graf; how he had planned on using it to expose the Covin's nefarious activities and collapse their criminal empire, and how he hid it inside a bookcase that he attempted to smuggle out of England aboard a ship named the *Greenwich*.

Fortunately, the Covin learned of his attempted sabotage and made sure the Greenwich never reached port in America. Graf mysteriously vanished, along with the information he'd collected and the bookcase that held it.

But unbeknownst to the Dampierre family, the threat didn't end there. Only recently, Edouard had learned of a second, matching bookcase, owned by the family of noted bookseller Henry Hammond, Nathan's Cole's grandfather. And just like the *Greenwich* bookcase, the Hammond twin contained more of the apothecary's incriminating information, which Nathan had discovered, leading to the arrest of Edouard.

Learning of the second bookcase struck at the very core of Ginette's senses like a broad axe. She exhaled, as if she'd been holding her breath the entire time. It was beyond belief that the apothecary's interference continued to haunt them after all these years. Then again, it was entirely possible that Pantano's source had misinterpreted her brother's words. More often than not, that was the case when information was passed from one person to another.

Stories got twisted.

Critical details changed.

Some parts dropped out altogether.

"How trustworthy is your source?" she asked.

"Very," Pantano replied firmly.

"You're sure of this?"

"He's never let me down in the past."

"This isn't the past," she said sharply. "I want you to go back and confirm what my brother told him. Make sure nothing was left out."

"All right," Pantano said, like it was a waste of time. "But I already know what he'll—"

"Do it!" she shouted, cutting him off. Her eyes were drawn to the window once again, her mind hard at work digesting this new information. Very slowly, her face broke into a smile.

"What?" Pantano asked.

"Perhaps your assessment is correct," she said, in a cooler tone. "A direct attack on the boy could make matters worse. But...what if it were an accident?"

"Yes," Pantano said, grinning. "That's perfect."

"Who do we have that can get it done quickly and quietly?"

"Leave it to me," Pantano said, matter-of-factly.

"No. You focus on your source at the prison. At the moment, he's the only means we have of communicating with my brother."

Pantano shrugged. *Whatever you say.* "As far as available assets, your brother used Trask," he said, referring to the Covin's architect of evil, an eccentric and unhinged man known for the most cruel and twisted constructions, each designed to inflict the maximum amount of pain and suffering on their enemies. "But there may be a problem there," he said.

"What are you talking about?"

"He helped your brother construct a trap for Cole. It's unclear how it happened, but the boy somehow managed to escape. Shortly after that, everything went south."

"What happened to Trask?"

"Unknown," Pantano said. "He could be laying low until things cool down. Then again, for all we know, he might've fled the country."

"Very well," she said curtly, pulling a burner phone from her purse, "I'll use one of my people."

"Can he be trusted?"

"She," Ginette replied, entering a series of numbers into the phone. "And yes, discretion is not an issue, although I believe she has a much more redeeming quality, one that suits her profession well."

"Which is…?"

"She's a chameleon. She can blend in anywhere."

"Hmm, sounds like my kind of girl," Pantano said, flashing both eyebrows. "I'd like to meet her."

"No," Ginette replied matter-of-factly, holding the phone to her ear. "You wouldn't."

Seconds later she heard a dull beep. There was no message that followed, no cheery greeting or promise of a call back. Just dead silence.

Niko was quirky like that.

Cautious to a fault.

When Ginette heard the beep, she uttered three words—a coded sequence that would identify her as the caller and ensure a return call within 30 minutes.

"Order for pickup."

David Cole, Nathan's father, was two blocks from home when he got Jameson's call. His phone emitted a sharp popping sound, like a ping pong ball being volleyed back and forth across the net at a feverish pace. The moment he heard it, he grabbed the phone from the center console. When he saw who was calling, he pulled over to the curb and took the call.

"Jameson," he said. "How's it going over there?"

"We have a serious problem," Jameson replied.

"I'm listening," David said. In the side mirror, he saw his wife Elizabeth approaching in the distance. As she drew nearer, she slowed, then signaled and pulled to a stop two feet from his rear bumper.

"Where's Nathan?" Jameson asked.

"At home, I assume," David said. "I just got out of work and I'm—"

"Find him," Jameson cut in. "As quickly as you can."

Elizabeth tapped on her horn but David ignored it. "Why? What's wrong?" he asked.

"We tracked Ginette Dampierre to a hotel in Lucerne, but she managed to elude us."

"She couldn't have gone far, right?" David said optimistically.

"That's why I'm calling," Jameson said. "She already left the country."

Elizabeth appeared at the side window and rapped on the glass.

"Jameson, hold that thought," David said. He lowered the window. "Get in," he said, showing her the phone. "You need to hear this."

Once she was seated next to him, he pressed the speakerphone button. "Jameson, Elizabeth is with me," he said. "What was that you were saying?"

"Ginette Dampierre is in the wind," Jameson said. "If our source is correct, she left Switzerland eight hours ago. I believe she's headed to the United States."

"How do you know this?" Elizabeth asked.

"I'll fill you in later," Jameson said. "But suffice to say, with the arrest of her brother, and the Covin's business in disarray, she'll be looking to set things straight."

"Set things straight," Elizabeth repeated. "What does that mean exactly?"

Jameson chose his words carefully. "It means that we need to be ready for the worst. I've got a safehouse in mind. I want you to take Nathan there and —"

"NO!" Elizabeth shouted, cutting him off. "Nathan has already been through enough."

David rested his hand on her forearm. "Honey…just hear him out."

"I will not!" she barked, pulling her arm away. "Nathan stays at home. Period. With any luck, the emotional and physical scars he has will have a chance to heal. Then, maybe, just maybe, he'll be able to live like an ordinary 12-year-old for a change."

"Jameson, she raises a good point," David said. "Maybe this time we just hunker down."

Jameson considered the idea momentarily. "One week," he said. "After that, barring any fatalities, the arrangement can stand."

"What do you need us to do?" David asked.

"Find Nathan. Find him now. And keep him in the house. Whatever you do, don't let him leave. He's not going to like it, but you need to make him understand the danger that Ginette Dampierre poses. She's even more cold blooded than her brother, and that's on a good day when her business is running smoothly. Now that Edouard is in custody, and the Covin's business dealings have suffered a considerable setback, she's going to come at us hard. Not that I'd use those words."

"You mean, make him understand the danger without scaring the living daylights out of him," David said.

"It's a little late for that," Elizabeth said. "Our son has been hunted by a lunatic, abducted by thugs, twice, and imprisoned in some sicko's house of horrors. And that's just in the past month."

"I've already called in reinforcements," Jameson said. "They should be arriving at your house at any moment. Beginning immediately, keep Nathan out of sight. He needs to stay inside until we have Ginette Dampierre in custody."

"Don't worry, Jameson," David said. "We'll make it happen."

Elizabeth turned away and shook her head. *Yeah, right...we'll see about that*, she thought.

Nathan was camped out in the garage, rifling through a pile of cardboard boxes. Each one was filled with a strange assortment of books, catalogs and magazines that had previously resided in the *Greenwich* bookcase, one of two identical bookcases built by Nathan's ancestor, Thomas Hammond, a master woodworker living in London during the mid 1800s.

Ever since recovering the bookcase from Edouard Dampierre earlier in the week, in a boarded-up old mill on Saco Island in Maine, Nathan had been obsessed with its contents. He knew that Dampierre was a major player in the Covin. He knew the Covin traded in a high-end stolen artwork. What he didn't know was why Dampierre

29

would keep Thomas Hammond's bookcase in his office, filled with such a strange collection of literature. It wasn't like he was an avid reader. A "book hound" as his mother liked to say. Dampierre was a criminal, pure and simple.

Adding to the mystery were the small slips of paper tucked inside every volume. Each one had a number scribbled at the top in fine black ink. Some were single digits, some were double, but many of them were triple-digit numbers. They followed no discernible pattern, which was confusing enough, but even more confusing was the fact that some of them were circled. Others were not. Was that just someone being sloppy, or did it mean something?

Sitting next to him was Gina McDermott, his best friend and next-door neighbor whom he referred to as "the puzzle master." It was a fitting nickname for a girl who craved word search puzzles, aced anagram word games, absolutely destroyed cryptograms, and would settle for nothing less than the most difficult crossword puzzle. He was pretty sure she did puzzles in her head while she slept.

With the afternoon wearing on, he sat back and eyed the open boxes. "Books, magazines, catalogs, brochures," he said, frustration in his voice. "It makes no sense." He reached into one of the boxes, pulled out a large paperback book, and read the title aloud. *Impulse and Improvisation, A Study of Abstract Expressionism in the 20th Century*, by Leslie Newman." He removed the narrow slip of paper tucked in the binding and read the number written at the top. "Three hundred fifty. Do we have that one yet?"

Gina checked the number against the list she'd been compiling in her small leather-bound notepad. "Nope. That's a new one," she said, adding it to the list

"It means something, but what?" Nathan asked.

She gestured with her hand. *Gimme.*

"What do you want?"

"The book?" she said. "Please?"

He tucked the slip back in the book and handed it to her, watching as she studied the pages for what seemed like an eternity.

"What is it?" he asked.

"Shhh!"

He flopped his head to one side and stared at her, tapping his foot impatiently on the floor.

"You're looking at me," she said.

"Fine, I won't look at you," he said. From another box he pulled out a copy of Vogue Magazine dated two years earlier. "Why would he keep a fashion magazine?" he said.

Gina glared at him. "Do you mind?"

He glared back...*well excuse me*...then buried his nose in the magazine and kept reading, taking great care not to make any noise. Heaven forbid she hear a page turn. Three houses away, a dog barked. Then, a car raced past the house. Other than that, silence.

The sound of Gina madly rummaging through one of the boxes made him stop reading and look up. She had a purposeful look on her face as she pulled out one volume after another, quickly flipping through the pages before moving on to the next. She was halfway through the box when a realization came to her. She stopped and looked over at him, eyes wide.

"What is it?" he asked.

"Can I take one of these boxes home with me?" she asked.

"Help yourself," he said. "Are you going to tell me why?"

"No."

She closed the flaps on the box, picked it up, and made a beeline for the door.

"Fine, don't tell me," he grumbled, as she pulled the door shut behind her. He opened the Vogue magazine and continued checking the pages, reading aloud as he went. "Ooh, the new Gucci collection. Lovely." He turned the page. "What's this? At home with a Hollywood director after his life-changing African safari? *That* could be interesting. Not!" Next page. "Okay, here we go. Surprises at the Versace autumn/winter show in Milan…"

His concentration was broken when his father burst through the side door of the garage.

"Nathan," he said. There was a clear-cut urgency in his voice. "Come with me. Right now."

"Uh…I'm kinda busy here, Dad," Nathan said.

His father walked over and pried the magazine out of his hands.

"Hey! Give me that!" Nathan shouted.

"It can wait," his father said. He dropped the magazine in one of the open boxes and herded Nathan out the door.

"What are you doing? Stop!" Nathan yelled as he was hurried across the yard and into the house.

"This way," his father said, leading him down the hallway toward the living room.

When they came to the entryway, he saw his mother standing in front of the fireplace with Jameson's daughter, Kendra. They were talking in hushed voices, a look of concern on their faces. At the sight of him, they stopped.

No greeting.

No wave.

Just forced smiles.

"Is someone going to tell me what this is all about?" he asked.

Just then, the front door opened and Gina stepped inside, followed by her aunt, Ellie. Gina was clearly annoyed and went straight over to Nathan's side. "What's going on?" she asked.

"No idea," he replied.

"Why don't we all take a seat," David said, gently ushering Nathan and Gina into the living room.

They plopped down in the matching overstuffed chairs that resembled two giant bell peppers. David and Elizabeth sat on the couch directly across from them, and Ellie and Kendra took up positions at the front windows, watching the street.

When everyone was settled, David sat forward with his elbows on his knees and his hands clamped tightly together. "Late this afternoon we heard from Jameson," he said.

At the mention of Jameson's name, Nathan sat up. "Where is he?" he asked. Since they'd raided Edouard Dampierre's warehouse on Saco Island earlier in the week, Jameson had simply vanished.

"He's been out of the country," David said.

"Did something happen to him. Is he all right?"

"He's fine," David said. "He's been working with the European authorities in an attempt to find Ginette Dampierre."

"She's Edouard's older sister," Elizabeth explained.

"Yes, Mom, I know," Nathan droned.

"What you may not know," David said, "is that the criminal organization that her brother ran here in America—"

"The Covin, Dad," Nathan said. "It's all right, you can say it."

"Yes, the Covin," David said calmly. "Their American network has a European *division*, I guess you'd call it, run by Ginette Dampierre."

"Jameson has some experience with the Covin," Elizabeth added.

Of course he does, Nathan thought, a spark of anger showing in his eyes. *They killed his wife.*

"Jameson told me they tracked Ginette Dampierre to a hotel in Switzerland, but she managed to escape," David said. "He believes she may have returned to the United States, intent on rebuilding the Covin's network."

"So?" Nathan said, unaffected. "What does that have to do with me and Gina?"

"Jameson fears that resurrecting the Covin's criminal empire is not the only thing on her agenda."

Nathan's jaw fell open. "What are you saying? She's coming after us? What did we do?"

Gina shot him a pathetic look. "Really, Nathan?" she said. "Think about it. You led the U.S. Marshals to that old mill in Saco. You exposed the Covin's shipping operation. And you got her brother arrested."

"Uh, excuse me," he said. "There were others involved too. It wasn't just me."

"Yeah, well, you started it." *So there.*

Nathan's shoulders drooped and he sank back into the chair like a punctured beachball. "Great," he muttered. "We get rid of Edouard and now I have to deal with his sister?"

"Not so fast," David said. "We don't know that for sure."

"Well...based on what Jameson told us..." Elizabeth began.

Nathan straightened in the chair. "What?" he demanded. "What did he tell you?"

"He said none of us are safe," Kendra called out from the far end of the room. "Ginette Dampierre is even more ruthless than her brother, which means she'll be gunning for everyone involved in Edouard's capture."

"You two don't have to worry," Elizabeth said, eyeing Nathan and Gina. "We're going to keep you safe right here at home, and Jameson is putting together a team of people to help protect you."

"And…" David said, prompting her to tell them the rest.

"And he feels it would be best if we all lay low until Ginette Dampierre is apprehended."

"Lay low?" Nathan repeated.

"Keep out of sight," David said. "That means we stay inside the house where none of Ginette Dampierre's thugs can ambush us."

"Us?" Nathan exclaimed, the anger inside him spilling out. "You mean, ambush *me!*"

With a look of resignation, his father slowly nodded his head. "I'm afraid so."

"What about me?" Gina asked.

David nodded again. "That goes for you, too," he said. He looked across the room at Ellie, who was peering through the curtains. "Ellie, did you work it out?" he said.

"I did," she replied, keeping her eyes on the street.

"Work what out?" Gina asked.

Ellie left the window and walked over to where Gina was sitting. "I can't hide you in some remote location again," she said, referring to their recent stay at Merrymeeting Lake in New Hampshire, an attempt to keep Gina safe from Edouard Dampierre's thugs. "It would raise too much suspicion with your parents."

"So…then…where are we going?" Gina asked.

"Nowhere," Ellie replied. "You heard what Nathan's father said. We're staying right here."

"We?"

"I'll be staying with you for an undetermined length of time," Ellie said. "A week. A month. We'll just have to wait and see how this all plays out."

"Do my parents know about this?" Gina asked.

"They do."

"O-kay," Gina said slowly, wondering what reason Ellie had given them for her extended stay.

"You and Nathan have been exposed to enough danger as it is," Elizabeth explained. "We thought it best to keep you both at home where we could protect you."

"I know this is all very sudden," David said. "Do you have any questions?"

"Yeah," Nathan said. "You're saying we have to stay in the house? We can't go anywhere?"

"That's right," Elizabeth said. "Not until Ginette Dampierre is captured. Why? Is there some place you need to go?"

"Well…no, but—

"But nothing," his mother cut in. "After what Edouard Dampierre and those monsters did to you, it's a miracle you're still alive. If you think we're going to let his lunatic sister do the same thing to you, think again. From this point on, you're confined to the house. Period. End of discussion."

True to form, Niko called back within the 30-minute window. Ginette gave her the name of the mark along with some other information she thought might be useful. In Niko's line of work, too much information, no matter how trivial it may seem, was a good thing. She'd once used her target's fondness for tropical fish to finish the job.

The call lasted for less than 10 minutes, and when it was over, Ginette sat back in the seat feeling the satisfaction that a hunter experiences after an easy kill. "So much for Mr. Cole," she said. Then, it was on to the next item on her punch list.

At 10:45 that night, Ray Pantano sat waiting behind an automotive restoratin business one mile from MCI-Cedar Junction in South Walpole—the maximum-security prison was where Edouard Dampierre was being housed while he awaited trial. It was also where Pantano's brother-in-law, Gary Moran, worked as a security guard.

Pantano was checking the time on his phone when he heard the sound of an approaching vehicle. Seconds later, a pair of headlights pierced the darkness as they crept around the far end of the building. He watched Moran's orange Dodge Challenger Demon roll slowly over the uneven dirt lot, the 808-horsepower engine emitting a deep cat-like growl.

Moran rolled to a stop alongside Pantano's car and lowered his window. "I don't have much time," he said. "What's up?"

"That information you gave me," Pantano said, getting right to the point. "You're sure that's what he said?"

"Of course, I'm sure," Moran said, with a disgusted look. He pulled a spent cigarette pack from his shirt pocket and shook out his last smoke.

"Look, I'm sorry," Pantano said. "I gotta ask. Orders from the top, you know?"

"I bet," Moran chuckled, reaching for a lighter on the dashboard. He knew full well what Pantano was up against. His former boss was in custody. The criminal network he oversaw was in disarray. And the feds were actively hunting down any remaining members of his organization. That kind of pressure would make even the calmest person come unwrapped.

He lit the cigarette, the flame lighting up his face momentarily, then blew out a stream of smoke that drifted lazily through Pantano's open window. "I'll say this about your man," he said. "He's one messed-up dude. Doesn't say much, but when he does, it's in this soft voice. It's like he's saving his energy, waiting for the right moment to gut you with a spike. It's totally creepy, man."

Tell me about it, Pantano thought. "Have you talked to him recently?" he asked.

Moran shook his head as he took another drag. "They moved him," he said, smoke leaking from the corners of his mouth as he spoke. "But he did manage to pass me this." He squirmed in the seat and pulled a folded piece of paper from his back pocket.

Pantano reached through the open window and took it from him, then used the light from his phone to read the short message.

Get the books

"Did he elaborate?" Pantano asked, trying to decipher the message.

"Nope," Moran said. "There wasn't time." He sucked in another lungful of smoke and then tipped his head toward the open window and exhaled, watching the smoke momentarily blot out the canopy of stars overhead. "Anything else?" he asked.

Pantano shook his head as he stared at the note, trying to make sense of the words.

"Alright then, I'm outta here," Moran said. He flicked his cigarette out the window, the glowing tip sailing over Pantano's roof like a shooting star.

Pantano waited until he was gone, then pulled out of the dirt lot and made the short drive to Rt. 95 North.

Get the books.

It could only mean one thing.

Edouard had an old bookcase in his office. During the handful of times he'd been there, he'd never paid much attention to it. Antiques were never his thing—he was more of an IKEA guy. But now, he was convinced that it held the very books that Edouard so desperately wanted. Why that was, he had no idea. Nor did he care. What Edouard wants, Edouard gets. Imprisoned or not.

He eased down the ramp onto 95 North and moved over into the left lane.

Next stop: Saco, Maine.

Midnight came and went.

Nathan tossed and turned in his bed, besieged with questions about the books from the *Greenwich* bookcase, the numbered slips of paper, why some were circled, and why some were not. Adding to his confusion was what Gina had found that would make her want to take one of the boxes home with her.

Feeling like his head was going to explode, he tiptoed out of his room and went downstairs. Ginette Dampierre or no Ginette Dampierre, nothing was going to keep him from finding the answers to his questions.

He hurried through the kitchen and down the back hallway stairs. Standing at the back door, he peered out through the glass, the refrain from one of his mother's favorite songs playing softly in the back of his mind. *Hello darkness my old friend, I've come to talk to you again.*

Moving quickly and quietly, he slipped outside and darted across the lawn. The cool night air clung to his skin like paint, and when he reached the side door of the garage he slowly eased it open. Just as he was stepping inside, a hand emerged from the darkness and grabbed the back of his neck.

3

Claire

Nathan was yanked back outside and slammed up against the side of the garage. He tried to shout for help when a huge hand clamped down over his mouth. He looked up and saw the face of his attacker—a hulking mass of a man named Beck, one of Jameson's ex-military associates who'd been brought in a week earlier to help protect Nathan from Edouard Dampierre. Now he was back, offering the same protection against Edouard's older sister.

Beck leaned down, his nose just inches from Nathan's. "Inside the house. Now!" He pulled his hand away and Nathan hobbled across the lawn. Beck followed him to the back door, surveying the backyard as he went. When he walked into the kitchen, Nathan was leaning on the counter with one hand. His other hand was pressed against his lower back.

"I'm only going to tell you this one time," Beck said. He was standing so close that Nathan had to tilt his head back to see the big man's face. "You stay in the house. Period. You got that?"

"We'll see about that," Nathan muttered under his breath.

"What was that?"

"Yes. Fine!" Nathan blurted out. "Happy now?" With some effort, he pushed off the counter, sidestepped Beck, and staggered over to the table. "You didn't have to toss me around like a rag doll," he said, as he eased down onto the chair. "You could've just tapped me on the shoulder…you know…like normal people do?"

"You're lucky I didn't shoot you."

"Very funny," Nathan grumbled.

"I'm serious," replied Beck. "Be thankful it was me. If it was one of Ginette Dampierre's goons, you'd be hog-tied in the trunk of a car right now, on the way to a landfill. Or did you forget what her brother did to you?"

A week earlier, Beck had been duped by a trained assassin who had hidden a camera in the woods behind Nathan's house. The information he'd been able to gather had put Nathan's life in mortal danger, and Beck had no intention of letting that happen again.

Fool me once, shame on you.

Fool me twice, shame on me.

Nathan offered no reply. The rough treatment he'd received at the hands of Edouard Dampierre's men had left a gaping wound in his memory, one that wouldn't heal anytime soon.

"This battle isn't over," Beck said. "We have a powerful new adversary. She's on a whole different level than her brother, and we have no idea what force she'll bring to bear. But make no mistake, she *is* coming…if she's not here already."

"Fine," Nathan said. "You really want to help protect me?"

"What kind of question is that? You know I do."

"Then teach me how to fight."

Ray Pantano drove across the bridge onto Saco Island and turned into the lot that separated the two 19th century brick mills known as Saco Mill #1 and Saco Mill #4. Each of the refurbished buildings was over 500 feet long and housed an assortment of apartments and commercial space. He drove to the end of #4 and pulled into the last parking spot. Overhead, the moon was darting in and out of the spotty cloud cover, casting irregular patches of light on the ground.

He followed a narrow dirt road down to the Hamilton Mill, one of many historic mills built on the banks of the Saco river. Up until a week ago it had served as the southern Maine depot for the Covin's flow of illegal contraband, a place where crates were received, repacked and rerouted to various locations in and out of the country. Situated on the top floor was Edouard's office.

Since the raid by the U.S. Marshals Service, every door had been reinforced with new locks to safeguard the ongoing evidence gathering process. Not that locked doors would deter Pantano. They could seal every doorway with cinderblocks for all he cared. He had another way in.

At the base of building on the southern-most end was a small opening in the foundation, obscured by several large bushes. He found it with ease and climbed inside, crawling on his hands and knees across the uneven dirt floor.

Once inside, he stood, hunched over in the low crawlspace,

breathing in the moist air that was heavy with the smell of decay. He swung the beam of his flashlight in a wide arc until he spotted the short wooden stairway that led up to the first floor. Standing on the top step, he used his shoulder to push open the heavy cast-iron trap door, ignoring the painful screech of the hinges.

As he stepped out of the hole, he noticed puddles of dried blood staining the floor. If the rumors he'd heard were true, they were Edouard's blood—a cruel reminder of the cast-iron door slamming shut on his forearms as he was attempting to capture Nathan Cole.

He pushed the thought from his mind and hurried over to the corner, to the stairway that led to the upper floors. As he walked, the sound of his footsteps echoed through the now-vacant building. Days earlier, the U.S. Marshals Service had secured an emergency order from the Governor's office allowing them to remove every piece of contraband. Those sealed wooden crates now sat in an armory three towns away, guarded around the clock by a team of National Guard troops armed with M4 carbines.

When he reached the top floor, Pantano killed his flashlight and stepped into Edouard's office. Guided by the moonlight filtering in through the large mill windows, he saw an empty space across from Edouard's desk where the bookcase once sat. He did a full sweep of the room, thinking it might have been moved, but it was nowhere to be seen. He checked the floor below, and the floor below that. After an exhaustive search of the rest of the building he took out his phone and sent Moran a text message.

Can't find the books
Find out where he hid them

Moran's reply came moments later.

Will do.

Pantano waited nearly an hour for a reply. It wasn't until he was pulling to the curb in front of his South End condo two hours later that he got a return text from Moran.

Check the kid's house

Still sore from his run-in with Beck, Nathan found it impossible to sleep. He turned on the light next to his bed and grabbed a book from his bedside table. It was nearly an inch thick and had the weight and feel of a textbook.

Castles by the Sea
The Grand Estates of the New England Coast
by
Margorie Crandell Hicks

The cover showed a panoramic view of the Atlantic Ocean, taken from the stone patio of a sprawling ocean-side home. Jameson had discovered the book in the *Greenwich* bookcase when it was still sitting in Edouard Dampierre's office. The look of shock on Jameson's face when he pulled it from the shelf would forever be stamped into Nathan's memory.

As Jameson had explained, it was a gift to his wife Claire. She'd had it with her on the day she perished, during an ill-advised visit to Whitehall, a grand estate in Portsmouth, NH, and one of many properties featured in the book. The fact that Dampierre had it in his possession proved his complicity in Claire's death, a truth he confirmed when they had him cornered in his office.

"We should've dealt with you long ago, just like we did with your companion at Whitehall."

Those words had set a fire burning in Nathan's gut, and hearing Jameson recall the details of that day only made the fire burn hotter.

How he was out of the country at the time.

The call he'd made to Claire from his hotel room.

The revelation she shared with him about the book: how she found something in it that tied the Covin to the historic Portsmouth estate, and her intention to visit the property for confirmation.

He had pleaded with her to await his return, but still she went. Alone.

And he never saw her alive again.

Ever since hearing Jameson's account, Nathan had been besieged with questions. Why did she ignore his plea? What was so pressing that she decided not to wait for his return? What had she learned about Whitehall, and how was it connected to the Covin?

Late into the wee hours of the morning, with a deathly hush permeating every room of the house, Nathan scoured the chapter on Whitehall. The massive home was a breathtaking example of fine 19th century Victorian architecture, and whatever clue Claire Jameson found had to be in those pages. Why else would she be so determined to visit the property—a reckless act that would eventually take her life?

He read and reread the chapter, and it wasn't until his third pass that he noticed something in one of the outer margins. It was just two words, written so lightly that they were nearly invisible to the eye. He held the book up to the lamp, angling it one way then another until he could make out the faint scrawl. It was as if someone had scratched the words into the paper with a needle, or written them with a pen that had no ink.

Lule
Caracci

The name held no meaning, but it filled his mind with yet more questions.

Did Claire etch it into the margin?

Were the words already there when Jameson gifted her the book, put there by someone else?

What significance did the name have to the property, or to the Covin?

It was impossible to know.

On Saturday morning, shortly before six o'clock, a wave of anticipation stirred Gina from her sleep. She scrambled out of bed, driven by the certainty that she was very close to solving the riddle of the *Greenwich* bookcase.

With her parents snoring in the room down the hall, she sat on her bedroom floor surrounded by the various periodicals she'd brought home from Nathan's garage. She examined each of them carefully, focusing only on the photos and jotting down a quick note about each one in her notepad. When she was done, she tiptoed downstairs to the living room and went to work on the computer, all the while referring to her notes.

Five minutes later she got the first confirmation of her theory. Shortly after that, she found another. Then another. "I don't believe it," she muttered under her breath. She slumped back in the chair, awestruck. "All this time, it was right there in front of our eyes."

The next morning, Nathan was chased from his dreams by a desperate voice calling to him in the dark. *"Is someone there? Anyone? Please, help me!"* He bolted upright in bed, his heart pounding, relieved to see that he was in his own room. It was morning. Everything was fine. As he was making his way downstairs, the doorbell rang. But when he opened the door, no one was there. He pushed his face against the screen door, looking to the right, then to the left. And that's when he saw her—a young woman in a gray sweat suit, standing at the far end of the porch, looking up the driveway toward the garage. "Uh…hello?" he said.

The woman spun around and smiled, embarrassed. "Sorry about that," she giggled. She had a round face and large brown eyes, with straight blond hair that fell just below her chin. "I was just admiring your yard," she said.

From the far end of the hallway, Elizabeth called out. "Nathan? Who are you talking to?"

"Mom?" he said, surprised to see her. "What are you still doing home? You're going to be late for work."

"I'm not going to work," she said, as she walked toward him. "I'm taking some time off."

The visitor peered through the screen door and waved. "Good morning!"

Elizabeth rested her hand on Nathan's shoulder. "Wait here," she said, then pushed through the door and stepped outside. "May I help you?" she asked.

"I certainly hope so," the woman said. She smiled and extended her hand. "My name is Bev."

Elizabeth stood firm. "Bev...?"

"Oh, silly me," the woman gushed. "McKinney. Bev McKinney."

"Elizabeth Cole," Elizabeth replied, studying Bev's face as she reached out and shook her hand.

"Nice to meet you Elizabeth," Bev said. "And let me guess," she added, looking over Elizabeth's shoulder at the door. "That must be Nathan."

Elizabeth spun around and said, "Nathan, close the door and go in the kitchen. Your father has breakfast waiting for you."

Yes! Saved by the mom, Nathan thought as he closed the door.

"I'm sorry," Bev said. "Did I do something wrong? I certainly meant no—"

"Bev?" Elizabeth said, cutting her off. "Is that short for Beverly?"

"Yes."

"You'll have to excuse us. Things are a bit hectic right now. We have a lot going on."

"Oh, of course, I fully understand," Bev said. "The last thing I want to do is intrude. It's just...I'm new to the neighborhood and I need help moving some heavy boxes into the attic. One of your neighbors mentioned your son's name and suggested I hire him for the job. I'll pay him well..."

"You say you're new to the neighborhood?" Elizabeth asked. "Which house?"

"Over on Henderson," Bev said. "The large white colonial?"

Elizabeth said nothing. She could think of three large white colonials on Henderson. What she couldn't remember was if any of them had a realtor's sign on the front lawn.

"You know, perhaps I should come back another time," Bev said. As she spoke, she moved backward toward the steps like she was easing away from a ticking timebomb that might go off with the slightest vibration. When she reached the bottom of the steps she stopped and looked back. "So, you'll ask Nathan about the job?"

"Nathan already has a job," Elizabeth replied.

"He does? At his age? Doing what, pray tell?"

"Sorting books," Elizabeth said.

"Huh," Bev said. "Does something like that pay well?"

"It's not about the money," Elizabeth said. "It's more like a favor for an old friend. Lots of boxes. Too many to handle by himself. I'm sure you understand."

"Well, *yeah*," Bev said, with a goofy look. "That's why I stopped by, remember?"

Elizabeth watched her walk across the lawn and meander up the sidewalk, studying the houses and flowering shrubbery on either side of the street. Only when she was completely out of sight did Elizabeth go back into the house.

"What was that about?" David asked, when she walked into the kitchen.

"New neighbor," Elizabeth replied. She poured herself a cup of coffee from the carafe on the counter and then took a seat next to

Nathan at the table. "From now on, no more answering the door," she said. "You leave that up to me or your father. Is that clear?"

"Fine by me," Nathan said, drowning his pancakes with syrup. He had better things to do than answer the door. Like, figuring out why the Covin had saved such a strange collection of literature; why there were slips of paper tucked in each one, Claire Jameson's book, and the riddle of Whitehall that attracted her like a moth to a flame, with the same grisly end.

"It's not punishment," his mother explained. "We're just trying to keep you safe."

"Speaking of that," he said, "why didn't you tell me about Beck?"

David was about to respond when Elizabeth waved him off. *I got this.* "Beck is part of the security team protecting us while we're here in the house," she said.

"You mean while we're *prisoners* here in the house," Nathan grumbled.

Elizabeth ignored the comment and continued. "We didn't tell you about him because, at the moment, you don't need to concern yourself with who's on the team, where they are, or what they're doing."

Nathan rolled his eyes. *Here it comes.*

"You need to focus on one thing and one thing only."

"Yes, I know," Nathan said in a tired voice. "Staying in the house."

"That's right. The last thing we want is a repeat of …you know," she said, referring to his recent abduction, orchestrated by Edouard Dampierre.

Nathan gave her an angry look. "Really, Mom?" he said. "Are we going to keep talking about it? It's bad enough that it happened in the first place. You don't have to keep reminding me."

"Yes, you're right. I'm sorry," Elizabeth said. "That was a painful experience and we don't need to keep rehashing it."

Nathan frowned. *Ya think?*

"It's just that…I need you need to understand the gravity of this new development."

"Oh, I understand just fine," Nathan fired back as he pushed his chair away from the table. The thought of being trapped in Edouard Dampierre's demented deathtrap still cut into his memory like a dagger. He put his breakfast dishes in the sink and went back upstairs to his room. As he was getting dressed his flip phone rang and he grabbed it off the bedside table. He checked to see who was calling, then sat down on the edge of his bed and took the call. "Hey," he said.

"It's me," Gina whispered.

"Yeah, I know. My phone has caller ID, remember?"

"Shut up," she said. The fact that he had a cell phone and she didn't still drove her crazy. The very idea was preposterous. Criminal, even.

"Why are you whispering?" he asked. "Please tell me you're not in the bathroom again."

"No!" she shot back. "I don't want my folks to hear me."

"Yeah, we wouldn't want that, would we?" he snipped.

Ever since they'd forbid her from spending time with him, she'd secretly done just the opposite. If they knew about her continuing escapades with him, each a near-death experience, talking to him on the phone would be the least of her worries. They'd lock her in her room and only let her out three times a day to eat and use the bathroom.

"I'm glad you called," he said. "There's something I need you to check out."

"Yeah, well, it can wait," she said. "You know those books I took home with me?"

"What about them?"

A sudden knock on the door made him pull the phone from his ear and shield it next to his body. "Yeah?" he called out.

"I need you to come downstairs," his mother said.

"Be right there," he told her. He held the phone inches from his mouth. "Gina, I gotta go."

"Wait," she said. "There's something I need to tell you."

"Nathan? Let's go!" his mother shouted from the far end of the hallway.

"Gina, look, I can't talk right now."

"Nathan Cole! Don't you even think about—"

Click!

When Nathan came downstairs, he saw his mom and dad standing in the living room talking to Richard Abbott. The well-seasoned book buyer, mentored years earlier by Nathan's grandfather, had agreed to employ Nathan to help him process the thousands of books he bought and sold each year. As usual, he was dressed in baggy chino pants the color of sand and a light blue Oxford shirt. A pair of round tortoiseshell eyeglasses hung from his neck on a thin leather cord.

"Ahh, there you are," he said, as Nathan entered the room.

Yeah, here I am, Nathan thought. *Prisoner #1.*

"How are you, my boy? It seems like weeks since I last saw you."

"Yeah, it's been awhile," Nathan replied. *You wouldn't believe what happened to me.*

"Indeed," Richard said. "I'm sorry to say that the barn has fallen into quite a state of disrepair during your absence."

"Disrepair?" Nathan repeated.

"Yes. Pallets of books unattended to. New ones arriving daily. Customers hounding me to no end with questions about their orders. It's all been rather unpleasant, which is why I stopped by. I had hoped you might be available to resume your duties."

Nathan looked over at his parents, wide eyed. *Well? Can I?*

David looked at Elizabeth and shrugged. *Why not?*

She took hold of his arm and pulled him close. "Could I speak with you in private?" she said softly.

David looked at Richard and said, "Would you excuse us for just a moment?"

"Why certainly," Richard replied.

In the kitchen, Elizabeth steered David into the corner and spoke in a low voice. "Tell me you're not serious about letting him do this."

"I'm very serious," David said.

She opened her mouth to protest when he raised an open palm. "Just. Hear me out. Please?"

She pursed her lips and crossed her arms tightly across her chest. "I'm listening."

"He's not going to stay in the house. You know this," David said.

"Oh really?" she shot back. "He will if I—"

"Just. Let me finish," David cut in.

54

She closed her eyes, mouth clamped shut, and exhaled through her nose.

"Going to Richard's barn to help with the books is fine...*if...* someone goes with him," David explained.

"Go on," Elizabeth said.

"One of us will drive him. We'll wait there until he's finished. Then we'll drive him home. At no time will he be left unguarded."

"One of us?" Elizabeth said. "Who, exactly?"

"I don't know. You? Me? We could ask Kendra. I'm sure she'd be happy to do it."

Elizabeth said nothing for several seconds as she mulled it over.

"If we don't find something for him to do, you know what will happen," David said. He didn't mention the conversation he'd had with Beck right before breakfast. How he'd caught Nathan sneaking out of the house in the middle of the night.

"Kendra," she said.

"Excuse me?"

"I'd prefer Kendra went with him."

"Alright then," he said. "Kendra it is."

Ginette Dampierre sat down behind the large mahogany desk as she waited for the others to take their seats. Three of them sat across from her in the French bergère armchairs, carved from dark brown walnut. The other two chose the Empire chaise positioned along the near wall.

The room was part of an elegant top-floor suite. There were no windows and it had the feel of a private study. To the left of the desk, a Victorian marble and bronze clock sat atop a Gilded Age step-back credenza. Antique statues were placed at strategic intervals around the room, and covering the floor was a large hand-knotted, pre-1900 Bakhtiari Persian rug.

Down an adjoining hallway was another meeting area, with sectional couches, mirrored walls, and a bar that ran the full width of the room. In one corner was a corridor that led to an exquisitely furnished master bedroom and private bath.

"Thank you for making the trip," Ginette said, once her guests were settled. "I know some of you came quite a distance. The reason I asked you to join me today is to assure you that, despite our recent setbacks, business will continue as usual. Up until now you've been dealing with my brother. From here on out, you'll answer directly to me."

For several seconds no one spoke.

"How *is* Edouard?" one of the men asked, tentatively. The measured tone in his voice suggested that he feared what the answer might be.

"All reports indicate he's doing fine," Ginette said.

"If I may," said Gerald Thorpe, the most senior of the men in the room and the owner of a high-end antique gallery in Camden, Maine. "Is it true what they're saying…about the authorities? That they're actively pursuing you from one corner of the globe to the other?"

"Yes," Ginette said calmly. "But don't let that concern you. My anonymity is secure. You should all carry on as if nothing happened."

"About the deliveries," said Carl Jaquith, seated next to Thorpe. He was a longtime friend of Edouard and owned a prestigious gallery in Wells, Maine. "Will they continue?"

"Yes," Ginette replied. "I expect the deliveries to continue just as before." She paused briefly. "There's much my brother kept to himself in that regard."

"Perhaps this will help," Jaquith said. From the inner pocket of his tweed suitcoat he produced a colorful trifold brochure that he'd received in the mail from a museum in Portland, Maine. He unfolded it and slid it across the table to her.

"What is this?" Ginette asked, looking at it without picking it up.

Jaquith leaned across the desk and tapped his finger on one of the images—a stunning Isfahan rug, featuring a central medallion surrounded by vines and flowers in red, blue and indigo on an ivory background.

Ginette looked at it with mild interest. "What about it?"

"I thought it might be of interest," Jaquith replied.

"Meaning what, exactly?"

"I thought it was something we could...uh...look into?"

"I'm not sure what you're talking about," Ginette said, pushing the brochure back across the desk, "and at the moment I have more pressing matters to attend to."

Jaquith glanced at Thorpe, sitting in the chair next to him. *She doesn't know.*

Thorpe nodded his head in agreement.

"What's wrong?" Ginette asked.

"You were right," Jaquith replied. "There is much that Edouard hasn't shared with you."

"Humor me," she said.

That's when he explained the deliveries.

And the Watchman.

4

Reckless

Kendra was only too happy to drive Nathan to Richard Abbott's home and wait until he was done sorting books in the barn. As a self-employed business owner, her schedule was her own. More importantly, the treatment Nathan had received at the hands of Edouard Dampierre and the madman Trask sickened her. She had vowed never to let him fall victim to such cruelty ever again.

When she got to Richard's house in North Cambridge, she pulled up the crushed-stone driveway, her battered blue Volvo chugging like a miniature tank. "How much time do you need?" she asked, coming to a stop in front of the barn.

"I couldn't tell you," he said, staring at the heavy wooden door, wondering what "disrepair" awaited him on the other side of it.

"Well, take as much time as you need," she said. "I'll be parked out front at the curb."

"Doing what?"

"Watching."

"Oh. Right."

He climbed out of the car and slid the barn door open, the cast iron rollers giving off their usual high-pitched squeak.

"Good! You're here," came a voice from directly behind him.

He looked over his shoulder and saw Richard walking toward him, clipboard in hand. They had just stepped into the barn, the cool air washing over them like a breath of January wind, when Nathan stopped short, his jaw hanging open in disbelief.

Running down the outer wall to his right was a long row of shrink-wrapped pallets, each one piled high with boxes of books. There had to be at least 10 in all. "You weren't kidding," he said.

His attention was diverted when a crimson-red BMW 3-series sedan rolled to a stop several feet from the open door. A woman got out and eyed the barn from top to bottom. She had wheat-colored hair cut in a straight bob with side-swept bangs, and was dressed in a sleek oyster-gray blazer, matching vest, with a blue and white-striped shirt and beige dress jeans. Hipster lawyer or millionaire businesswoman, Nathan couldn't decide.

She walked as far as the open door and paused, her slender body casting a long shadow across the sunlit plank floor.

"Ah...perfect timing," Richard said, as he walked toward her. "Miss Prescott, I presume?"

"You can call me Jordan," the woman said, looking over his shoulder into the barn.

Richard extended his hand. "Richard Abbott, at your service."

She ignored the gesture and walked past him. "These are the books?" she asked, pointing at the row of untouched pallets.

"Yes," Richard said. "They've been arriving all week and...uh... I'm a bit behind on sorting them."

"I can see that," Prescott said, less than enthused.

"However, I'm happy to report that help has arrived!" Richard said triumphantly. He extended his arm graciously in Nathan's direction. "May I present, my able-bodied assistant, Nathan Cole. He'll be helping me sort and classify the books."

Prescott considered Nathan like she was examining a scratch in her antique armoire. "Are you sure he's up to the task?" she asked.

"Oh, I assure you, Mr. Cole is quite competent," Richard said. "He comes from a long line of seasoned book collectors. You must've heard of his grandfather, Henry Hammond?"

"Can't say I have," Prescott said, sizing up Nathan once again.

"I'll have him put your order at the top of the list," Richard said. He walked over to one of the pallets and inspected the slip of paper tucked inside the clear plastic wrap. "Nathan, I believe Ms. Prescott's book will be in this lot."

"One book?" Nathan said, shocked. *Are you serious?* Most of Richard's clients placed orders for dozens of books, if not more.

"Yes. A very intriguing title," Richard said. "Yesterday, when Ms. Prescott called to inquire about it, I remembered seeing it in an exquisite collection of books I purchased from a retired doctor in Brookline." As he spoke, he flipped to the last page on the clipboard where the most recent orders were listed. "Let's see..." he said, running the tip of his finger down the titles. "Ah...here it is...*A General Introduction to Psychoanalysis*, by Sigmund Freud. First edition, second printing. And in excellent condition I might add."

"Nathan!"

The voice came from just beyond the open door, and when Nathan looked, he saw Kendra standing in the driveway.

"Everything okay here?" she asked, eyeing Jordan Prescott suspiciously.

"Yeah? Why wouldn't it be?" he said.

"Just checking." She made a mental note of the BMW's plate number, then walked back down the driveway.

"Ms. Prescott, you're welcome to wait in the house while Nathan looks for your book," Richard said.

"That won't be necessary," she said. "I'm happy to wait here. If what you say about the boy is true, it shouldn't take him that long. Isn't that right, Mr. Cole?" she said, her eyes boring into his.

"Uh, yeah," he said nervously, feeling like he was caught in the grip of an alien tractor beam.

"Well then, I'll leave you to it," Richard said cheerfully. He excused himself, citing the need to catch up on a mountain of paperwork, then promptly left the barn.

In the awkward silence that followed, Nathan grabbed a utility knife from the long farmer's table that stretched down the middle of the room and used it to cut the plastic wrap from the pallet.

Prescott looked up studying the ceiling, then walked the perimeter of the room, inspecting the scarred plank floor in the glow of the overhead lighting. "What was that Richard said about your family?" she asked, from the far side of the room.

"My family?" Nathan said. He balled up the plastic wrap and tossed it aside.

"He said you come from a long line of book collectors?"

"Oh, that," Nathan said. "Yeah, I do."

"Tell me about them," Prescott said. She stopped in the back corner and studied an old grain chute. The opening was roughly three feet square and looked down into the lower barn, which was completely obscured in darkness.

"What can I say?" Nathan said, pulling open the first box. "My family likes books. They always have."

"I see," replied Prescott. "And does that apply to you as well? Do *you* like to collect books?"

"Uh…yeah…I guess," Nathan said nonchalantly, like he hadn't given it much thought.

"Interesting," Prescott said. "Do you have many?"

Nathan pictured the boxes from the *Greenwich* bookcase that currently resided in his garage, packed with all types of printed matter. Add them to the books in his grandfather's bookcase, hiding in the attic, and he had a pretty serious collection—not that he could talk about it with a random stranger like Jordan Prescott.

"Mr. Cole?"

"Oh…sorry," he muttered, snapping out of his funk. "Do I have many books? Uh, yeah, I have a few," he said.

"I'd like to hear about them," Prescott said. She came to a narrow wooden stairway that led up to the second floor. She studied it momentarily, then made her way up it, the treads creaking beneath her feet.

Nathan dug through the box, examining each of the titles wedged inside. Because they'd been packed spines up, he was able to make his way through them in a matter of seconds. As he dug through the next box, he could hear the floorboards creaking overhead. *What is she doing up there?* he wondered, fearing she might come crashing down on him at any moment.

In the third box he found the book. "Freud…psychoanalysis," he said, reading the spine aloud. He checked it off the list and was bringing it over to the table just as Prescott came down from the second floor.

"It appears Richard was correct in his assessment of your book skills," she said.

Nathan handed her the book but said nothing.

"Perhaps I'll come by another time and you can tell me about your collection," she said.

Nathan shrugged. "Yeah, whatever." *Please don't.*

Forty five minutes later, Kendra appeared at the door again. "You ready for lunch?"

He tossed the clipboard on the table. "I thought you'd never ask," he said. "Where should we go?"

"There's a great place just down the road," she said. "They make an outstanding Cuban."

"A what?"

"A Cuban," she repeated. "Don't tell me you've never had one."

"Nope."

"Well then," she said. "Prepare to be amazed."

Kendra's great place was a small diner just off Mass Avenue in Porter Square. By the time they walked in the front door the lunch rush was already in full swing. The smell of fried onions and garlic filled the air, and the room was alive with the clamor of the Saturday lunch crowd. It took a few minutes, but they were finally seated at a small table next to the wall.

"So...a Cuban," Nathan said, scanning the laminated menu. "What is it, exactly?"

"Only the best sandwich ever," Kendra said. "Trust me, you'll love it."

A waitress who looked older than the building appeared at their table, pen in one hand, an order pad in the other. "What'll it be, folks?" she asked.

"Two Cubans, fries, and two large colas. Whatever you have is fine," Kendra said.

"Excellent choice," the waitress said, scribbling furiously.

After she left, Nathan drummed his fingers on the tabletop. "When does Jameson get back?" he asked.

"This afternoon," Kendra said.

"Then what?"

"I'm sure he'll tell us. Whatever it is, do us all a favor and don't... you know..."

"Don't what?" he asked.

"Don't be you."

He gave her a hard look. "What's that supposed to mean?"

"You know exactly what it means."

"No, as a matter of fact I don't," he shot back. "Why don't you spell it out for me? And be sure to use small words so I don't get confused."

She rolled her eyes. *Oh brother.* "Okay fine," she said. "It's no secret that you and trouble go hand in hand."

"Oh really," he said. "How do you figure?"

"You're impulsive."

"Impulsive," he repeated, scratching the side of his head. "Can you spell that?"

"Stop it," she said.

"Sorry. It's just that I've never been called that before."

"Well it's true," she said. "You're reckless. And sometimes, just sometimes, you're hotheaded." *Like right now*, she thought.

"So, let me get this straight," he said. He counted on his fingers as he spoke. "I'm impulsive. I'm reckless. And I'm hotheaded. Did I leave anything out?"

"Forget it," Kendra said.

"Oh, no, by all means, continue," he insisted. "I want to hear it all."

She looked away, mumbling to herself. "I shouldn't have said anything."

He leaned forward and spoke in a voice only she could hear. "Do you understand anything about my family?"

"More than you know," she replied.

"No. I don't think you do. I don't know how much Jameson told you, but the bookcase in my attic, the one I got from my grandfather? The one he got it from his father? Who got it from *his* father? It's not just an ancient relic filled with old books. It's a legacy in my family. And now it's been passed on to me. Do you understand what I'm saying? I was chosen to safeguard it, and to use it just like everyone before me did."

"Yes, I'm aware of that," she said.

Nathan kept on.

"Ever since it came to America, members of my family have

filled it with unsolved mysteries—accounts of people who were falsely accused, shamed, or worse. Why? To reveal the truth. To set the record straight. Call it what you will."

She said nothing and let him talk.

"It's a tribute to my ancestor Thomas Hammond, who built the bookcase, along with its twin, the *Greenwich* bookcase. After he was falsely accused and hung, the generations of my family that followed have been using the Hammond bookcase as a force for good, knowing there are people in the world that are working for an opposite cause."

Kendra knew the story all too well, having heard it from Jameson years earlier. *Oh, if you only knew the rest,* she thought, slowly shaking her head.

"What? You don't believe me?"

"Oh, no," she said quickly. "Just the opposite."

An ambulance screamed past the front windows with its light bar flashing, the siren momentarily drowning out the chatter of the boisterous lunch crowd. After it passed, Nathan said, "Jameson explained the history of the bookcase to me—things my grandfather would've told me if he were still alive. He also made me recite an oath that every keeper of the bookcase abides by."

"Which is…?" she asked.

"Careful. Watchful. Unseen."

"HA!" Kendra blurted out. "You have *not* been careful."

The woman sitting at the next table shot Kendra a disapproving look, then continued cutting into her wedge salad.

"I know," Nathan said. "I'm trying to get better at that. But I can't stop doing what I'm supposed to do. What my grandfather *chose* me to do."

"Of course," Kendra said. "All I'm saying is, you need to work harder. You need to be more careful and less impulsive. More watchful and less hot headed. And you need to be *way* less noticeable. I'm not joking when I say that your very life depends on it."

Neither one spoke for several seconds. All around them, the roar of the lunch crowd continued with loud voices and laughter, and the constant *whumph* of the swinging doors that led to the kitchen, as the waitstaff ferried trays of food to their waiting customers.

"I'm not sure if you know this," Nathan said, breaking the verbal stalemate, "but Jameson told me something else, too."

"About the bookcase?"

"No. About Claire."

The look of regret that fell over Kendra's face did little to mask the crippling sadness she had buried deep inside—a burden she would carry for the rest of her life, knowing that her stepmother was gone forever. "I'm surprised he did that," she said softly. "It's not something he likes to talk about."

"I don't think he could help himself," Nathan said.

"Why do you say that?"

"He found the book she had with her on the day she went to Whitehall."

"What?" she exclaimed.

Salad lady gave her another nasty look.

Kendra glared at her. "Really?" she said. "Would you like us to write it down for you? Would you? That way, you won't miss a word."

Nathan rapped on the table. "Excuse me," he said. "Are you done?"

Kendra snarled at the woman, then looked at Nathan. "Sorry," she said. "You were saying?"

"Claire's book was in the *Greenwich* bookcase. In Edouard Dampierre's office."

"Are you serious?" Kendra said. She clenched her teeth and grabbed both sides of the table like she might hoist it in the air and hurl it across the room.

Nathan nodded his head, then looked around to make sure no one was listening. "After he found it, he told me the whole story. How Claire discovered something in it that linked the property to the Covin, and how she went there all alone to check it out."

Kendra's shoulders slumped and she sat back in the chair. Like a punishing storm that leaves irreparable destruction in its wake, that day would forever unleash a torrent of grief and heartbreak for her father. Losing the woman he loved to a criminal organization with no conscience. No soul. The very thought of what they'd done to Claire made her blood boil.

"I want to go there," Nathan said.

"Excuse me?"

"I want to go there, to Whitehall. If she really did find something, I want to know what it was. Don't you?"

She nodded her head slowly. *More than you know.*

"Well then? What are we waiting for?" he said. "Let's go."

She gave him a look.

"What's wrong?" he asked.

"Right there," she said, jabbing a finger at him. "That's reckless."

"How is that reckless?"

"You have no actual proof, only suspicion."

"So?"

"By my way of thinking, that's reckless."

"So, I guess that means you won't drive me there."

"Absolutely not," she said. "On the other hand…if you were to bring me definitive proof, then maybe, just *maybe* I'd consider it. Until then, for your own safety, you need to stay clear of the place. And it's best if you didn't talk about it around my dad."

Nathan stared absently across the room, thinking. *Definitive proof.* And that's when the realization hit him. Maybe he already had the proof. It was just buried, and all he had to do was dig it up.

Or get someone else to do it.

Kendra drove Nathan back to Richard Abbott's house and waited in front of the house like she had before. Nathan's plan was to work another hour before calling it a day, and since their return she'd seen nothing suspicious. No one had driven slowly past the house. No one was parked nearby, checking it out. No one had so much as pulled into the driveway to reverse direction.

Thirty minutes had passed when her phone rang. She checked the caller ID, saw her father's name, and took the call at once. "Hey," she said. "Did you land?"

"Fifteen minutes ago," Jameson said.

"I'm glad you made it back safely," she said. In the background she could hear an announcement echoing through the terminal, something about pre-boarding for a flight to Cleveland.

"In the morning, I'll fill everyone in on what we know," Jameson said. "But first, I need you to meet me as soon as possible."

"Sure. What's up?"

"I'll explain when I see you. How soon can you be at my place?"

She checked her watch. If Nathan held to his plan, they'd be at Richard's for another 30 minutes. By the time she dropped him off at home it would be almost three o'clock. "How about 3:15?" she said.

"Perfect. I'll see you then. And Kendra?"

"Yeah?"

"Bring Nathan with you."

"Just Nathan?"

"Yes. Just Nathan. No one else can hear what I'm going to say."

After Nathan's abrupt dismissal on the phone, Gina gathered the books and magazines from her bedroom floor and began repacking the box. "What a jerk," she muttered. "Hangs up on me just as I'm about to tell him what all of this means." She was gathering the last of the periodicals when she saw one of the numbered slips lying on the floor. When she picked it up, she noticed something peculiar about it—something she'd failed to see before.

"Well, that's interesting," she said, holding it up to the light.

Nathan was standing at the long table in the barn, sorting books two stacks at a time—a trick he'd developed months earlier. With two piles of books positioned in front of him, he would read each title, then search for both of them on the pages of Richard's clipboard. He'd become so good at it, he was toying with the idea of looking for three titles at a time.

He was checking the list when he heard the muffled sound of his flip phone ringing. He pulled it from his pocket and answered as he turned to the next page on the clipboard. "Yeah?" he said.

"Yeah? *That's* how you answer your phone?" Gina crabbed. "Remind me to give you a lesson in phone etiquette. And…uh…if it's not too much to ask, would you please refrain from hanging up on me this time?"

"Sorry about that," he said. "I'm trying to finish up here. What's going on?"

"I figured out what they mean," she said.

"They?"

"The slips of paper. I know what they mean."

"Seriously?" he exclaimed. He set the clipboard on the table and walked over to the open door, where the humid afternoon air hung like a wet curtain just beyond the sill.

"Uh-huh," she said. "That's not all. I discovered something else too. And before you ask me, the answer is no, I'm not going to tell you what it is. I have to show it to you in person."

Nathan's curiosity spiked. "Let's meet up after I get home," he said. "In the meantime, I need you to help me with something. Two things, actually."

She let out a tired breath. "Fine. What are they?"

Nathan chose his words carefully. If his hunch was correct, once she heard them, she'd be powerless to say no. "I'm trying to solve a riddle and I've pretty much hit a wall," he said.

"Go on," she said, intrigued.

"There's a property in Portsmouth, New Hampshire. It's called Whitehall. I need to find someone who can tell me everything about it."

"In Portsmouth, New Hampshire?" she asked. *How hard could that be?*

71

"Yeah."

"Hang on a minute," she said. She went over to her desk and grabbed her notepad. To the casual observer it might look like any other jotter, but this one was a special gift from her grandmother. It was linked to a dangerous secret that she'd entrusted to Gina, and it was so perilous that she couldn't share it with anyone. Not Ellie. Not even Nathan.

"All right," she said, turning to the first blank page. "Give me the name again."

Nathan pumped his fist in the air. *Yes!* "Whitehall," he said.

"You sure?" she asked, hesitating before she wrote it down.

"Positive."

"Street?"

"Uh…I don't know…I mean, I do know, I just can't tell you right now."

"What are you babbling about?"

"I don't have the address with me, but I can tell you when I get home."

"Don't bother," she said. "I'll find it. What's the other thing?"

"Lulo Caracci."

"Excuse me?"

"Lulo. Caracci," he said again, pronouncing each word slowly. "See if you can find out who that is."

"Spell it for me."

"First name, Lulo…L-u-l-o."

"And the last name?"

"Caracci…C-a-r-a-c-c-i."

"Got it," she said, closing her notepad. "What's this all about?"

"A monster."

5

Chessman

Just after three o'clock Kendra pulled away from the curb in front of Richard Abbott's house, tires chirping on the pavement, and nearly collided with a FedEx delivery van that was speeding up the street. The driver leaned on the horn as he swerved to avoid her.

"OH YEAH?" Kendra shouted out the window. "TRY SLOWING DOWN YOU MORON!"

Nathan held tightly to the edge of the seat with both hands, his feet pressed firmly against the footwell, as she hit the gas and sped through traffic, cursing at anyone who got in her way. She was three blocks from Nathan's house when she cut the wheel and took an abrupt left turn, slicing through an intersection just as the light turned red.

"Uh, where are you going? My house is that way," Nathan said, pointing over his shoulder.

"Yes, I know that," she said. "But Jameson called. He wants to see us."

"He's back?" Nathan asked.

"No. There's a private jet waiting for us at Logan Airport, ready to fly us to Switzerland. Of course, he's back!"

"And he wants to see us?" Nathan asked, ignoring her sarcasm.

"Yes. Both of us."

"O-kay," Nathan said, slowly. "What's up?"

"We're about to find out," she said as she coasted through the front gates of Birch Meadow, the rambling retirement facility that Jameson called home. The driveway stretched through a dense forest of tall birch trees where bands of afternoon sunlight were piercing the emerald-green canopy overhead, giving the land a soft, dream-like appearance. When they reached the main building, Jameson was sitting on an oak bench near the front entrance waiting for them.

At the sight of Kendra's car, he stood.

She parked nearby, and as they walked across the pavement she noticed that he looked different. Something in his expression was off.

"He looks tired," Nathan said.

"Tell me about it," Kendra replied.

"Thank you both for coming so quickly," Jameson said, as they stepped up onto the sidewalk. "Come, there's much to discuss."

"Is everything all right?" Kendra asked.

"No. Things are far from all right, and I'm afraid to say that time is not our friend."

He escorted them through the lobby and the grand front room, expertly decorated with oriental rugs, plush chairs, and large leafy plants in oversized pots. As they walked, no words were spoken. Any resident or staffer who passed them received a polite smile. Nothing more. When they reached his room, he hustled them inside and quickly shut the door.

At that, Kendra and Nathan exchanged a troubled look.

"As I reported yesterday," he told them, "Ginette Dampierre escaped several hours before we raided her penthouse suite in Lucerne. At the time, based on information we were able to gather, I feared she may have left the country aboard a direct flight to Boston."

"And…" Kendra said.

"My fear was confirmed when my contact at Interpol reviewed the airport security tapes and spotted a woman who he believes was Ginette Dampierre. If his assessment is correct, we need to move quickly if we're going to catch her."

"Why? Is she going somewhere?" Nathan asked.

"Yes," Jameson replied.

"Good," Nathan quipped. "Let her go. As far away as possible. And let's hope she never comes back."

"I wish it were that simple," Jameson said. "But the threat she poses to all of us, especially you, is far too great. Only with her in custody can we eliminate the carnage she's sure to inflict on those who crippled her family's criminal enterprise."

Nathan said nothing. He did what he did. They caught the bad guy and exposed his criminal dealings. By his way of thinking, if he had the chance to do it again, he would, without a second's hesitation.

"We can assume that she'll be meeting with key associates from here in the northeast," Jameson said. "She'll want to erase any doubts they may have about the future of the Covin. And given the size of their operation, this is just the first of several meetings she'll be having here in the United States. Based on the information I've gathered over the years, she'll be holding similar meetings in Miami, Phoenix, Los Angeles, and Chicago. And those are just the hubs I know about. There may be more."

"What are you thinking?" Kendra asked.

"We have to find her, and fast. We have no idea how long she'll be here in the Boston area."

"And you have a plan for doing that?" Kendra asked.

Jameson gave her an uneasy look. "I'm working on it," he said. "She's very cunning, so we need to devise a foolproof trap, just like we did for her brother."

Nathan stepped back and raised both hands defensively. "Don't look at me."

On the car ride home, Nathan stared absently out the side window, the word 'trap', cutting through his thoughts like an acetylene torch. After his recent near-death experience, where he volunteered to be the bait in an elaborate trap to capture Edouard Dampierre and the elusive assassin Karl Odom, he had no interest in being used again to snare an international fugitive, or anyone else for that matter.

"Are you all right?" Kendra asked, breaking the silence that had filled the car since they left Birch Meadow.

"I'm fine," he lied. "Now I know why your father insisted on a private meeting. If my mother hears the word 'trap' again, her head will explode. I'm serious. It will actually shoot off her neck and burst like a piñata."

"That's why it's absolutely critical that you say nothing to anyone until my dad comes up with a plan," Kendra said, slowing to turn onto Nathan's street. "Whatever he devises, your safety will never come into question. I promise."

"Really?" he said looking over at her. "That's what the U.S. Marshals told me last time, and we know how *that* turned out."

"This won't be like last time, trust me. But until a plan is made, not a word to anyone. Understood? That includes your mom and dad. Gina, too." She pulled into his driveway and stopped near the end of the front porch. "Same time tomorrow?" she asked.

"Sure," he said, envisioning the long row of pallets waiting for him in Richard's barn.

"See you in the morning then. And remember, not a word."

"Yeah, I got it," he grumbled.

He was watching her back down the driveway, Jameson's words still stewing in the back of his mind, when he felt a tap on his shoulder. He flinched, then turned around and saw Gina standing there. Grinning. Without a word she grabbed him by the arm and dragged him toward the garage.

"Hey! What are you doing?" he exclaimed, swatting at her arm to free himself.

She let go but kept walking. "You'll see. Follow me."

They went into the garage and she quickly shut the door. From her pocket she took out a small zip-lock baggie. Through the clear plastic Nathan could see small strips of paper.

"Are those what I think they are?" he asked.

'Yes. Now don't talk. Just listen. These came from the box I took home with me."

"Right!" he said, suddenly remembering her phone call. "You told me you found something."

"What did I say about talking?"

"Sorry," he said softly.

She set the baggie on the workbench and dug out one of the slips. "These numbers?" she said, pointing to the top of the slip. "They're monetary values."

"Huh?"

"They're dollar figures that correspond to something in the specific book, or catalog, or magazine they were put into."

"You lost me," Nathan said.

"The Covin buys and sells stolen artwork, right?"

"Right."

"I think these boxes are filled with things they wanted to acquire, or did acquire—all pieces of rare and extremely valuable art. The slips of paper were used to record the estimated value of those items."

Nathan stared at the slip in her hand, awestruck. "But, how did you…?" he started to say.

"Figure it out?" she said, finishing his question. "I don't know why, but the book you found on abstract expressionism gave me the idea. When I got home I went through the box and checked each of the bookmarked pages, making notes about any pieces of artwork shown. Then I checked the market value of each item against the number on the slip. My first confirmation was in an auction catalog where I saw a rare oil painting by Roger Godchaux. The appraised value was a perfect match of the number on the slip. That's when I knew I was on to something."

"You did all that in one day?"

"Please," she said, smirking. "It wasn't that hard."

Not for you, he thought.

"As I was researching the various pieces of art," she said, "I also checked their current status."

"Their status?"

"Where they currently reside?" *Hello?*

"Oh," he said, nodding.

She gave him a pathetic look. *Try reading a dictionary sometime.*

"You were saying? About the status?"

"Some of the artwork is on display in a museum or a gallery. Other pieces are privately owned. The rest are reported stolen, or their current whereabouts unknown." She dug into the baggie and pulled out two slips, one with a circled number and one with an uncircled number. "These circled numbers match a piece of art that is missing or reported stolen. Now, that could mean anything, but if you ask me, I think it's a code, a kind of checkmark the Covin used to label the item as something they had acquired."

"You mean something they stole."

"Yes. The uncircled numbers matched artwork with a known location. In other words, still out there and still available to steal."

Nathan shook his head, amazed. "They were cataloging the things they wanted to steal, and using the bookcase as a kind of tracking system."

"That's exactly what I think," Gina said.

Nathan looked over at the boxes on the floor. "They must have an army of thieves," he said. "I mean, look at all these boxes. They're filled with hundreds of potential things to steal. That's way too much for it to be just one guy."

"What if it was a team of thieves being directed by one person?" Gina asked.

"You mean, the one identifying and selecting only the most valuable items?"

"It makes sense," she said. "He knew what to steal and where it was located."

"It had to be Edouard Dampierre," Nathan said. "That would explain why he had the bookcase in his office."

Gina shook her head back and forth slowly.

"No?" Nathan said. "What makes you so sure?"

"That's what I couldn't tell you on the phone. I have to show you."

Nathan's dad was trimming the rhododendron bushes that skirted the front porch when a car he didn't recognize pulled into the driveway. He stopped trimming and started across the lawn when the driver's door opened and a woman climbed out holding a brown pastry box.

"Hi there," she said in a bubbly voice. "Don't mean to intrude. Just wanted to drop this off for your wife."

"I'm sorry," David said. "Have we met?"

"Oh, silly me," the woman said, feigning embarrassment. "I'm Bev McKinney. I stopped by yesterday and spoke with your wife. It's Elizabeth, right?"

"Yes, that's right. I'm her husband David."

"Nice to meet you David." She gave him a sheepish look and spoke as if she didn't want anyone else to hear. "I think Elizabeth and

I got off on the wrong foot," she said. "I was feeling bad about that so I thought I'd drop off this pie as a sort of…well…peace offering."

"That's very kind," David said, "but totally unnecessary I assure you."

"You'll see she gets it?" Bev said.

"Of course."

She gave him a playful look. "You're not going to sneak out back and eat it yourself are you?"

"No," he said, chuckling. He tucked the clippers under his arm and took the pie from her. "I'll be sure to let her know you dropped it off."

She craned her neck and looked at the front door, then turned and looked up the driveway toward the garage.

"Is there something else I can help you with?" David asked.

"I was hoping to speak with Nathan," she said. "As I explained to your wife yesterday, I'd like to hire him to move some heavy boxes into the attic for me."

"I see," David said. "Why don't I speak with him and then one of us will get back to you?"

"Thank you," she said, relieved. She placed her hand on his arm. "You're very kind."

She started back toward the car when David called out, "Would you like to leave a number where we can reach you?"

"No, that's okay," she said without turning around. "I'll stop by again."

He watched her back out into the street and drive away when Elizabeth stepped out onto the porch.

"Who was that?" she asked.

"Bev McKinney. She said she spoke to you yesterday?"

"Oh, her," Elizabeth said. "She just moved in over on Henderson Street. She's very, how shall I say…enthusiastic?"

"Not the word I'd use but it'll suffice," David muttered as he walked up the stairs. When he reached the top step he handed her the pastry box. "She dropped this off for you…called it a peace offering."

"A peace offering?"

"Her words."

"Oh, right," Elizabeth said. "I was a little short with her. I'll have to stop by her house and thank her. She really didn't have to do that."

"She said something about hiring Nathan to move some boxes."

"What do you think?" Elizabeth asked.

"Fine by me," David replied. "She seems harmless enough."

Gina cleared a space on the workbench and dumped out the slips. Nathan watched as she picked through them, spreading them out and arranging them in a long row, side by side.

"Take a look," she said.

He stepped up to the bench and considered the slips briefly. "Yeah? What am I looking for?"

"Closer," she said.

He bent down until his face was inches from the bench, then eyed each of the slips slowly from left to right. And that's when he saw them.

Letters.

Printed in a fancy cursive font.

Embossed onto the paper.

They were grouped in twos and threes, some letters pushed to the left, some pushed to the right. A few of them were partially cut off but still readable.

"Weird, right?" Gina said.

"What do they mean?"

"Nothing," she said, "until you do this."

She edged him out of the way with her elbow and rearranged the slips, pulling out any duplicates and shoving them back in the baggie. When she was done, only half a dozen slips remained. She pushed them together so they were touching. "Now tell me what you see."

He looked again and froze. "Huh?" The letters, once a jumble, now spelled a name. "Arthur Chessman," he said, pronouncing the name slowly. "Who is *that?*"

"If I'm not mistaken, he's the one who made all these slips."

"What makes you say that?"

"Because they were cut from sheets of *his* stationery."

"Stationery?" Nathan said, skeptical. "Are you sure?"

"It has to be," she replied. "What other type of paper has a person's name embossed on it?"

He stared at the name as he pondered her question.

"Think about it," she said. "He's combing through all these books and magazines and what-have-you, and he sees something that interests him, some extremely valuable piece of art that fits the Covin's clientele. But before he puts the book in the bookcase for safe keeping, he cuts a little strip of paper from whatever he has handy. He writes the item's value on it..."

"And then tucks it in the book," Nathan said, finishing her thought.

"Now do you understand why I had to show you?" she asked.

He looked down at the slips, an idea percolating in the back of his mind, when the door opened and Ellie poked her head inside.

"Hey, you need to come back home," she told Gina. "Your folks are looking for you."

Gina rolled her eyes. "What now?" she moaned.

Ellie gave her a look. *Does it matter?*

"Go," Nathan said, nudging her with his elbow. "This can wait."

After she left, he pulled out his flip phone, and with the press of a button he speed-dialed Jameson.

"Nathan?" Jameson said, answering after the second ring.

"I know how we can do it," Nathan said.

"Do what?"

"Set the trap."

Ginette Dampierre was sitting in her Pullman limousine, parked at the curb outside Ray Pantano's South End condo. She checked her watch for the second time in as many minutes, then lowered the tinted privacy divider. "You *did* tell him that I'm here, right?" she asked the driver, a short, overly friendly man named Anthony.

"Oh, yes, ma'am, I did," he said, with utmost sincerity.

Since her arrival in America, the limo had become her traveling office. It gave her quicker access to the people she needed to see, and with seemingly every law enforcement agency scouring the globe in search of her, the tinted windows provided optimum privacy.

"Would you like me to call him again?" Anthony asked.

Before she could respond, the side door opened and Pantano climbed in. "Sorry about that," he said, sliding onto the seat across from her. "Couldn't be helped."

"Don't ever keep me waiting again," she said. "Is that clear?"

The question hit Pantano like a gut punch. Who did this woman think she was, speaking to him like that? Edouard never treated him that way.

"I asked you…is-that-clear?" she repeated, emphasizing each word.

There it was again.

"Yes," he said, holding back the anger that was stirring inside him.

"I certainly hope so," she said. She took the notepad from her purse and flipped to the list of questions she'd been compiling. "What do you know about someone called the Watchman?"

"The what?"

"The Watchman," she repeated, louder.

"Never heard of him," he said, turning his attention to the side window. Through the tinted glass he watched a young woman climb out of the car parked in the next space.

Ginette pressed. "My brother never mentioned him?"

"No" Pantano said. The woman stood at his window, straining to see through the glass, or checking her hair in the reflection. The smoky glass made it hard to tell.

Ginette tried a different approach. "Are you sure? Take your time. Think back," she said calmly, as if he had the aptitude of a finger puppet.

Pantano felt a wave of anger warming his face. People who insulted his intelligence did so at their own peril, as more than one sorry individual had learned over the years. "I told you," he said, trying to stay calm, "I've never heard of him."

So much for humility, Ginette thought. "Then, here's what you're going to do. Talk to your contact at the prison. Have him ask my brother about it. And make sure you explain that timing is of the essence. Do you think you can remember that or should I write it down?"

In that moment, Pantano envisioned himself springing across the space that divided the two seats, pulling the knife from his ankle sheath, and driving the blade deep into the side of her neck.

"Hey," she said, snapping her fingers at him.

The image faded and he smiled. "No problem," he said with false sincerity. "Is there anything else?"

"Yes," she said, reading from her notes. "Who's our contact at the landing?"

"Soto."

"Soto?" she repeated. "S-o-t-o?"

"Yes."

"Interesting name," she mumbled, as she wrote it down. She checked the rest of her questions but none of the them involved Pantano, so she closed the notepad and slipped it back into her purse. "That's it for now," she said. "Talk to your contact. We need to find this...*Watchman*...as quickly as possible. I expect an answer by this time tomorrow. Understood?"

"Loud and clear," Pantano said. He climbed out of the limo, Ginette's words like an inferno burning in his gut. *I expect an answer by this time tomorrow...understood?*

That's when the idea came to him.

In his state of anger, he'd completely forgotten to tell her about the books, and Edouard's directive to retrieve them. Ordinarily, he'd call her right back and share the information. But not this time. His omission presented an opportunity that could make him a very wealthy man. *I wonder what she'd pay for those books?* he asked himself as he walked back up the steps of the seven-story high rise. The late afternoon sun was inching lower in the sky, making the arched windows on the top floor sparkle like a diamond tiara.

He pushed through the front doors of the building, mapping out a plan as he walked. *First, I go to the kid's house and find the books,* he thought. *How hard could that be? They're just books, not nuclear warheads. It'll be a simple grab n' go.*

He figured if Edouard wanted the books so bad, they must be worth quite a bit. And once he had them, he knew just the right person to broker a deal with Ginette Dampierre—someone just as tough as she was, who wouldn't flinch at the first death threat she uttered.

Standing at the elevator that would take him up to his 5th floor condo, he imagined how his friend's conversation would go.

"Listen up and listen good because I'm only going to say this once. I have a collection of books from your brother's office. You know which office I'm talking about—the one that just got raided by the U.S. Marshals. Rumor has it that your brother is obsessed with getting them back before the authorities get their hands on them. Why? I don't know and I don't care. So, here's the deal. And this is a one-time offer. You want the books? It's going to cost you. I'll call you back in an hour with a time and place. After that the deal is off. The next time you hear about the books will be on the six o'clock news."

The elevator doors opened with a soft *ding!* and Pantano stepped inside. As the car slowly made its way upward, he calculated a hefty asking price for the books. Then he doubled it.

Shortly before 5 o'clock, when Beck arrived for his nightly guard duty, Nathan was waiting for him on the front porch. He watched Beck's truck chug up the driveway, the dual tailpipes growling like a caged tiger. By the time Beck opened the door, Nathan was standing on the lawn, several feet away.

"What's up?" Beck said, as he climbed down from the cab.

"You were going to teach me how to fight, remember?"

"Right," Beck said plainly, like he was having second thoughts. He stood there thinking, then lunged forward, grabbed the front of Nathan's shirt with both hands, and hoisted him up in the air like has made of balsa wood.

"Whoa, whoa, whoa," Nathan exclaimed, making a futile attempt to break free.

Beck held him up for several more seconds and then lowered him to the ground. "Lesson #1," he said. "Be ready for anything."

"That's it?" Nathan said. "Be ready for anything?"

"Uh-huh," Beck said. "What did you think? I was going to teach you a bunch of jump kicks and leg sweeps?"

"Well...*yeah!*"

"No," Beck said, shaking his head. "You're too young for that."

"Too young? I'm 12-years-old!"

"That's right," Beck said. "Twelve is much too young for attack moves, or even blocking techniques for that matter."

"Why?"

"Because your body isn't ready for that kind of pain," Beck said.

"Until you get bigger, and *stronger*...much stronger...your best approach to fighting should be not to fight at all."

Nathan smirked. "What's that from, *Karate for Dummies?*"

"No, it's from the school of common sense. At your age you need to learn evasive techniques, like leaning to the side or stepping back. When you do that, no matter what your attacker throws at you, they can't hit you because you'll be out of their range. Even if they try hitting you with a combination of blows, they'll keep missing. They'll waste energy and tire out more quickly. So...Lesson #2 is...?"

"When someone attacks me, get out of the way."

"Very good. Now, evasion is a powerful weapon, but it won't work if you're slow or unable to get out of the way quickly. Lesson #3: be fast and light on your feet."

"Fast and light on my feet," Nathan repeated. "Got it."

"Remember," Beck said. "If they can't hit you, they can't hurt you."

"So, how do I get fast?" Nathan asked

"Jump rope. Shadowbox. Both are excellent training tools."

"Jump rope?" Nathan said with a sour look. "Are you serious?"

"Yes," Beck replied, matter-of-factly. "What do you think championship boxers do?"

"Oh...yeah...right," Nathan said softly.

"When you get fast, you'll be ready for Lesson #4."

"Why not just tell me now?" Nathan asked.

Beck exploded at him again, but pulled up at the last second. It was so sudden that Nathan stumbled backward, tripped, and fell to the ground.

"Any more questions?" Beck asked.

"No," Nathan grumbled, as he slowly got up off the ground.

Out in the street, Kendra's faded blue Volvo cruised past the mailbox and then swerved into the driveway, coming to a squeaking stop behind Beck's truck.

"Hey guys, what's going on?" she asked through the open window.

Nathan was bent over, brushing grass and dirt off his pant legs. "Don't ask," he muttered.

She and Jameson were getting out of the car when David and Elizabeth came out the front door of the house and started down the porch steps.

"Well this is a nice surprise," Elizabeth said, as she walked up to Jameson and Kendra. "We were just about to make dinner. How about you join us? That includes you, too, Beck."

"We'd be delighted to," Jameson said. "But first, there are some things Beck and I need to discuss. It should only take a few minutes."

"Take as much time as you need," she said. "When you're done, come inside. I want to hear all about your trip."

He waited until Elizabeth and David went back in the house to start dinner, then said to Nathan, "We only have a few minutes. You have something to tell us?"

"Actually, something to show you," Nathan said.

They followed him up the driveway to the garage. Once they were all inside, he pulled a gallery catalog from one of the boxes and held it up for them to see. The gallery in question specialized in rare rugs and tapestries. On the cover was the photo of a reddish-orange Oushak rug.

"This is how we can trap Ginette Dampierre," he said.

"With a catalog?" Beck said, frowning.

"Uh-huh," Nathan said. "This catalog, and every other book, magazine, and brochure in these boxes."

"Go on," Jameson said, intrigued.

"Everything in these boxes is a blueprint for the artwork the Covin is planning to steal…or has already stolen." He pulled the slip of paper from the pages of the catalog and handed it to Jameson. "The number on that slip is the value of a piece of artwork in this catalog," he said.

Jameson pulled the slip closer and read the number aloud. "Four five zero?"

"That stands for $450,000," Nathan said.

"How do you know that?"

"Gina," Nathan said. "She researched some of the items from this collection on her computer. She figured out that the number written at the top of each slip is the monetary value of a piece of art shown in that particular volume."

Jameson stared at the slip, amazed, as if he was holding a rare gold Florin from the 14th century.

"Gina and I think Edouard Dampierre was using the bookcase as a sort of filing system," Nathan said. "That way, he could keep track of the items the Covin was channeling into their network."

"If that's true," said Kendra, "then somebody's going to want all these boxes back."

"Somebody like Ginette Dampierre, perhaps?" Nathan replied.

A smile creased Jameson's face. "It's perfect," he said.

"Uh…I think you're forgetting something," Beck said. "If what you say is true, then, technically, these boxes are evidence. Critical evidence. The kind the authorities are going to need when they prosecute Edouard Dampierre and other members of the Covin."

"So we don't tell them," Kendra said.

"Well, maybe not right away," Jameson countered, the workings of a plan taking shape in his mind.

"You sure you want to do that?" asked Beck.

"Yes," Jameson replied. "I've been chasing members of the Covin for too many years with nothing to show for it. I'm not about to let a chance like this slip away. This collection gives us an opportunity to end them once and for all."

"And it's not like we're going to just hand it all over to Ginette Dampierre," Nathan pointed out. "It's just the bait."

"The question is, how do we pull it off?" Kendra asked.

"Easy," Nathan replied. "We do it just like we did with her brother. We use someone she trusts."

"And who might that be?"

Nathan smiled. "I know just the guy."

6

Street Urchin

Early Sunday morning, just after 2 a.m., Pantano parked one block away from Nathan's house. Dressed in a black tee, jeans, and a knit cap that made him nearly invisible in the murky gloom of early morning, he used fences and arbors, garden sheds and detached garages as cover as he crept through the residential neighborhood. Not that anyone would see him. The people who lived in this part of town weren't the kind to be standing at their window at two o'clock in the morning, watching the blanket of clouds, like sheets of ginned cotton, crawl slowly across the night sky.

He stayed off the street and approached Nathan's house from the neighbor's yard. When he reached the property line, he paused at the thick stand of lilacs. Through the tangle of branches, he could see the back of the house. Diagonally across from it was the garage— a likely place for someone to store extraneous items. Like books. If they weren't there, he'd check the house. But first, the garage.

He moved to his left, following the lilacs to the back corner of the neighbor's lot. From there, he slipped into the thick band of woods that lined the back of the Cole property.

As he neared the back of the garage he heard a soft rustling sound. He stopped short and surveyed the trees from left to right. It had to be a racoon or a fox, he reasoned. Or the wind. He looked up at the treetops overhead and froze. In a narrow gap between the branches, set against the pale gray cloud cover, he saw a massive shape descending from the sky like a prehistoric bird of prey.

Jameson was confident that Nathan's plan would work. But to pull it off they'd need everyone's help, just like before, when they set the trap for Edouard Dampierre. Through dinner he said nothing of Nathan's idea, figuring it best to save the fireworks show for the next day. But as he and Kendra were leaving, he pulled David aside. "If it's not too much trouble," he said, "I'd like to get everyone together for a meeting first thing tomorrow morning."

"Sure. Any special reason?" David asked.

"We may have found a way to lure Ginette Dampierre out of hiding and end this Covin threat once and for all."

"*Lure* her out of hiding? Uh…I don't know," David said nervously. "After that fiasco with her brother, I can tell you right now, Elizabeth won't allow Nathan to be put in harm's way. Not again."

"The plan I have in mind poses zero risk to Nathan," Jameson explained. "In fact, he won't be anywhere near Ginette Dampierre or any of her thugs when it goes down."

"Oh…well…in that case…" David said.

The next morning, Jameson and Kendra arrived early. As the Volvo came to a stop in front of the garage, Beck emerged from the side door and stopped at the corner of the building, waiting like a dog at the end of his chain. The look on his face was more serious than usual.

"What's with him?" Kendra asked, pulling the key from the ignition.

Jameson climbed out and made his way around the front of the car. "Is something wrong?" he asked.

Beck waited until Jameson was closer, then said, "We had a visitor."

Jameson's expression darkened. "When was this?"

"Early this morning," Beck said. He walked to the back of the Volvo and eyed the trunk from side to side, doing a quick computation in his head.

"What are you doing?" Kendra asked.

"You'll see," Beck said. "Do me a favor. Wait here and make sure no one comes in the garage. And I mean, no one."

"Whatever you say," she told him.

As he walked back up the driveway he nodded for Jameson to join him, and together they went into the garage. Lying in a heap in the far corner was Pantano. He was bound and gagged, his face severely bruised.

"Who's that?" Jameson asked.

"One of Edouard Dampierre's goons. He's working for Ginette now. Says his name is Pantano."

"Pantano," Jameson repeated, the name emerging from the depths of his memory. "I know that name. I'm surprised he was forthcoming with it."

"People have a way of speaking the truth when the right pressure is applied," Beck said, using his thumb to wipe away a spot of blood between the knuckles of his left hand.

Jameson turned his back to Pantano and spoke quietly. "Was he here for Nathan?"

"No," Beck said. "He was looking for the books."

"He told you that?"

Beck nodded.

"Well, so much for our trap," Jameson said.

"Why do you say that?" Beck asked.

"If Ginette sent him here looking for the books, it means she knows that we have them not the supposed thief who's going to claim she stole them."

"She doesn't know," Beck said.

A spark of hope lit Jameson's face. "How do you know that?"

"Pantano said he learned about the books from Edouard, through one of his contacts at the prison. He never told Ginette about them because he was planning to use them to extort money from her."

"And you're sure of this," Jameson said.

"Positive," Beck replied, cracking the knuckles in both hands.

Jameson let out a long breath, relieved that their plan still had a pulse. "The question is what to do with *him*," he said, looking over his shoulder at Pantano.

"We sit on him until this is over," Beck replied. "For two reasons."

"I'm listening."

"First, our enemy is down an asset, which is a gift that helps our side."

"And the second?"

"I don't return gifts."

"Do you need a place to stash him?" Jameson asked. "We have several safehouses you can use."

"No. I'm all set with that," said Beck. "But my truck is parked two blocks away and we need to get him out of here before the others arrive."

"Take the Volvo," Jameson said.

"My thought exactly," Beck said. "The trunk might be a little tight but I'll make it work."

"Yes," Jameson said under his breath, giving Pantano a sorry look. "I'm sure you will."

By nine a.m. everyone had arrived. Jameson stood at the fireplace, waiting, as they took their usual seats: Nathan and Gina in the overstuffed chairs, Elizabeth and David on the couch, Ellie and Kendra at the front windows, watching the street.

Jameson was set to begin when Beck appeared in the entryway. When their eyes met, Jameson raised his head slightly. *Is it done?*

Beck nodded once. *Done.*

Jameson returned the nod...*good*...then addressed the group. "Thank you all for taking time out of your Sunday morning," he said. "I called you all together today because a recent development has presented an opportunity that we can't pass up."

"What development?" Elizabeth asked.

"Nathan and Gina have made a rather remarkable discovery," he replied. "One that gives us an excellent chance to capture Ginette Dampierre."

Gina, still groggy from being yanked out of bed so abruptly, leaned over the arm of the chair and whispered to Nathan. "What's he talking about?"

"Just listen," he said.

"Through some very diligent work by Gina," Jameson said, "we've learned that the contents of the *Greenwich* bookcase are of considerable value to the Covin. In fact, they may represent a major cog in their process of acquiring and distributing stolen artwork. For that reason, it goes without saying that they'll want them back."

Gina sensed what was coming and gave Nathan a hard look.

"What?" he asked.

"You lied to me," she said.

"What are you talking about?"

"You said the boxes could wait."

"That's right," he said. "Technically, that wasn't a lie. I just didn't tell you what I was thinking."

"Same difference," she snarled. She saw Jameson watching her, waiting for her to finish, and quickly averted her eyes. "Sorry."

"No apology needed," Jameson said. "Your excellent detective work has paved the way for us to trap an international fugitive who's been evading the authorities for the past 20 years."

"Trap?" Elizabeth said. "Oh, no...we are not doing that again!"

David rested his hand on her shoulder. "Honey? You need to hear him out. It's not what you think."

"David is correct," Jameson said. "This is not going to be a repeat of last time. At no time will Nathan be in danger."

"Gee, where have I heard that before?" Elizabeth grumbled.

"Jameson, why don't you tell us what you have in mind," David said, trying to ease the tension of the moment.

"Nathan has given us the name of an associate of Edouard Dampierre," Jameson said. "His name is Carl Jaquith. He runs a high-end antiques gallery in Wells, Maine."

"And how is it that you know this man?" Elizabeth asked Nathan.

"Edouard Dampierre was using him to try and lure Richard Abbott to Maine in hopes that I would tag along," Nathan explained.

Elizabeth's eyes went wide at the thought of how that might've turned out.

"It should be noted that Nathan saw through the ruse from the very start," Jameson said. "As such, Edouard's plan failed."

Elizabeth sensed there was more to the story than they were telling her, but she let it pass. Nathan was sitting across from her, alive and well, and that was all that mattered.

"So, about this plan?" David said. "You say the Covin will want the contents of the bookcase. How do you intend to use them to trap Ginette Dampierre?"

"We're going to let Jaquith know that the collection is available to buy. But we have to do it in such a way that he won't get suspicious. We start by sending someone into his shop, a person who appears to be, let's just say, not a friend of the local police. In a very casual manner, that person will let it slip that they have a collection of literature for sale. Very unusual literature acquired from a certain mill on Saco Island. Notably, the one that was recently raided by a team of U.S. Marshals."

For several seconds no one spoke.

"I'll do it," Ellie said, breaking the silence.

Gina jumped up from the chair. "No!" she cried out, worried what could happen to her favorite aunt at the hands of a mad women like Ginette Dampierre.

Ellie walked over and gave her a hug. "Gina, my dear, you are very sweet," she said, "but you don't have to worry about me."

"But…it could be dangerous," Gina said.

Ellie held her at arm's length. "Gina, Gina, Gina. There's so much about me you don't know."

Soto eased his pearl-white Chevy 1500 into the vacant spot next to Ginette Dampierre's limousine and killed the engine. The State Park was unusually quiet for a Sunday morning. The ocean was the color of tin, and thin lines of waves were gently lapping the shoreline. The parking spaces that ran along the sea wall were nearly empty, and only a handful of locals were wandering the beach.

He climbed down from the truck and paused to look up at the tufted clouds overhead, their steel-gray color resembling the thick mane of an Arctic wolf.

Rain was coming.

He could feel it.

Which explained the deserted beach.

By modern-day standards he was considered a bulky man. A giant, by some interpretations. With some effort he leaned down and squeezed through the door of the limousine.

"Good morning," Ginette said, forgoing a handshake.

"Ma'am," he said, settling back in the plush seat. The supple leather brought back fond memories of his first saddle, expertly crafted in full-grain crazy horse leather, that his parents had given him on his sixth birthday.

"Thank you for meeting me so early, and on such short notice," Ginette said. "Given recent events, I felt it was important that we meet as soon as possible to discuss the road ahead."

"I agree," Soto replied, his eyes sweeping the interior of the car like a curious child.

She pulled the small spiral notepad and a pen from her purse and began flipping through the pages. "I'll forgo any details of my brother's incarceration," she said. "Right now, I'm more concerned with any needs you may have."

"I have no needs," he told her. "Other than the obvious, of course."

"Ah, yes…product," she said, nodding. "We're working on that. Tell me, what do you know about the Watchman?"

"Say again?"

"The Watchman?" she repeated.

Soto shook his head. "I have no knowledge of that person."

"Huh," she said, tapping the pen on her notepad. Nobody seemed to know this guy, and of the few who did, they didn't know his name or where he could be found—only that he existed. *Why would Edouard keep the identity of the man secret?* she wondered. *Especially from Soto of all people.* She pushed the thought away and glanced down at the next item on her list. "Let's talk about the pipeline. Any issues there?"

"No," Soto replied. "Our storage area is secure, transfers are running smoothly, and all of our equipment is in perfect working order. I have a regular maintenance schedule to ensure that it stays that way."

"Very good," Ginette said. She crossed off that item and moved to the next. "How are you set for manpower?"

"Also, good. My men know what is expected of them. For this reason, they are fiercely loyal and extremely hardworking."

"Not to mention well paid," Ginette noted.

"Yes. That, too."

She ran a line through that entry, leaving only one. "What about currency?"

Soto waved off the question. "All set."

She pulled back, surprised. No one ever refused the money. "Are you sure?" she said. "We have plenty, you know."

"The offer is very kind," Soto replied, with a polite nod. "Years ago, my answer might've been different. But over time I've learned that there are more effective ways to influence people and secure their cooperation."

"Indeed," Ginette said, closing the notepad. She smiled and said, "I think you and I are going to get along quite well."

She waited until he exited the limo and then checked her phone messages. There was nothing from Pantano. Only a short message from Niko.

In position

The words brought a smile to her face.

Things were starting to happen.

Finally.

She glanced at her checklist, then lowered the privacy divider and gave Anthony their next destination.

While Elizabeth and David put out a buffet of sweet breads and fresh-brewed coffee in the kitchen, the rest of the group remained in the living room to discuss the details of the plan.

"Tell me about the books," Ellie said, looking directly at Nathan and Gina. "Are they new? Old? Hardcover? Softcover?"

"Actually, they're a mix," Gina said.

"What she means is, they're not just books," Nathan explained.

Ellie eyed each of them, confused. "What do you mean, not just books?"

"It's *mostly* books," Gina said. "Art history and art collecting guides, things like that. But there's also a bunch of auction house catalogs, art gallery brochures, museum leaflets—"

"Don't forget fashion magazines," Nathan added.

"Tell her about the strips of paper," Jameson said.

"What strips of paper?" Ellie asked, looking back and forth from Jameson to Nathan.

Nathan explained how each periodical had a narrow slip of paper bookmarking a specific page. After that, Gina explained the meaning of the number scribbled at the top of each one.

"So, wait a minute," Ellie said, when Gina was done. "Does Jaquith know about this collection? These books and brochures and catalogs and what not?"

"We don't know," Jameson answered.

"Does it matter?" Nathan asked. "The whole collection could be worth, what, a million dollars?" he said, looking over at Gina.

"More than that," she said. "Much more."

"Even better," Nathan said. "Whether Jaquith knows about it or not, he's looking at a huge payday. Is he really going to walk away

103

from something like that?"

"Nathan's right," said Beck. "The question is, will it be enticing enough to make him contact Ginette Dampierre?"

"I guarantee it," Jameson said. "Remember, she's here to rebuild their network. To do that she's going to need product. This is one way she can get it."

"When do you want to do this?" Ellie asked.

All eyes turned to Jameson.

"We can't afford to wait," he said. "Ginette Dampierre could finish her business dealings at any time. Once that happens she'll simply vanish again, so the sooner she knows about the collection the better."

"In that case I'll go tomorrow," Ellie said. "I'll check to see what time Jaquith's shop opens and plan my visit accordingly."

"About that," Beck said. "You have these books, which you got how, exactly?"

"I'll tell Jaquith I broke into the building after the U.S. Marshals left, saw the bookcase and thought what was in it might be worth something."

"So, you're a night burglar?"

"That, I am," Ellie said proudly.

"In that case, you should wait until after lunch to meet with Jaquith. And when you go in the shop, you should look tired, like you just woke up. Remember, you have no job. You're a thief who operates after dark. Most days, you don't get back home until the crack of dawn."

"Night time is the right time, baby," Ellie joked.

Kendra gave her a high five. "You got that right, sister!"

Beck gave them both a pitiful look. *Really?*

"So, let's review," Jameson said. "You'll wait until after lunch to enter the shop. You'll want to dress appropriately. I'm thinking scuffed shoes, worn out jeans, maybe an untucked shirt…"

"Ah, yes," Ellie said. "A street urchin."

"I'd go with grunge," Kendra said. "Yeah. Definitely grunge."

"What if he wants to see the books?" Nathan asked.

"Too bad," Beck replied. "Money first. Then the books. And don't be afraid to use those words. After all…"

"I know, I know," Ellie said. "I'm a thief."

"But wait," Gina said. "Isn't he going to want some kind of proof?"

"Oh, trust me, he'll want proof," Jameson said. "And we'll give it to him."

"How do you propose we do that?" asked Beck.

"Take him a sample. Find the slip with the biggest number, the most valuable piece of artwork in the collection. Show him the book, and the slip, and that should convince him."

Nathan looked at Gina and said, "Where's your list?"

"What list?" Jameson asked.

"She made a list of all the numbers."

"Of course she did," Kendra said, fist-bumping Gina.

"So…I show him the book and the slip, and we discuss a price…" Ellie began.

"I'd be firm on a price," Jameson said. "But if he pushes, you could give a little."

"Agreed," Beck said. "Let him think he's getting the better of you. After that, you take the book and you leave. Tell him you'll be in touch the following day with a time and location for the exchange."

"Be sure to remind him that nothing happens until you see the money," Kendra said.

"And no cops!" Gina blurted out.

Nathan rolled his eyes. "Oh brother," he mumbled.

"Be quiet," she said. "I saw it in a movie."

Nathan looked at Kendra and smirked. "She saw it in a movie." Like that made it a thing.

Gina reached over and flicked him in the ear.

"All right you two, let's go," Ellie said, herding them toward the hallway. "We've got books to look at."

"They're not just books," Nathan said.

"She knows that," Gina sniped.

"Enough!" Ellie said.

The intoxicating aroma of fresh-brewed coffee pulled Kendra and Beck, like siren song, into the kitchen. Jameson remained in the living room and called Eric Fuller, a deputy marshal with the U.S. Marshals Service in Portland, and a member of the Special Operations Group. One week ago to the day, Fuller had assembled his team in South Berwick, Maine, to help apprehend Edouard Dampierre and the killer-for-hire Karl Odom. Jameson assumed it was still a sore subject with Fuller, given how his plan had unraveled. Still, protocol demanded that he contact him and apprise him of the situation.

True to form, Fuller answered on the first ring. "Jameson," he said, all business. "How did you make out?"

"Sorry to say, not as we would've liked," Jameson replied. "We thought we had her cornered but she managed to slip past us. Fortunately, we know where she went." In the background he could hear the sound of children playing, their voices shrieking with excitement. He envisioned them running through a sprinkler in the yard, arms flailing wildly.

"Hold on," Fuller said. "Let me go inside." Moments later, he came back on the line. "Sorry about that," he said. "You were saying?"

"We have confirmation from Martin Bishop that Ginette Dampierre entered the United States shortly after five p.m. on Friday."

"I wasn't aware of that," Fuller said. "Go on."

"She's obviously come here to rebuild the Covin's pipeline after the recent arrest of her brother, not to mention the confiscation of hundreds of crates of product. To catch her, we're going to use a trap, much like we did with Edouard. But since we have no idea how long she'll be in the Boston area, timing is critical." He paused briefly, then said, "Truth be told, the plan was Nathan's idea."

"Why am I not surprised to hear that?" Fuller said. "How *is* Nathan?"

"As good as can be expected, given what he went through," Jameson replied, implying that Nathan's near-death experience at the hands of Edouard Dampierre was going to leave an indelible mark on his psyche.

"He's an amazing kid," Fuller said. "I could use a few more like him up here in Portland. Now, this plan," he said, getting back on topic. "Did I hear you right? You're planning to set a trap for Ginette Dampierre?"

"Yes," Jameson said taking a seat on the couch. He gave Fuller a full rundown, starting with Gina's discovery with the slips of paper, Nathan's suggestion of using Carl Jaquith as a pawn, and Ellie's offer to set the hook.

"Sounds good," Fuller said. "Does Ginette Dampierre know you have the books?"

"No."

"That's good, but there's another matter you need to consider."

Jameson sensed what Fuller was about to say.

"This literature," Fuller said. "You say it was in Edouard Dampierre's office in Saco?"

"Yes."

"And it's linked to thefts committed by his organization?"

"That's right."

"Then Martin Bishop and the rest of Interpol are going to need it as evidence."

"The thought had crossed my mind," Jameson said.

"Have you told Bishop about it?" Fuller asked.

Elizabeth appeared in the entryway with a carafe of coffee and a clean mug. *Coffee?* she mouthed, raising the carafe in the air.

Jameson waved her off. *None for me, thanks.*

"Jameson?"

"Yes, I'm still here," he said. "To answer your question, no. Martin's not aware of the collection, its value to the Covin, or that we have it."

"Knowing how elusive Ginette Dampierre can be, I can provide manpower to help you apprehend her," Fuller said. "But I suggest you give Bishop a call. The sooner the better. With any luck, once he hears about your plan, it may buy you some time."

"Let's hope so," Jameson said.

"What's your timeframe?" Fuller asked.

"We go tomorrow afternoon."

"Very good. I'll get to work right away on assembling my team."

Jameson ended the call and then dialed Martin Bishop. "Martin" he said, after Bishop picked up. "It's Jameson. I need a huge favor."

Ellie stood next to the cube of boxes Nathan had constructed, her hand resting on the top layer. "This is all of them?" she asked.

"Yup," Nathan said.

"All right," she said. "Where's that list you were talking about?"

Gina pulled her notepad from her back pocket, turned to the list of numbers, then handed it to Ellie.

"Wow," she said, turning the pages slowly. "You said you had a list, but this looks more like a phone book." When she came to the last page, she handed the notepad back to Gina and said, "Find me the biggest number. While you're doing that, Nathan and I will open the boxes."

Five minutes later the boxes were opened and arranged in a row on the floor.

"Okay, what are we looking for?" Ellie asked.

"The number we want is 40.7."

"Forty point seven?" Ellie asked, making sure she'd heard it right. "That's the biggest number?"

"Oh, no, wait," Gina said. "It's 40.7 with a small 'm' after it."

"As in, 40.7 million dollars," Nathan explained.

"That's more like it," Ellie said.

Working quickly, the three of them went box by box, pulling out each periodical and checking the numbered slip tucked inside.

"Found it," Nathan called out, several minutes later. "In his hands was a copy of *Antiques & Fine Art* magazine, dated 1989.

Ellie took it from him and opened to the bookmarked page. She saw the photo of a painting on display at the Metropolitan Museum of Art in New York City. "*Au Lapin Agile,*" she said, reading from the photo caption. "Oil on canvas, by Pablo Picasso. Sold recently at Sotheby's for $40.7 million dollars."

"That's crazy!" Nathan said.

"Apparently not...for some people," Ellie muttered. She set the magazine on the workbench and grabbed the roll of packing tape. "Here," she said, tossing it to Gina. "You cut the tape. Nathan and I will reseal the boxes. And Nathan? When we're done, we need to cover them with a blanket or a tarp, to keep them hidden from prying eyes."

"You really think...?" Gina said, then paused for fear that saying it might make it come true.

"Better safe than sorry," Ellie said. Up to now, the kids hadn't noticed the spots of blood on the floor in the opposite corner. She was surprised Beck had missed them. After all, a man with his resume should know—you always clean up.

With the boxes sealed, and draped in a blue tarp Nathan found stored in the rafters, they left the garage and walked back to the house. Ellie pulled open the back door and stepped inside, and that's when Gina grabbed Nathan's arm and pulled him back.

"Hey, what are you doing?" he asked.

She put a finger to her lips. *Shhhh.*

What? he whispered.

"I found him," she said.
"You found who?"
"Arthur Chessman."

7

Natalie

Nathan awoke with a start, once again tormented by a woman's voice calling to him in his dreams. *"Please! Someone! Help me!"* He sat up and kicked away the covers as the voice, like an echo down a deep canyon, slowly faded away. He was rubbing the sleep from his eyes when a curious sound from somewhere nearby made him pull his hands from his face. He sat perfectly still, listening.

…SHH…

It sounded like two sheets of sandpaper rubbing together, but it was so faint and so brief that he wondered if he'd imagined it. Until he heard it again.

…SHH…

He surveyed the room from right to left, running his eyes over every surface.

...SHH...

When he discovered the source of the sound.

On his bedside table, Claire Jameson's book was inching toward the edge as if being nudged by an invisible hand.

...SHH...

It teetered momentarily and then fell to the floor with a loud *THUNK!*

From out in the hallway, his mother called to him. "Nathan? Are you all right?"

He scrambled out of bed and snatched the book off the floor when the door suddenly opened and she ducked her head inside.

"Nathan?"

"I'm fine Mom. I just dropped something, that's all."

"Well, that's a relief," she said. "I could've sworn you fell out of bed."

He waited until she closed the door, then climbed back in bed and opened the book. This wasn't the first time he'd seen a book launch itself off a table, or fall out of a bookcase all by itself. Strange things like that had been happening ever since he first discovered his grandfather's bookcase in the attic. At this point he was well past any feelings of shock or fear at the sight of such occurrences. Even if he wanted to, there wasn't anyone he could talk to about it, other than Gina. No one else would believe him.

Seeing the book plummet to the floor only confirmed his curiosity about the Whitehall property and Claire Jameson's suspicion about it. He leaned back against the headboard and plowed through the Whitehall chapter again. When he was done, he pored over every picture of the giant castle-like structure: the lush grounds;

clay tennis courts, the flower gardens, all meticulously maintained; the upper terraces that overlooked the ocean, and the enormous granite and bluestone patio that stretched along the back.

Equally impressive was the interior, with its cathedral ceilings, cavernous formal dining room with Tudor-style oak paneling, and the twin staircases that curved upward to the second floor like the horns of a Moulton ram.

Sprinkled throughout the pages were historical pictures that showed the building's architectural timeline through the years. In one, there was an old carriage house at the back corner of the property, seemingly untouched by the ravages of time and the harsh New England weather.

He pored over every picture, every word, but nothing stood out. He couldn't find a single thing linking the structure to the Covin. But a clue was buried somewhere in those pages, he was sure of it. Unless there was something Jameson hadn't told him.

Just after ten o'clock, Elizabeth was bringing a basket of laundry up from the basement when the doorbell sounded. She opened the front door and saw a young woman in her mid 20s, dressed in a crisp slate-blue pantsuit. In her hand was a single Manila folder. She had a narrow face with almond eyes and thick brown hair that fell loosely over both shoulders.

"May I help you?" Elizabeth asked.

"Elizabeth Cole?" the woman said nervously.

"Yes?"

"Hi, I'm Natalie?" she said, as if seeking permission to have that name. "The school hired me as a temp while…you know…you're out."

"Good!" Elizabeth exclaimed. "That means I won't find my desk buried under a mountain of paperwork when I return. Natalie was it? Please, come in." She pushed the screen door open and Natalie stepped inside.

"I have some papers that need your signature," Natalie said, "and…well…I thought I'd bring them by because that way I could… you know…introduce myself."

"Of course," Elizabeth said, trying to put the girl at ease. "Why don't we go into the living room. Can I get you some coffee?"

"Coffee? That would be great," Natalie gushed. "That stuff they serve at school…it tastes like…I don't know…"

"Pond water?" Elizabeth joked.

Natalie giggled, then nodded her head. *Yes.*

"Well, you won't find any pond water in *this* house," Elizabeth said. "We have a good friend who owns a coffee shop, and she keeps us stocked with only the best. Now, the living room is right through that entryway," she said, pointing. "Why don't you have a seat while I brew us a nice fresh pot."

Natalie offered a sheepish nod, then went into the living room and sat down on the end of the couch. She hadn't been there long when Nathan came bounding down the front hall stairs. He raced past the entryway, then skidded to a stop on the hardwood floor and took several steps back.

"Hello," he said, eyeing Natalie with a confounded expression. *Who are you and what are you doing in my house?* he was tempted to ask.

Natalie gave him a short wave. "Hi…um…I'm Natalie."

From the kitchen came the snarl of the coffee grinder as it

chewed through a generous helping of Ethiopian Sidamo coffee beans.

"I'm Nathan."

"Sorry," Natalie said. "What was that?"

"NAY-THAN," he said, nearly shouting.

The grinder stopped and silence filled the room.

"Oh," she said, embarrassed. "I thought you said Nason."

He gave her a curious look. *Nason? Is that even a name?*

"I'm here to…uh…see your mom," Natalie said. "She's making us some coffee."

Nathan nodded slowly. *Yup, I kinda figured that out already.*

"Are you excited to…you know…start school next month?"

Nathan stared at her, flat faced. *You're kidding, right?*

"I loved school…I mean…when I was your age," she said. "Not that…you know…I don't like working there now."

Love? School? Nathan thought. Never.

His mother appeared at his side. "Oh good, you're up," she said. "When do you have to be at work?"

"Not until one o'clock."

"Well, that doesn't give you much time. You need to eat, shower, and get dressed, so I suggest you get a move on." She watched him bolt down the hallway to the kitchen, then shook her head. "Boys," she said.

"A job? Wow," Natalie said. "What I mean is…that's impressive… you know…for someone his age."

"Our good friend has hired him to help sort books in his barn. Books are a big thing in our family, so when Richard offered him the job, it was hard for Nathan to say no."

"Sorting books...that sounds like...I don't know...a dream job," Natalie said. "Not that...you know...working in an office is a bad thing."

As Nathan sat at the kitchen counter devouring one English muffin after another, he could hear the two women talking in the living room, their chatter echoing down the hallway for what seemed like an eternity.

"And just one more," Natalie said, sliding the last document across the coffee table.

Elizabeth reviewed it briefly and then scribbled her name at the bottom. "How are things at the office?" she asked.

"Crazy," Natalie said, like she couldn't believe she'd agreed to the job. "But for you...I'm guessing...you know...it's normal, right?"

"It's like swimming in an icy river," Elizabeth joked. "You have to numb up to it."

Natalie took the last sip of her coffee and set the mug on the table. "Well, I should, um, get back," she said. She pulled a small piece of notepad paper from the folder and handed it to Elizabeth. "This has my cell number," she said. "It's the quickest way to...you know...reach me if you have a question, or if you...I don't know... remember something you forgot to do." No sooner had the words left her lips than a look of dread crossed her face. "I'm not saying that...you know...you're sloppy or anything. Your office is...like... super organized. I just meant that...well...if there's something—"

"That's fine," Elizabeth cut in, taking the note from her.

Natalie closed the folder and stood up like she wanted to run from the room and never return. As they walked to the front door, she said, "Do you know when you'll be back?"

"Uh…" Elizabeth said, guessing. "I want to say…Friday?"

"I hate to ask this but…um…until then…do you mind if…you know…I call you if I have a question?"

"Please," Elizabeth said, like it was a silly question. "Call me anytime. I'm happy to help."

Natalie let out a sigh of relief. "Thank you."

Ellie walked into the kitchen dressed in a pair of unwashed blue jeans that she pulled from the laundry hamper that very morning, along with a ratty Wailers tee shirt. The beat-up sneakers on her feet came from the bottom of the gym bag she kept stashed in the back seat of her car, and the slightly soiled gray hoodie came from the trunk.

She had skipped her regular morning shower and hair regimen and had the look of someone who had just crawled out from under the porch, or simply didn't care about the way they appeared to others.

Gina was sitting at the table, pencil in hand, her face buried in a book of word-search puzzles. Lying on the table nearby was a 9" x 12" catalog envelope with the information she'd collected for Nathan.

"What do you think?" Ellie asked, doing a quick pirouette.

Gina eyed her from head to toe. "Lovely," she said, smirking. "Think he'll buy it?"

"I guess we'll find out," Ellie replied. "The more important question is, what am I going to do with you?"

"Uh…I *can* stay home alone, you know."

"Not gonna happen," Ellie said.

"Fine, then take me with you."

"*Absolutely* not gonna happen." Through the window on the far wall she could see Kendra's Volvo parked in Nathan's driveway. Right behind it was another car she didn't recognize. "I know," she said. "Follow me."

They crossed the lawn and were approaching the back door of Nathan's house when Ellie spotted a woman she didn't recognize standing at the side of the garage door, peering through the window. "HEY!" she shouted, making a bee line for the garage. "What do you think you're doing?"

Bev McKinney spun around, saw Ellie in her street urchin attire, and raised both hands in surrender. "I'm sorry, I'm sorry," she said. "I was just looking for Nathan. Have you seen him?"

"No," Ellie said. "What makes you think he'd be in the garage?"

The fierce look on Ellie's face made Bev take a step back. "Uh… I'm not really sure," she said. "I guess I thought— "

"Who are you?" Ellie demanded, cutting her off.

"Bev McKinney. I'm new to the neighborhood. Perhaps Elizabeth mentioned me?"

"No, as a matter of fact she didn't."

"Hmm, that's odd. I spoke with her about hiring Nathan to move some boxes for me."

"What kind of boxes?" Ellie asked.

"Oh, just some things I need to put into storage."

"Good luck with that," Gina muttered.

The back door slammed and they all turned to see Kendra walking toward them.

"What's going on here?" she asked, pushing her sleeves up as she made her way across the lawn.

"Somebody looking for Nathan," Ellie replied, never taking her eyes off of Bev. Something about the woman just seemed off.

"Nathan is unavailable," Kendra said, stopping inches away from Bev.

"You know," Bev said, "I can come back another time." She eased between Ellie and Kendra and walked briskly to her car. She was backing out of the driveway when Nathan came out the back door.

"Who was that?" he asked.

"Some woman who wants to hire you to move boxes," Gina said. "I told her you only move really heavy ones, and you don't mind smelly basements or spider-infested attics."

Nathan gave her a tired look. "Very funny."

"She told us she spoke with your mom about it," Ellie said.

Nathan shrugged. "That's news to me."

"Yeah, well, let me know if she comes around again?"

"Whatever you say."

After lunch, Kendra, Nathan, and Gina piled into the Volvo. Kendra liked the idea of bringing Gina because it would give her someone to talk to while she waited.

They were backing out of the driveway when a red BMW sedan approached from the far end of the street. Kendra pulled over to give it room to pass, but the driver slowed to a stop next to her, lowered the window, and made a circular motion with her finger, signaling Kendra to do the same.

"Who's this?" Kendra muttered, as she reached for the window's crank handle.

Nathan leaned forward to take a look and recognized the driver

120

at once. "You don't remember?" he asked.

"No," Kendra said, defensively. "Should I?"

"Well...*yeah.*"

"Good afternoon," Jordan Prescott said, through the open window.

Suddenly, Kendra remembered. "Oh, I remember you," she said. "Richard Abbott's barn, right?"

"Very good," Jordan replied, looking annoyed that it took Kendra so long to figure it out. She looked past Kendra and saw Nathan sitting in the passenger seat. "Mr. Cole," she said. "I wanted to thank you for your help. The book was even better than I had anticipated."

Nathan flashed a thumbs up. "Happy to help," he said.

"Give me a break," Gina muttered under her breath.

Nathan shot her a nasty look.

"Perhaps I'll stop by again," Jordan said. "I have several other titles in mind."

Nathan shrugged. *Sure, whatever.*

"Until next time, then?"

The window went up without a sound and the car pulled away.

"Someone has a girlfriend," Gina said in a sing-song voice.

"It's not like that," Nathan said.

"Oh really? Did you give her your home address?"

"No." *Why would I do that?*

"Then how come she knows where you live?"

"An excellent question," Kendra said, as she pulled away from Nathan's driveway. She checked the rearview mirror expecting to see Prescott's car in the distance, but the road was clear.

Gina leaned forward and tossed the catalog envelope into

Nathan's lap.

"What's this?" he asked, examining both sides of it.

"Uh…the information you asked me to find?" she said. "Remember?"

"Oh, yeah, thanks. How did it go?"

"The first thing was a piece of cake," she replied. "The second thing? Not so much."

Kendra came to a stop at the end of the street and glanced at the envelope. "Is that something I should be worried about?"

"I'll let you know," Nathan said. He tucked it under his seat, then twisted around to face Gina. "What was that thing you said about Arthur Chessman?"

"Arthur Chessman? Who's that?" Kendra asked. She looked both ways, then cranked the wheel to the right and punched the gas. Gina grabbed hold of the armrest with both hands and waited until the car had straightened out before answering.

"He's the one who made all those little slips of paper," she said.

"How do you know that?" Kendra asked.

Gina explained the embossed letters on the back of the slips, how they'd been cut from pieces of stationery, and by working and reworking them she'd come up with only one possible name: Arthur Chessman.

Suddenly, Kendra leaned on the horn and shouted, "JUST TURN ALREADY!"

Gina looked back and saw the driver shaking his fist at them through his open window.

Kendra saw it in the rearview mirror and yelled, "GET OVER IT YOU CLOWN!"

"Must you?" Nathan asked, giving her a disapproving look.

"The guy was taking all day to turn," she said. "What was I supposed to do?"

"I could think of several things," Nathan muttered under his breath.

"I'm sorry, what was that?"

"Never mind," he said. He looked back at Gina, who was still clutching the armrest. "You said something about finding Arthur Chessman. Was that for real?"

"Of course," she said, frowning. "What did you think? I made it up?"

"No, it's not that," he said quickly. "It's just…I have a few questions I'd like to ask him, that's all." He waited a beat, then said, "So, how'd you do it?"

"I started by doing a computer search for his name."

"And you found him? Just like that?"

"Not even close," she said. "There were, like, a million listings for Chessman in Massachusetts, New Hampshire, and Maine. It was crazy."

"But…" he said, prompting her to continue.

"One of them stood out," she said.

"And that was…"

"Arthur Chessman, in Wolfeboro, NH."

"And he was different from the others because…?"

She gave him the death stare. "You keep doing that and I won't tell you."

"Okay, fine, I'll stop," he said. He waited several seconds, then spoke like they were two old friends swapping juicy bits of gossip over lunch. "So, tell me," he said. "Arthur Chessman. You know, the one from Wolfeboro, NH? What's *his* deal?"

Sometimes she could just slap him.

"He owned an antiquarian bookstore," she said.

A knowing look fell across Nathan's face. "Of course," he said. "Bookstore owner. Combing through books looking for art to steal." Then his expression changed. "You said 'owned'."

"Yeah. I tried calling the number but it was no longer in service. Luckily, I was able to reach someone in the fabric store across the street."

"Wait," Kendra said. "How did you know there was a fabric store across the street?"

"I used a map program on the computer," Gina explained.

"Cool."

Nathan and Gina exchanged a look. *Old people.*

"So…back to the person in the fabric store," Nathan said.

"Her name was Marge. She was very nice. Kept calling me 'dear', like she was my grandmother. She said the bookstore closed over a year ago."

"Did she say anything about Arthur?"

"Yup. The last she'd heard, he was living in Weston, Massachusetts, at some place called Boxberry Green."

Ellie left for Maine at 11 o'clock. By her calculations, Wells was a little over an hour away. Factoring in a lunch stop in Ogunquit, at whatever seafood restaurant had the shortest wait time, she'd arrive at Jaquith Antiques just before one o'clock. Sitting on the passenger seat next to her was the *Antiques & Fine Art* magazine, with the slip marked 40.7m.

She was cruising up Rt. 1 in Ogunquit when she spotted Olson's, a small dilapidated clam shack that wasn't much bigger than the bathroom in Gina's house. It sat back from the road on a rough dirt lot with a rectangular sign on the roof that boasted "Maine's Best Clams." Much like the dingy white shingles on the outside of the structure, the red lettering was faded and flaked with age. Picnic tables were scattered about beneath the overhanging branches of the towering pine trees that lined the back edge of the property.

She pulled into the small dirt parking lot and within 15 minutes she was seated at one of the picnic tables, staring down a heaping plate of soft-belly clams. She had just started attacking the pile when, out of nowhere, Beck appeared. He straddled the bench seat across from her and sat down, making the whole table rock.

"Well, well, this is a surprise," she said.

He took one look at the clams and shook his head, sadly.

"What?" she asked defensively.

"I never took you for the soft-belly type."

"They were out of filet mignon," she said, pulling a clam from the top of the pile. She flashed him a smile and then shoved it in her mouth, her eyes clamped shut as she savored every delicious moment.

Beck shifted his position on the bench so he could watch the street. He looked left, then right, taking note of the landscape, the people, and the serpent-like parade of cars crawling along Rt. 1 in both directions.

"Looking for something?" Ellie asked as she reached for another clam.

"Always," he replied. He watched a jacked-up Dodge Ram pull

into the lot, leaving a cloud of dust in its wake. The doors squeaked open and two boys barely 20 years old jumped down from the cab and shuffled over to the shack.

"Fishermen," Ellie said.

"Excuse me?"

"Those two guys," she said, nodding in their direction. "They're fishermen."

"You think so, huh?"

"Yup," she said. "Want to know how I know?"

"Do tell."

"The rubber boots," she said. "I'll bet you a crab cake dinner that those two spent the morning pulling lobster traps." She dipped another clam in the small plastic container of butter and then popped it in her mouth. As she chewed she pointed at the plate. *You want one?*

"No thanks, I'm good," Beck said, then turned back to the passing traffic.

"Not a clam guy?" she asked.

"Mahi-mahi is more my style."

"Why does that not surprise me?"

Several seconds passed and neither of them spoke, the obvious question hanging in the air between them. The two guys from the truck appeared, carrying plates of seafood, and sat down two tables away.

"So…are you going to tell me?" Ellie asked, breaking the silence.

"Tell you what?"

"Why you followed me here."

Kendra drove up the crushed stone driveway past Richard Abbott's house and came to a stop in front of the barn. The humid summer air seemed to be stuck in time, refusing to move, carrying with it the heat of the day which had already climbed into the mid 90s.

"How long?" she asked.

"Give me an hour," Nathan said. "I'll see how far I get."

As Kendra backed down the driveway, he walked over to the barn door and paused. It was partially open, and through the narrow opening he could see two new pallets of books that hadn't been there when he left the day before. "Great," he said. "More pallets."

When he slipped inside, the new pallets were blocking the light switch and he had to squeeze between them to reach it. He gave it a flick with his finger and nothing happened. He tried again. Still nothing.

"You're late," Niko said.

Nathan spun his head around, expecting to see someone standing behind him. But all he saw was a wall of solid black. "Who is that?" he called out.

There was no answer.

Just the sound of footsteps moving quickly across the old plank floor.

He turned back to the wall and tried the light switch again, flicking it repeatedly.

"Don't bother," Niko said.

She was closer now.

When the barn door began to close, he pried himself free of the two pallets and lunged at it, trying to stop it before it closed completely and sealed off what little light there was.

Too late.

It rambled shut, and try as he might, he couldn't get it to open—something was holding it shut.

"Relax," Niko said, her voice eerily calm. "I'll make this quick."

8

Periodicals

Beck looked down at his watch. It was almost 12:45 p.m. "It's about time you got going, don't you think?" he said.

Ellie pushed what was left of the clams away and used a cheap paper napkin to wipe her hands. "You still haven't told me what you're doing here."

"I'm your shadow."

"My shadow?" she said. "Don't tell me you're worried about me."

"Worried about you? No. Not in the least. I'm here to see what Jaquith does after he hears what you have to say."

"Smart," she said, nodding her approval.

"I have my moments."

Yes, you do, she thought. She finished wiping her hands and tossed the spent napkin on top of the plate. "So, you're going to hang around and watch?"

"Something like that."

"And what if it all goes sideways?"

"It won't," he said.

"What makes you say that?"

"Because I won't let it."

As Nathan's eyes adjusted to the dark, he began to make out vague shapes. Rough outlines in muted shades of black and brown. The only one that concerned him at the moment was the silhouette of the woman standing less than 10 feet away.

"Why are you doing this?" he asked, slowly inching away from her.

"Why am I doing this?" Niko repeated. She moved with him step for step as if they were connected by an unbreakable cord. "Honestly, I have no idea. She didn't tell me the reason."

She.

Suddenly it all made sense.

This was Ginette Dampierre's revenge. The very thing Jameson had foreseen. How this woman had come to find him was disturbing, but Jameson had warned them in no uncertain terms—payback was coming. Lethal payback.

The actual word he used was "carnage."

"You should know...there are people coming to check on me," Nathan said. "They'll be here any minute."

"You mean the woman and the girl who dropped you off? You told them to come back in an hour, remember?"

A stab of dread rocked Nathan's body. Whoever this woman was, she had obviously snuck into the barn before he arrived, which explained the partially opened door. From that vantage point, she was able to hear everything he'd said to Kendra.

"I wouldn't count on your friends," Niko said. "By the time they come to check on you it'll be too late."

That voice, Nathan thought. *I've heard it before, but where?* He considered shouting for help but quickly dismissed the idea. There was no way Kendra or Gina would hear him. Or anyone else for that matter. Blinded by the darkness, and unable to clearly see his attacker, he was left with only one option.

Lesson #2: if someone attacks you, get out of the way.

He turned and ran toward the back of the barn, the layout imprinted in his memory from long days of sorting books.

Pallets on the right.

Farmers table on the left.

Empty pallets and flattened cardboard boxes piled against the back wall.

He'd gone less than ten feet when he felt a hand grab his shoulder. The fingernails, like pointed razors, digging into his skin through the fabric, stopping him in his tracks.

"So, what now?" Gina asked. "We just sit here and wait?" She had moved up to the front seat and rolled down the window. For what good that did. Even though the car was blanketed by the shade of two giant oak trees in front of Richard's house, it still felt like she was sitting under a heat lamp.

"Yup," Kendra said. "We wait and we watch." She eyed the oncoming traffic, then checked the side mirror. Seeing nothing suspicious, she pulled her phone from the cup holder in the center console and checked for any messages. There was no word from Jameson about Ellie's visit to Jaquith Antiques, but it was early yet. She put the phone back in the cup holder and resumed her vigil, watching the seemingly endless flow of traffic. "Tell me more about this Arthur Chessman guy," she said, trying to make conversation.

"What's to tell?" Gina said. "He was the one who identified the artwork that was ultimately stolen by the Covin. And I'm talking about real valuable stuff. Some of the most expensive artwork on the planet."

"So, he identifies it," Kendra said, trying to understand. "He determines its value. But who ran the crew?"

"You mean, who told them what to steal, and where, and when?"

"Yeah."

"Who knows?" Gina said. "It could've been anyone. Edouard Dampierre. Arthur Chessman. Maybe someone we don't know about. There's really no way of knowing...unless..." "Unless what? Kendra asked.

"We could always go ask him," Gina said.

"Who are you talking about?"

"Arthur Chessman."

"*What?*" Kendra snapped. "You want to drive to Blueberry Lane and—"

"Boxberry Green."

"Huh?"

"It's called Boxberry Green," Gina said.

"Oh, excuse me...*Boxberry Green*," Kendra said with a smirk. It sounded like the kind of decorative roping people strung across their mantle at Christmas time. "You think you can just march in there and start asking him questions?" she asked.

"Why not?" Gina said.

"Well, let's see. First of all, he works for the Covin. You do remember them, right? International art thieves? Ruthless killers?"

"He's not like that," Gina said. "At least, not anymore."

"What makes you say that?"

"Boxberry Green is a CCRC."

"A what?" Kendra asked.

"A continuing care retirement community."

"O-kay," Kendra said, confused. "Why is that important?"

"Because according to Marge, the nice lady in the fabric store? They're one of the top-rated memory care facilities in the country."

"Memory care," Kendra repeated.

"Uh-huh," Gina said. "Arthur Chessman may be a lot of things, but dangerous isn't one of them. Trust me."

Nathan tried to break free, but Niko yanked him backward, tripping him with her leg and slinging him face-first onto the hard plank floor. He tried to get up but she ground her knee into his back, then leaned down until their heads were almost touching. When she spoke, he could feel her hot breath on the side of his face.

"You should be more careful," she said. "Running in the dark like that? You could have an accident. Now, *let's go!*" she growled. She yanked him up off the floor like a hooked fish and dragged him through the darkness toward the back of the barn.

As they passed the row of pallets, his hand brushed an open box of books. Ignoring the pain that stung his shoulder, he planted his foot on the floor and pulled back, stopping her long enough to pull a thick hardcover book from the box.

"Come along now," she said, like they were window shopping. "We're almost there."

She jerked him forward and he lurched headlong into the dark, holding the book low at his side. As they neared the back wall, he raised the book in the air and slammed the spine down on her wrist with a hard tomahawk chop. She grunted in pain and her hand went limp, giving him the opening he needed.

He dropped the book, balled his fists and charged, pushing her across the floor. As she staggered backward, she spun her body and used both hands to fling him against the back wall.

He hit it head-first and blacked out, then dropped to the floor like a wet towel.

Jaquith Antiques was housed in an old Federal-style building that once served as a carriage stop and tavern along the Kennebunk Road, the coastal route that connected Massachusetts and Augusta, Maine. The entire structure was bone white, with a gabled roof, traditional six over six double-hung windows, and flat lintels. A set of thick granite steps led up to the four-paneled front door that featured a semi-elliptical fanlight and narrow sidelights.

Ellie drove past it slowly, then pulled to the curb several hundred feet down the street. Before she got out of the car she tucked the art magazine inside her hoodie, ruffled her hair, and then pulled the hood over her head.

As she walked back down the sidewalk, she stopped periodically to check the street in both directions. Seeing nothing suspicious, she continued on to the antique shop, climbed the granite steps, and pushed through the front door. Once inside, she swept her eyes from left to right, making a mental inventory of the layout.

She was in a small foyer. Positioned in the corner to her left was an antique mahogany stand-up desk. To her right, through an arched entryway, was a large open gallery. Directly ahead was a carpeted stairway leading up to the second floor, and to the right of that was a central hallway that stretched to the back of the building.

"Well good morning," came a voice from the top of the stairs.

She looked up and saw a man in his mid 30s, dressed in a shiny French-blue dress shirt and gray dress slacks. His thick-flowing brown hair was combed back in a wave, giving him a decidedly preppy look.

He came down the stairs, studying her from top to bottom with an uncertain look. "How may I help you?" he asked.

"I need to speak to the owner," Ellie said. The tone in her voice indicated that she wouldn't take no for an answer.

"And who are you?" the man asked.

"You first," she said, playing the tough girl role.

"My name is Charles," he said graciously.

"Are you the owner?" she asked, knowing full well that he wasn't.

"The owner? Oh, no," Charles said, rolling his eyes. "Don't I wish."

"Right. So here's what you're gonna do, *Charles*. Go find your boss. Tell him I have something he needs to see."

"Can I tell him what it is?"

"No."

"I see," Charles said. "Well, at the moment I believe Mr. Jaquith is in conference with a client."

"You believe?" She took a step forward, crowding him. "How about you go find out for sure?"

"Uh…yes, of course," Charles stammered, inching backward.

"Oh, and one more thing," Ellie said. "When you talk to him, be sure to mention the Hamilton Mill."

"I'm sorry?" Charles said.

"The Hamilton Mill," she said again, slower. "In Saco."

"The Hamilton Mill in Saco," Charles repeated carefully, as if answering a test question aloud. "You wait here and I'll go see if Mr. Jaquith can make time for you."

"Yeah, you do that," Ellie said.

Charles hurried back up the stairs and followed the hallway to Jaquith's office. When he walked through the open door, Carl was seated behind his late 1800s French ormolu-mounted mahogany pedestal desk. In his hand was a large wood-handled magnifying glass that he was using to inspect an original manuscript leaf from Sir Arthur Conan Doyle's *The Hound of the Baskervilles*, valued at roughly $100,000.

Jaquith heard Charles enter the room but didn't look up. "Yes?" he asked.

"There's a young lady downstairs who insists on speaking with you."

"Did she give you her name?" Jaquith asked, leaning closer to inspect the rough edge of the manuscript.

"No," Charles said.

"Did she say why she needed to speak with me?"

"Uh…yes and no."

"What does that mean?"

"She said to tell you she has something you need to see."

"Did she say what it was?" Jaquith asked, moving the magnifying glass slowly across the paper.

"No, but she wanted me to mention the Hamilton Mill in Saco."

Jaquith stopped what he was doing and looked up, his face momentarily frozen. "You're sure she said the Hamilton Mill?" he asked.

"Yes."

Jaquith set the magnifying glass on the desk, then gently placed the manuscript in a side drawer. "Where is she?" he asked, pushing his chair away from the desk.

"Waiting in the front hall," Charles replied.

Jaquith stood and made his way toward the door, straightening his tie as he walked. "If anyone calls," he said, "take a message."

Nathan regained consciousness just as Niko was rolling him over onto his back. She hooked her hands under his arms and dragged him backward across the floor. As they passed a tall stack of wooden pallets, he turned his foot and caught the corner, stopping her in her tracks. She pulled once, then again. When that didn't work, she muttered something under her breath and dropped him on the floor.

As she leaned across his body, trying to dislodge his sneaker, he unleashed a vicious kick to her head with his left foot. The impact sent her tumbling backward, clutching her face in her hands. Before she could regain her balance, he climbed to his feet and charged forward, driving his shoulder into her stomach. The force sent her staggering backward into the corner where she fell through the open hole in the floor, into the darkness below.

Ellie was peering out at the street through one of the sidelights when Jaquith came down the stairs, the creaking of the treads muffled by the blood-red Persian carpet runner.

"Good afternoon," he said, when he reached the bottom step.

She turned from the window and quickly sized him up. Medium height. Expertly coifed hair. Slate-gray Brunello Cucinelli pinstripe suit. Turnbull & Asser silk tie. Berluti calf-leather oxfords. The man was literally bleeding money.

"My name is Carl Jaquith," he said. "How may I be of assistance?"

"You got a place we can talk…just you and me?" Ellie said, keeping her language purposefully crude and unsophisticated.

"Why, certainly," Jaquith replied. He gestured toward the entryway to his left. "Right this way."

He led Ellie through the large gallery, weaving his way past a stunning collection of fine antiques that were tastefully arranged on the floor. The walls were decorated with an equally impressive selection of paintings, gilded mirrors, and war memorabilia.

He walked to the far end of the room, to a set of ornate 19th century French doors that opened into a private viewing room. Inside were a pair of paintings by 18th century Italian artist Antonio Joli. They were displayed on separate easels that were set a few feet apart and angled inward. Each featured a different view of the Gulf of Pozzuoli in Naples, Italy. The first, from the northeast, with the islands of Capri and Ischia in the distance. The second, from the southwest, showing the island of Procida.

Jaquith showed her into the room, then closed the doors. "Now, what brings you to my shop today?" he asked. "Charles mentioned something about the Hamilton Mill?"

"Yeah. That's where I got this," Ellie said, fishing out the copy of *Antiques & Fine Art* magazine from inside her hoodie.

"Ah, yes, a very fine publication," Jaquith said, eyeing it with mild interest.

"That old mill?" she said. "You know it got raided last week, right?"

"Yes, I...uh...seem to recall hearing something about that," Jaquith said.

"Well, I went in for a little look-see after the marshals were done going through the place. In the office on the top floor I found an old bookcase filled with all kinds of books and magazines...everything to do with old furniture, paintings, you name it."

Jaquith said nothing. He remembered seeing the old bookcase during his visits to the mill, but Edouard never spoke of it and he had never bothered to ask. He just assumed it was some curious artifact Edouard had used to cover the rough brick wall between the windows.

"You say you actually went into the mill?"

Ellie nodded.

"Curious," he said. "Someone told me the U.S. Marshals had it locked down tight."

"Please," Ellie said, frowning. "Like that could stop me." She opened the magazine to the photo of Picasso's *Au Lapin Agile*, with the small slip of paper wedged into the binding, and handed it to him.

Jaquith gave the photo a cursory glance, then removed the slip. "What's this?" he asked.

"You tell me" Ellie said. "Everything from the bookcase has one.

They're like…what do you call them?"

"Bookmarks?" Jaquith said.

"Yeah, that's it, bookmarks."

Jaquith pulled the slip closer and read the uncircled number: 40.7m. Something about it seemed vaguely familiar. *Where have I heard that number before?* he asked himself.

Then he remembered.

And it sent a jolt through his body.

It was years earlier, during a conversation he'd had with Edouard. They were discussing the healthy flow of new arrivals when Edouard revealed that he'd recently hired a scout, a man he referred to only as "the Watchman," whose sole job was to locate priceless pieces of art.

Edouard's words were charged with excitement because the Watchman's most recent discovery stood to reap millions of dollars for the Covin. While he never mentioned the Picasso painting by name, the dollar figure he quoted was 40.7 million.

Unfortunately for the Covin, the acquisition never happened. An undercover policeman overheard the thieves talking about the robbery days before the job was to take place and the thieves were subsequently caught as they attempted to break into the museum. Ever since that day, the painting continued to hold a place of prominence in the Metropolitan Museum of Art—a painful reminder of the Covin's abject failure.

Jaquith blinked hard as the realization hit him. This "Watchman" was scouring books and magazines in search of priceless antiques, and Edouard was stockpiling them in the old bookcase. Then, one by one, he had systematically orchestrated the robberies of those pieces, lining the Covin's pockets with hundreds of millions of dollars.

Jaquith couldn't help but wonder what other treasures lay hidden in the Watchman's collection. "You say every periodical from the bookcase has one of these slips?" he asked.

"Periodical?" Ellie asked, feigning ignorance. "What's that?"

"The books, the magazines…"

"Yeah, they all have one," Ellie said. "I couldn't tell you what they mean, but they look important."

"How many more do you have?" Jaquith asked.

"I have all of 'em…everything from the bookcase."

He closed of the magazine and stared at the cover, his suspicion kicking in. "Why me?" he said.

"Why *not* you?" she shot back, pretending to be annoyed by the question. "You buy and sell antiques, right?"

"Yes," he said. "We're an eclectic shop with a specialty in—"

"Yeah, yeah, yeah, I get it," she cut in, like she was in no mood for a tiresome elevator speech. "These… *periodicals*…are all about antiques, so I figured you might want 'em. But, hey, if you don't, no problem," she said, plucking the magazine out of his hand. "I'll find somebody else."

"No, that won't be necessary. I'll take the entire collection," he said. "How much?"

"Twenty thousand."

"Five," he said.

"Ten," Ellie countered.

He reached for her hand. "Done."

After they shook, Ellie said, "I'll call you with a time and place for the exchange. You got a card or somethin'?"

Jaquith pulled a business card from his coat pocket and scribbled his cell phone number on the back. "Best to call me at this number," he said, handing her the card.

She glanced at it briefly and then shoved it in the back pocket of her jeans. "I'll be in touch. And just so we're clear. No money? No *periodicals*. Understood?"

"Of course," Jaquith said, like he dealt with petty thieves on a regular basis. "I look forward to your call."

Minutes before Ellie stepped through the front door, Beck had snuck in the back of the building through a metal door that opened into small utility room. From there, he made his way to the main hallway and hid behind a recently acquired 1800s linen press cupboard that stood over six feet high. From there, he watched Ellie's interaction with Charles, followed by her conversation with Jaquith.

When the two left the foyer and went into the private viewing room, Beck moved across the hall, to an adjoining set of doors used for bringing large pieces in and out of the main gallery. With his ear pressed against the door, he listened to their conversation, picking up only muffled bits and pieces.

At the conclusion of the meeting, while Jaquith was escorting Ellie to the front door, Beck ducked back behind the linen cupboard. Jaquith let Ellie out, then stood at the window and watched her walk away. When she was out of sight, he pulled his phone from his pocket and made a call, his words finding their way down the long hallway.

At the conclusion of the call, after Jaquith had gone back upstairs, Beck slipped out of the building like a ghost, leaving just as quietly as he had entered.

Ginette Dampierre was sitting on the balcony of her hotel suite enjoying a bowl of Som Tum Thai. Considering how her morning had gone thus far, the spicy papaya salad was the only bright spot in an otherwise lackluster day. It was Monday afternoon and she still hadn't heard from Pantano, whom she assumed was face down on the floor of his condo, passed out after a weekend of too much single malt whiskey.

Her pursuit of the man her brother called "the Watchman" had hit a dead end, and the mood among the shopkeepers was growing sour. Business had been good under Edouard's watchful eye, but now they were openly cautious around her. *Probably wondering if Edouard's older sister has the moxie to run the family business*, she told herself.

She was finishing the last of the salad when her cellphone buzzed on the small glass-top table next to her chair. When she read Carl Jaquith's name on the screen, grumbled something under her breath, and then reluctantly took the call. She was in no mood to hear about a smelly Persian carpet. "What is it, Carl?" she asked impatiently.

Jaquith explained his mysterious visitor, and the potential goldmine that had just fallen into his lap—one that Edouard had kept a secret for years. As he spoke, she set the empty salad bowl aside and smiled.

Maybe this day had promise after all.

Gina began to fidget. Her back was aching and she couldn't believe she hadn't brought a puzzle magazine with her. Something, anything, to pass the time. Finally, she couldn't stand it any longer.

"Can I get out and stretch my legs?" she asked.

"Of course," Kendra said.

Gina opened the door and climbed out. As she doing a standing calf stretch on the sidewalk, she saw Nathan come running down the driveway. Something about his face was all wrong. He looked as scared as she'd ever seen him, and he was unsteady on his feet, moving like his legs were made of rubber and might give out at any moment. "Uh, Kendra?" she said, watching him cut across the front lawn.

"Yeah?"

"Something's not right."

Kendra jumped out of the car and saw Nathan charging toward them, waving both hands wildly in the air as if the house was set to explode and they should get as far away as possible. "Gina, get in the car, *now!*" she barked, then slid back behind the wheel. She had just started the car when the back door opened and Nathan launched himself onto the back seat.

"What's wrong?" she asked, seeing the look of fear on his face.

He pushed himself up into a sitting position and pulled the door shut. "GO!" he shouted.

"Alright, I'm going, I'm going," she said. She stomped on the gas pedal, sending the Volvo rocketing forward into the street ahead of an approaching electric company bucket truck.

Gina wrenched her body around in the seat. "What happened?"

Nathan looked back and saw no one chasing them, then faced forward again, trying to catch his breath. "Ginette Dampierre happened…that's what," he said.

"What are you talking about?" Kendra asked. She came to

144

Rindge Avenue and headed west.

"There was a woman waiting for me inside the barn," he explained. "She was sent by Ginette Dampierre."

"You're sure it was a woman?"

"Positive."

"What makes you think Ginette Dampierre sent her?" Gina asked.

"She told me as much before she tried to throw me down the old grain chute."

"Are you hurt?" Kendra asked. "Should we take you to the hospital?"

"No! Just keep driving. We need to get as far away from here as possible."

"Agreed," Gina said. "If that crazy woman sent one person, who's to say there aren't more out there?"

Nathan looked over his shoulder, checking the traffic behind them. "I need to hide, like, right now!" he said.

"Either hide," Gina said, "or go someplace where she'd never expect you to be."

"And where might that be?" Kendra asked, as they approached the Alewife Brook Parkway.

"I know the perfect place," Gina replied. "Take a left at the light."

Kendra leaned on the gas and shot through the intersection just as the light turned red.

"At the circle, take a right on Concord Ave," Gina said.

"Where are we going?" Kendra asked.

"You'll see."

145

They rode for another two miles when they came to an s-shaped section of road. Kendra zigzagged through it as horns blared all around her. "OH YEAH RIGHT!" she shouted at the rearview mirror. "LIKE YOU DON'T DRIVE LIKE THAT!"

"At this next intersection, turn left," Gina said.

"Left?" Kendra repeated, growing more impatient by the second. She checked her side mirror, then changed lanes and cruised through the intersection without incident. "Gina?" she said, the pitch of her voice rising. "What are we doing?"

"Relax," Gina told her. "Where we're going is the last place Ginette Dampierre or any of her thugs would ever expect Nathan to hide."

"Why is that?"

"Because they know he wouldn't be that dumb."

9

More Than One Promise

Gary Moran slept in. After working the entire weekend, which included two grueling 12-hour shifts, he was in desperate need of a day off. Just after 1:30 p.m. he rolled over, blinked his eyes open, and looked at the clock on his bedside table. "NO!" he shouted, when he saw the time.

Edouard had been very specific during their conversation the night before. It was right after Moran explained that he'd gotten no update from Pantano, and that the man had seemingly vanished into thin air.

"In that case there are two things I need you to do," Edouard had told him in his soft, eerily calm voice "Do the first one in the early morning. The closer to sunrise the better. The second one? It's best if you wait until the afternoon. And don't breathe a word of it to anyone."

Moran reached over and grabbed his cell phone off the table, then punched in the private number Edouard had given him, reading it off the inside of his forearm where he'd scribbled it in black ink.

Ginette was sitting on the balcony reviewing notes from her various meetings when Moran's call came through. Without a second thought, she picked up the phone, tapped the talk button, and continued reviewing her notes. "Yes?" she said.

"Is this Ginette?"

"That depends," she replied calmly. "Who is *this*?"

"Gary Moran."

"I'm sorry to disappoint you Mr. Moran, but I know of no person by that name. Good day to you."

"WAIT!" Moran barked. "Your brother gave me this number and told me to call you."

"Is that a fact?" Ginette replied. "And what brother might that be?"

Moran let out a tired breath. *Fine, lady…you want to play*, he thought, *let's play*. "What brother? That would be the one I spoke to last night outside his cell. The Massachusetts Department of Corrections has him listed as prisoner #W114501. Does that number ring a bell?"

Ginette's heart raced as she realized who she was talking to. "You're Pantano's contact at the prison," she said.

"That's right. Have you seen Pantano recently?"

"I was going to ask you that same question," Ginette said.

"The last time I saw him in person was Friday night, right before my shift," Moran told her. "He texted me on Saturday, but since

148

then…nothing."

"Did you check his condo?"

"I did. He wasn't there. The maintenance guy said he hasn't seen him in days."

Ginette set her notepad down and sat back in the chair, staring at the view to the east. The cloudless sky was cobalt blue and the towering skyscrapers of Boston's busy financial district were gleaming in the bright afternoon sunlight.

It was time to move on from Pantano. She could simply assign another asset to find him, but why bother? With so much remaining to do, and plenty of manpower to help her get it done, Pantano no longer mattered. "All right, you've got my attention," she said. "Why did Edouard give you my number?"

"He wanted to know if Pantano gave you the books."

The whine of a jumbo jet overhead, making its final approach to Logan Airport, made her clamp her free hand over her ear. "Say again?"

"The books," Moran repeated. "Did Pantano give them to you?"

"What books?" she asked.

"I don't know. All he told me was that Pantano was supposed to get them."

"Huh," she said, watching the jet dip below the rooftops in the distance. "What else did my brother tell you?"

Kendra merged onto Trapelo Road, slicing through the sea of cars around her, when her curiosity bubble finally burst. *That's it*, she told herself. She braked hard and took a sharp right turn into an apartment complex with several large red-brick buildings set at various angles to one another. She navigated through them to the resident's parking area in the back and pulled into the first empty parking space she saw.

"What are you doing?" Gina asked.

Kendra killed the engine and looked over at her. There was no joy in her face. "Nothing," she said. "We're going to sit here until you tell me where we're going."

"Weston," Gina said, without hesitation.

"You cannot be serious!"

"What's in Weston?" Nathan asked.

"I'm *totally* serious," Gina said.

Kendra looked at her, dumbstruck. "That's crazy!"

"Uh, guys? What's in Weston?" Nathan asked for a second time.

"It's *not* crazy," Gina said. "Think about it. Does Ginette Dampierre know about the bookcase from her brother's office? Does she know what he kept in it? I doubt it. She spent the last 20 years hiding in Europe. Even if by some miracle she does find out about it, she can't possibly know that we figured out what the slips of paper mean, or that they were made by Arthur Chessman, *or* that we know where he lives. And…there's no *way* she'll think we'd actually go there."

"GUYS!" Nathan shouted. "What-is-in-Weston?"

Kendra and Gina replied in unison. "Arthur Chessman!"

"Oh…right," Nathan mumbled. In all the excitement, he'd completely forgotten Gina's revelation about finding Chessman's current whereabouts. "I agree with Gina," he said. "We need to go there."

"Not you too," Kendra groaned.

"Are you serious?" Nathan asked. "You really don't want to go there?"

"No, I really don't."

"Well I *do*, because I have questions for Arthur Chessman."

"What questions?" she asked.

"Well, for starters, what does he know about Whitehall? Claire Jameson suspected it was linked to the Covin. The question is, how? With any luck, we might be able to trick him into telling us."

"That is a monumental assumption," Kendra said.

"Maybe, but we won't know unless we try. Have you forgotten what they did to her?"

Kendra eyed him in the rearview mirror, the emotional scar she had from that tragic day showing through eyes of rage. "I will never forget, nor forgive, what they did to her," she said in a low growl. "And don't you *ever* ask me that question again."

"I'm sorry," Nathan said, suddenly regretting the question. "But I want answers, and I know you and Jameson do too. This may be our one and only chance to get them. Besides, it's like Gina said, Weston is the last place Ginette Dampierre's killer will expect me to be. Right now, she probably thinks I went back to…"

His words fell off and his face froze in panic.

"What's wrong?" Kendra asked.

"My parents!" he exclaimed, reaching into his pocket for his flip phone.

"No," Kendra said, taking her phone from the cupholder. "Let me."

"But…"

"Nathan?" she said, her voice firm. "Listen to me. I know what you're thinking, but it's better if I do it."

After Jameson got an update from Ellie, he called Eric Fuller. Ellie's successful visit with Carl Jaquith had set the fuse. Now it was time to prepare the charge.

"Jameson," Fuller said, answering right away. "How'd it go with Jaquith?"

"Nathan's plan worked just as we hoped it would," Jameson said. "Jaquith wants the entire collection and he's willing to pay to get it back. Best of all, he called Ginette Dampierre right after the meeting."

"So, we're on?"

"We are," Jameson said, "which means we have to move quickly."

"My team is ready to go," said Fuller. "Have you decided on a location for the exchange?"

"Not yet. I was hoping you could suggest one."

"I'll get working on that right away. Did you talk with Martin Bishop?"

"I did," Jameson said. "He agreed to give me a couple days before turning over the evidence, but then I had an idea."

"Go on."

"The original collection is too valuable to lose," Jameson said. "So, we don't bring any of it. Instead, we create a dummy set that resembles the real thing."

"Good thinking," Fuller said. "Will it work?"

"I don't see why not. Jaquith has only seen one of the items from the bookcase. He has no idea what the rest of it looks like."

"Good point," Fuller said. "Give me some time to confer with my team about a possible location."

Jameson's phone beeped, indicating an incoming call. When he saw Kendra's name on the screen, he said, "Eric, I have to take another call. How about we set up a video conference for an hour from now?"

"Perfect," Fuller said.

Jameson ended the call and then switched lines. "Kendra?" he said, unsure why she was calling.

"We have a serious situation," she said. "I would've called you sooner but we had to leave Richard's house in a hurry."

Jameson sat up in the chair. "What happened?"

"When I dropped Nathan off, there was a woman waiting for him inside the barn. She attacked him and tried to throw him down the old grain chute. From what she said to Nathan, it appears she was sent by Ginette Dampierre."

Jameson stood and began to pace. "Is Nathan all right?"

"He's got a few bumps and bruises but he'll be fine. Someone needs to go to his house and check on David and Elizabeth, in case this woman goes there looking for him."

"Where are *you*?" Jameson asked.

"Someplace safe. I have Gina with me too."

Jameson didn't bother to ask where they were. He had complete trust in Kendra, and at the moment he was embroiled in the plan to apprehend Ginette Dampierre. "This is exactly what I feared," he said. "I'll deal with David and Elizabeth. Meanwhile, Nathan has to disappear, and I mean totally vanish. If Ginette Dampierre is trying to eliminate him, it's the only way we can guarantee his safety."

"Consider it done," Kendra said. "By the way, how did it go with

Ellie?"

"Nathan's plan worked to perfection," Jameson said.

Kendra cupped her hand over the phone and looked back at Nathan. "Jaquith took the bait."

Nathan pumped his fist. *Yes!*

"What happens now?" she asked Jameson.

"We move on to phase two: setting up the meet. Your job is to safeguard Nathan and keep him from any harm. You know all the safehouses and how to get into them. Use whichever one you like, but it's imperative that you keep Nathan hidden. And Kendra? I want regular updates."

"Understood."

"Tell Nathan not to worry," Jameson said. "We'll make sure his parents are protected. And be careful!"

With that, he clicked off the call and immediately hit the speed dial number for Beck, who answered on the first ring.

"Jameson," he said. "Did Ellie call you?"

"She did," Jameson replied, talking faster than normal. "Where are you right now?"

"Headed back from Wells. What's wrong? You sound different."

"Ginette Dampierre sent an assassin after Nathan. She was waiting for him at Abbott's barn when Kendra dropped him off."

"She?"

"Yes."

Beck considered that briefly then let it pass. "What about Nathan?" he asked.

"According to Kendra, he's a little roughed up but none the worse for wear. She's taking him to a secure location as we speak. I need you and Ellie to go to the house and check on Elizabeth and David in case Ginette's asset goes there looking for him."

"Do they know about the attack?" Beck asked.

"No, not yet. I'm going to call them now."

"Ellie is a few minutes ahead of me," Beck said. "I'll call her and let her know she could be walking into an ambush."

"Do that," Jameson said. "And stay in touch."

He had just clicked off the call when he was blindsided by a horrifying realization. It sent a wave of panic through his body and with shaking hands he frantically dialed another number. "Come on, come on," he muttered, as he waited for the call to connect.

Three rings later, Russ McCullough answered. "Hi, this is Russ."

"Russ, it's Jameson. I need your help."

Russ had been repairing an old wooden chair in his garage, but upon hearing the desperation in Jameson's voice, he set down the clamp he was holding. When Jameson explained what he needed him to do, he raced into the house to get his truck keys.

And his old service revolver.

Kendra dropped her phone into the cupholder and started the car. She had the look of a woman with too many things to do and not enough time to get them done.

"So? What else did he say?" Gina asked, as Kendra backed out of the parking space.

"Do you know who Harry Houdini was?" she asked, ignoring Gina's question.

"Yeah, he was that magician guy."

"That's right. Did you ever hear about his vanishing elephant trick?" She reached the street, did a quick check of the oncoming traffic, then pulled out and continued toward Weston.

"Vanishing elephant? No," Gina said.

"He made an elephant disappear in front of, like, 5,000 people."

"Seriously?" Nathan said, from the back seat.

"Well, the crowd certainly thought so," Kendra said.

"Why are you telling us this?" Gina asked.

"Why? Because just like Houdini's elephant, we need to make Nathan disappear."

"I thought that's what we were doing," Gina said.

"I'm not sure *what* we're doing," Kendra said, still questioning the go-to-Weston-and-talk-to-Arthur Chessman idea. "But at least it'll give me some time to come up with a plan."

"What about me?"

Kendra was lost in thought and said nothing.

"Hey!" Gina said, snapping her fingers in the air.

"I'm sorry, what was that?" Kendra said.

"What about me?"

"What about you?"

"You can't just stash me somewhere."

"You're right," Kendra said, realizing she hadn't thought that far ahead. She grabbed her phone from the cupholder and speed-dialed Ellie.

"Kendra!" Ellie said, worry in her voice. "Beck just gave me the news. How's Nathan? Is he hurt?"

"He's fine. The kid's a warrior."

"Jameson said something about you taking him to a safe location?"

"Yeah, that's why I called. What's the plan for Gina?"

"Oh, right," Ellie said. "I forgot all about her. How about we find a safe place to meet, preferably a location where Ginette Dampierre's people won't find us?"

"We've got that covered," Kendra said. "Hold on a sec." She handed the phone to Gina. "Give her the name of that Boxwood place."

"Boxberry!" Gina said, rolling her eyes as she took the phone. *Write it down, already!*

She gave Ellie the name and address, reciting it from memory, and then listened as Ellie read it back to her.

"Dare I ask what's in Weston?" she asked Gina.

"I'll explain when I see you," Gina said.

"Is it going to be dangerous?"

"No," Gina said. "Not in the least."

Jameson took in a deep breath and let it out, trying to settle himself before calling Nathan's parents. Of his two choices, David or Elizabeth, he chose David, whom he suspected would handle the news without a complete meltdown.

David was cleaning out a flower garden along the side of the house and it took several rings before he picked up. "Jameson," he said, wiping his brow with his shirt sleeve, "any word from Ellie?" He walked over to the garage and stood in the cool shade to escape the blazing afternoon sun.

"Yes," Jameson replied. "But first, are you and Elizabeth all right?"

"We're fine," David said, watching Ellie turn into the driveway. Seconds later, Beck's truck appeared.

"David?" Jameson asked.

"Sorry about that," David said. "Ellie and Beck just pulled in."

Jameson breathed a sigh of relief.

Ellie scrambled out of the car and ran to the garage. "Where's Elizabeth?" she asked.

"She's inside. Why? What's going on?" David asked.

Beck jumped down from his truck and raced over to join them. "Is everybody okay?"

"Elizabeth's in the house," Ellie said.

"Go check on her. And take David with you. I'll do a perimeter sweep."

"Come on," Ellie told David, nodding toward the house.

David held up his hand…*wait*…then pressed the phone to his ear. "Jameson?" he said. "Is there something you'd like to tell me?"

Russ McCullough parked his truck at the curb, then got out and cut across Richard Abbott's front lawn. When he reached the side of the house, he took out his gun and crept along the privet hedge that marked the property line. At the back corner of the house he stopped and peered into the backyard. Such as it was.

There was no grass, no patio, and no barbeque grill—only a large circular parking area lined with crushed stone. Richard Abbott's car was nowhere to be seen. At the far side of the lot sat the barn. The door was partially open, and from what he could see, none of the inside lights were on.

He ran across the crushed stone and edged up to the opening, listening for any sound coming from inside. Hearing none, he grabbed the edge of the door and rolled it open as far as it would go. He was about to step inside when he heard a vehicle coming up the driveway. Seconds later, Richard Abbott's car rolled into view and stopped 10 feet away.

Russ placed a mental checkmark next to the first item on his agenda: check on the status of Richard Abbott, then he ran to the car and ducked down next to the driver's window, keeping his gun out of sight.

"What's the meaning of this?" Richard demanded.

"I'm here on behalf of Nathan's family," Russ said. "My name is Russ McCullough. I'm a retired police officer, and I need you to evacuate the area while I search the barn."

"Search the barn? For what purpose?" Richard asked.

"Earlier today you had an intruder," Russ said.

"An intruder? Here?" Richard asked, his confusion compounding. During all his years in the book business, no stranger had ever set foot on his property without an invitation. And none of them had the slightest interest in stealing anything. He craned his neck, trying to see into the barn. "Was Nathan here?" he asked. "Did he see who it was? I certainly hope he wasn't harmed by this person."

Russ responded just as Jameson had instructed. "Nathan's fine," he said. "When he arrived this afternoon, the intruder was already inside the barn. Luckily, Nathan was able to escape without serious harm."

"Shouldn't we report this to the police?" Richard asked. "Certainly they'll want to know about it."

"You leave the police to me," he told Richard. "Right now, for your own safety, I have to ask you to wait at the bottom of the driveway while I search the barn."

"Why? Do you think this trespasser is still inside?"

"I highly doubt it, but I need to be sure."

Richard eyed the gun in Russ' hand and then promptly backed down the driveway.

Russ waited until he reached the street, then stepped into the barn. In one hand was a small mag-light. In the other, his service revolver. He did a thorough search of the first floor, including the grain chute in the back corner. Through the opening, he saw a large impression in the soft dirt floor. Other than that, the lower level was clear. After checking the second floor and finding nothing, he walked down the driveway, put his gun back in his truck, and went to speak with Richard, who was parked at the curb.

"I gather from your relaxed demeanor that the intruder has fled," Richard said through the open window.

"Yes," Russ said. "Having years of experience with such situations, I'd say this was a one-time thing, but I'd keep an eye out for any suspicious persons. You might want to install a lock on the barn door, and some security cameras wouldn't be a bad idea either."

"What about David and Elizabeth?" Richard asked. "Are they aware of this intrusion?"

"They are."

"Very well, then," Richard said, starting his car. "Russ was it? I thank you for your help with this matter. Why anyone would want to break into my barn is beyond the scope of my understanding. Nonetheless, I'll take your suggestions under advisement."

"I'm happy to help," Russ said. "Now, before I go, there's just one more thing."

"Oh? What might that be?"

"I need to ask a favor."

It took the better part of 30 minutes and more than one promise to calm down Elizabeth and David. Sitting in the living room, huddled around David's phone, they listened to Jameson explain how Nathan was safe, and with Kendra's help he'd be as good as invisible to Ginette Dampierre and any of her thugs. After that he quickly shifted gears.

"Ellie's visit with Carl Jaquith went well," he told them. "The contents of the *Greenwich* bookcase represent a huge monetary payoff to the Covin and because of that, Jaquith wants it all. In just a few minutes Eric Fuller and I, along with Beck and Ellie, are going to work out the next phase of the plan. By this time tomorrow, Ginette Dampierre will no longer be a threat. But to pull it off, there's an important matter I need your help with."

"We're listening," Elizabeth said.

"The boxes in your garage are valuable evidence that tie the Covin to years of criminal activity," Jameson explained. "Martin Bishop has agreed to let me keep them until end of day tomorrow, by which time we should have Ginette Dampierre in custody. After that, we'll turn all of the boxes over to him so Interpol can build their case against Edouard, Ginette, and the rest of their organization. Until then, I've assured Martin that all of the evidence will remain safe."

"And how do you plan to do that?" David asked.

"With a subtle sleight of hand."

David nodded his head slowly, a smile forming on his lips. "You're not taking Jaquith the actual contents of the bookcase, are you?" he said.

"That's right," Jameson replied. "At first I thought that using the

161

originals wouldn't be a problem. Not with Eric Fuller's team deployed all around the exchange site. But the more I thought about it, the more I realized that any hope we have of shutting down the Covin once and for all lies in those boxes. They're simply too valuable. So…I came up with an alternate plan."

"And just to reiterate your earlier promise," Elizabeth said. "This will not include Nathan, like last time. Correct?"

"Correct," Jameson said. "Nathan has no part in what we're planning. You two, on the other hand, will play an important role."

"What do you need us to do?" David asked.

"Ellie?" Jameson said.

Ellie was standing in the entryway with Beck. At Jameson's prompt, she walked over to the couch with the copy of *Antiques & Fine Art* magazine. She pulled the narrow slip of paper from the binding and handed it to Elizabeth.

"What's this?" she asked.

"That right there has the power to put Edouard and Ginette Dampierre behind bars for the rest of their lives."

"One little piece of paper?" Elizabeth asked, with a skeptical look. If this was a joke, she could hardly wait to hear the punchline.

"Not just that one," Ellie explained. "All of them."

"I don't understand," Elizabeth said.

"Ellie and Beck will explain while you and David make copies of that slip," Jameson said.

"Copies?" Elizabeth asked.

"Uh-huh," Ellie said. "A whole bunch of 'em."

"What about the other thing," Beck asked.

"On its way," Jameson said.

Boxberry Green was set back from the road on a large parcel of farmland near the Wellington Farm Historic District. From the street, it looked like a far-off village, the rooftops barely visible behind a forest of 100+ year-old hardwoods. As Kendra drove down the long driveway, edged on either side by open fields, the facility slowly revealed itself.

It was actually one massive structure, with adjoining sections of varying architectural style. Some were clapboarded, others were shingled, with different colors and window styles, making it look like a collection of random buildings that had been swept up in a tornado and dropped in the middle of an old hay field.

"Here we are," Kendra announced, as she pulled into visitor parking. "Boxford Place."

Gina exhaled in frustration and flopped her head forward. *I give up.*

To their left was the front entrance. It had a large gabled portico with thick Doric columns that were roped with pink and purple rhododendrons. A narrow porch hugged the perimeter of the building and was home to long oak benches and cream-colored Boston rockers with striped cushions. Lavish hanging baskets, overflowing with petunias, begonias, and portulaca, hung at eight-foot intervals along the edge of the overhang. A young family was sitting on one of the benches, visiting with a gray haired woman in a wheelchair—smiles all around.

"What's the plan?" Kendra asked. "And if you think you're going to just walk in the front door and start asking around for this guy, think again. If he's as important as you say, the Covin probably has someone keeping an eye on him."

Nathan studied the front entrance momentarily, then said, "I have a better idea. Let's go."

"Go? Where?" Kendra asked.

"I'll show you."

She backed out of the parking space and he directed her to the opposite end of the parking lot.

"Where are we going?" she asked.

He leaned forward and extended his arm between the seats. "There," he said, pointing at a narrow service road that disappeared around the far end of the building.

Kendra followed it down to a lower parking area that was reserved for employees and deliveries. "All right," she said, coming to a stop. "Where to?"

"Now we park," Nathan said, like he was a driving instructor and this was Kendra's first time behind the wheel. As she rolled forward, crawling past a long row of parked cars, he craned his neck, looking back at the building. What he saw gave him an idea.

Kendra looped around into the next row, muttering under her breath, then suddenly cranked the wheel and shot into an empty parking space. "There, we parked," she said, turning off the engine. "Now what?"

Nathan didn't answer.

He had already pushed the door open and was climbing out of the car.

David sat at the kitchen table cutting the paper. Elizabeth sat across from him, pencil in hand, giving each strip a random number. "Do you think it'll work?" she asked.

"It will," Beck told her. "Jaquith will inspect each box, that's a given. A man in his position, with Ginette Dampierre breathing down his neck? He'd be a fool not to. But he'll just be checking to make sure every book or magazine has a little slip."

"Why do you say that?" David asked.

"Because in his mind, they're the ticket to millions of dollars of potential revenue."

From the back hallway they heard the screen door slam. Seconds later, Russ McCullough walked into the kitchen, both arms wrapped around a sealed cardboard box.

"How'd it go?" Beck asked.

Russ shook his head, amazed. "We hit the jackpot," he said.

Nathan zig-zagged his way through the parked cars, making his way toward the back of the building. Parked near a gray metal door that led to the kitchen was a large food service truck. He stopped at the end of the row 70 feet away and crouched down behind a black SUV. From there, he watched the driver take boxes off the back of the truck and load them onto a tall aluminum dolly.

"What are you doing?" Gina called out, as she and Kendra came up behind him.

"Yeah, what *are* you doing?" Kendra chimed in. "I thought we talked about you being less impulsive."

He spun around and put a finger to his lips...*Shhhh!*...then turned back toward the building. When he saw the driver wheeling the dolly toward the door, he stood up said, "Let's go."

"Wait!" Gina said, grabbing his arm. "Go where?"

He pulled his arm free. "Just follow me," he said, then darted across the pavement, stopping at the back of the truck.

"Uh…Nathan? I'm not sure this is such a good idea," she said nervously, when she and Kendra caught up with him.

He watched the delivery driver standing at the door, ringing the service bell. "Any second now," he said.

Just then, the metal door opened and a member of the kitchen staff appeared.

"Here we go," Nathan said.

The two men spoke briefly, then the kitchen guy stepped outside and held the door all the way open.

"Get ready," Nathan said, pushing his hair back behind his ear.

The kitchen guy watched the driver back the dolly into the building, then let go of the door and followed him inside.

"Now!" Nathan said.

10

Lyman

Nathan managed to catch the edge of the door just before it closed. Very slowly, he eased it open and ducked his head inside. Straight ahead was a narrow corridor that ran for roughly 10 feet, to a steel door with a large rectangular window set in the middle. He looked left and saw a hallway that led to the kitchen. Halfway down on the right, the kitchen guy and the driver had stopped at a large walk-in cooler. Nathan waited until the kitchen guy opened the door, which effectively blocked their view, then motioned to Kendra and Gina with his free hand. *Come on!*

They slipped inside and followed him down the corridor to the steel door. Through the window he saw a tiled hallway that stretched in both directions. There was no one in sight. "All clear," he said, then pulled the door open and they ducked into the hallway.

The blotchy gray floor tiles looked like oatmeal and the walls were an equally bland cream color. Overhead, classical music played softly from small speakers mounted in the ceiling.

"Okay, here's the plan," Nathan said. "We blend in."

Gina gave him a pathetic look. "Blend in? *That's* your plan?"

"You have a better idea?" he asked.

At the far end of the hallway, a member of the kitchen staff appeared, pushing a stainless-steel cart loaded with gray plastic tubs. Each one was overflowing with dirty dishes from the dining room.

"Yes, I believe I do," Gina said. "Follow me." She brushed past Nathan and walked toward the staff member. When he saw the three of them approaching, he steered the cart toward the wall to make room for them to pass.

"Uh, excuse me," Gina said, reading the name on his I.D. badge. "Thomas?"

"Yes?" he said, eyeing each of them briefly.

"Can you help us?" Gina said, sounding pitiful. "I think we took a wrong turn."

"Oh, sure," Thomas said, like it happened all the time. "The front desk is one floor up. Just follow this hallway to the elevator. It'll be on your right. When you reach the first floor, take a left. The front lobby is right there. You can't miss it."

Nathan tugged on Gina's sleeve. "May I?" He stepped around her and said, "Actually, we're looking for Arthur Chessman's room."

"Mr. Chessman?" Thomas said. A flash of recognition dawned on his face. "Oh, right, he said you might be stopping by."

Nathan and Kendra exchanged a look but said nothing.

"Tell you what," Thomas said. "Wait here. I'll be right back."

Russ McCullough set the box on the kitchen counter with a look of amazement on his face. "You won't believe it," he said.

"What are you talking about?" Beck asked.

"I did just what Jameson said. I asked Richard for ten boxes of books, preferably any that had to do with antiques, fine art, or art history."

"And...?"

"He looked at me like I was nuts. When he asked me why I wanted such a random collection of literature, I said it was a special favor for David and Elizabeth Cole."

"That was smart, using our names," Elizabeth said. "I'm not sure if you know this, but my father brought Richard into the book business. He mentored him and basically taught him everything he knows about buying and selling books."

"Well, he came through big time. It just so happens that he had a whole pallet of boxes from a museum gift shop in Chicago. Apparently it closed after a fire at the museum, and not long after that, Richard bought every book and magazine they had. You wanted books about art and art history? Check these out." He pried open the flaps on the box and began pulling out random items. "Look at this...art history books, museum guides and collections, books on fashion, exhibition catalogs, coffee table books, you name it."

A short time later they had the boxes arranged on the kitchen floor. Ellie helped Elizabeth and David insert the strips of paper into each volume, and when they were done Beck took the phone from his pocket and called Jameson.

"How's it going there?" Jameson asked.

"You won't believe what Russ brought back from Abbott's barn,"

Beck said.

"How do they look?"

"They're exactly like the originals. Jaquith won't suspect a thing."

"Excellent," Jameson said. "I just sent Elizabeth a video link for a conference call with Eric Fuller. I need all of you on the call so we can finalize the plan for tomorrow."

"Understood," Beck said. "Hold on a second." He pulled the phone from his ear and relayed the information to Elizabeth, who went to the living room to turn on the computer. "All right, Jameson, we should be linked in momentarily. Any word from Kendra?"

"No, but I'm not worried," Jameson said. "Nathan's in good hands."

Nathan, Gina, and Kendra waited in the hallway while Thomas wheeled the metal cart into the kitchen. Huddled together next to the wall, they looked like three lost travelers stranded in the wrong part of town.

"I don't like this," Kendra said, shaking her head slowly.

Nathan nodded in agreement. "We might be stopping by?" he said, repeating Thomas' words. "What does that even mean? Did we miss something?"

"Both of you need to calm down," Gina said.

"Calm down?" Kendra repeated. "What if someone knew we were coming and tipped him off? For all we know, there could be a couple of Ginette Dampierre's goons waiting for us in his room."

"Who?" Gina asked calmly.

"Huh?"

"Who knew we were coming?" Gina asked. "Do they know we

have Chessman's books, or that we figured out his numbering system? On the way over here, did you see anyone following us?"

"Uh...not that I can remember," Kendra said.

Gina gave her a look. *Well then...?*

The door to the kitchen swung open and Thomas emerged without the cart. "Sorry about that," he said. "You said Mr. Chessman, right?"

"Yes," Nathan replied.

"It'll be easier if I just take you up there myself," Thomas said. He assumed since they were already in the building, they'd signed in at the front desk, which all visitors were required to do.

"Thank you," Gina said, as they started down the hallway.

"No problem," Thomas said over his shoulder. "I know he's anxious to see you."

Elizabeth found Jameson's email and clicked on the link. Seconds later, Jameson and Eric Fuller appeared on the screen, each in their own frame. Elizabeth fiddled with the screen layout, adding a third frame that showed her in front of the monitor with David, Beck, Ellie, and Russ standing behind her.

"Elizabeth, it's good to see you again," Fuller said.

"Eric," she said, acknowledging him with a nod. Few words had passed between them since Nathan's recent abduction and near-brush with death at the hands of Edouard Dampierre, a scenario that Fuller had promised couldn't possibly happen. By Elizabeth's way of thinking, the fact that Nathan was still alive was nothing short of a miracle, no thanks to Fuller.

"Well, let's get started," Eric said. "How are you set on your end?"

"We have a duplicate set of books that Beck assures me will be more than adequate," Jameson said.

"Very good, and nice work folks," said Fuller. "I've spoken with my deputies, and after exploring several possible locations, we settled on an old sand pit in the town of Lyman. It's remote, which eliminates any potential interference from curious onlookers."

Ellie leaned down so that her face showed on the monitor. "We're meeting in a *sand pit*?"

"We won't actually be *in* the sand pit," Fuller explained. "It's only accessible by a long dirt road, lined on both sides by heavily wooded land. The optimum spot would be halfway down."

"Is the pit currently in use?" asked Beck.

"Do you mean will there be heavy equipment using the road?" Fuller asked.

"Yes."

"The pit sees sporadic use, but we'll contact the company that owns it and have them cease operations for the day. Ellie, did you give Jaquith a time?"

"Not yet. He's awaiting my call."

"Thoughts?" Fuller asked the group.

"Make it in the afternoon," Beck said. "As far as Jaquith knows, Ellie's a one-man team. That means she has to go to wherever she stashed the boxes, load them into her vehicle, then make the drive to Lyman."

"Makes sense," Fuller said. "Can we agree on three o'clock tomorrow?"

"Works for me," Ellie replied. "I'll call Jaquith when we're done here and set it up."

"Good. I'll text you the directions to the sand pit. We'll leave a marker on the shoulder. When you see it, pull over and park your vehicle. I'll have two teams deployed there, one on each side of the road. Two more teams will be posted at key positions along the main road as spotters."

"Question," Ellie said. "You mentioned a marker?"

"It'll be something you wouldn't think twice about. A branch? Maybe a large rock?"

"How about a crumpled McDonald's bag?"

"Oh, my team will love that," Fuller said. "Now, once you make the exchange, my guess is Jaquith will let you leave first. Probably won't want you following him. Just take the money and go. Once you're clear, one of two things will happen. If Ginette Dampierre is there, we'll move in and arrest her. If she's not, the people I have positioned on the main road will follow Jaquith and the books, in case he's planning to meet her at a remote location. Knowing how elusive she is, my money is on the latter."

"What about protecting Ellie?" Jameson asked.

"I'm sorry?" Fuller said.

"During the exchange," Jameson said. "What if things get rough?"

"Ellie has nothing to worry about," Fuller replied. "I'll have snipers surrounding the exchange site, ready to respond at the first hint of trouble."

Beck looked over at Ellie. "You good with that?"

"Are you kidding?" she joked. "My own team of snipers? What more could a girl ask for?"

Beck rolled his eyes. *Oh, brother.*

173

"There's another matter we need to discuss," Fuller said. "And Jameson, this is directed solely at you."

Jameson knew what was coming. He was surprised that Fuller had waited this long to mention it.

"During the recent arrest of Edouard Dampierre," Fuller said, "you stationed your people around the perimeter of the target area as a second line of defense."

"That's correct," Jameson said, offering no reason for his actions, which he'd kept from Fuller at the time. As it turned out, it was his decision to deploy a second team on the outskirts of Beale Brothers Antiques, as well as Ellie's quick thinking, that had ultimately saved Nathan's life.

"There'll be no need for that this time," Fuller said. "There's only one road in and out of the sand pit and my team will be ready for any eventuality. That said, if you'd like, I'll meet you before the exchange and give you a radio so you can listen in to what's happening."

"Fair enough," Jameson said.

"Is there anything else?" Fuller asked.

No one replied.

"All right, then. Ellie, we'll do a final briefing tomorrow morning. In the meantime, if any of you has a question, don't hesitate to contact me."

After Fuller signed off the call, there was a brief lull.

"So, what do you think?" Elizabeth asked Jameson.

"I think Eric Fuller's team will be well positioned and ready for anything," Jameson replied. "With additional marshals posted on the main road, I don't see how Ginette, or anyone she brings with her will escape."

"Uh…about the vehicle," Ellie said, hinting that she was having second thoughts about using her own car.

"I've been thinking about that," Jameson said. "As we've already witnessed, Ginette Dampierre is quick to dish out retribution to anyone who crosses her or her family. Therefore, it's imperative that the vehicle you use not be traceable back to you in any way."

"So, what you're saying is, I need a bogus vehicle."

"Exactly."

"I think I can help you there," Russ said.

On the elevator ride up to the first floor, Nathan stared blankly at the front of the car. Overhead, classical music continued to play softly from an unseen speaker, but he didn't hear it; he was too busy thinking about what he was going to say to Arthur Chessman. It wasn't like he could just walk in the room and start asking him questions about Whitehall and Claire Jameson.

"Yeah, hi, I'm Nathan Cole. We haven't met before but I just wanted to stop by and ask you a few questions about Claire Jameson. Nothing major, really. I'm just wondering what she found at Whitehall that you guys didn't want her to know about. It had to be something important, right? I mean, why else would you kill her?"

If only it could be that easy.

It was a foregone conclusion that Chessman wouldn't readily admit to anything about the Covin, especially to three complete strangers. What they needed to do was get him talking. Listen for clues. Get him to reveal the truth without realizing he was doing it, even if it leaked out in tiny bits and pieces.

The elevator reached the first floor and glided to a stop. As the door opened, Kendra extended her right arm, holding Nathan and Gina back, while motioning to Thomas with her left hand. "After you," she said.

As he stepped out of the car, she said to Nathan and Gina, "When we get to the room, you two stay behind me. I'll scope it out and then you can go in. *Only* then. If I tell you to run, you run. We meet back at the car. Got it?"

"We'll be *fine*," Gina assured her. She grabbed Nathan's arm and dragged him out of the car just as the doors were starting to close.

From the elevator, they followed Thomas down a wide hallway that ran away from the front desk. They passed one suite after another, eventually coming to a set of heavy wooden doors. Each had a narrow window running down the middle that offered a view into the next section of the building.

Thomas punched a four-digit number into the keypad that was mounted on the wall. He waited for the lock to click then pushed through the doors.

Gone was the classical music. The walls were painted bright white and were adorned with black and white photographs of Beacon Hill, Faneuil Hall, the Old State House, Quincy Market, Fenway Park, the USS Constitution, and other popular Boston-area landmarks.

Unlike the bland oatmeal-colored tiles on the bottom level, the floor in this section of the building was covered with pea-green carpeting and had a repeating pattern that resembled stringy river weeds swaying gently beneath the surface of the water.

When they came to the nurse's station, Thomas gave the nurse on duty a short wave and then turned left down an adjoining hallway.

Fifty feet later he stopped at a door on the right. "And here we are," he said. He rapped on the door and then eased it open. "Arthur?" he said loudly. "Your visitors are here."

Carl Jaquith stood in the main gallery admiring his most recent acquisition: a stunning late 18th century Italian gilded console table with truncated pyramid legs, exquisite carvings, and a Portoro marble top. Weeks earlier, Edouard had alerted him that it would be arriving but had said nothing about how or where it had been acquired. Like a number of other ornate pieces that had been delivered to his shop, Jaquith suspected the table had been smuggled into the country from one of the Covin's European dealers.

"It truly is exquisite," Charles gushed.

"Indeed," Jaquith replied. He turned and surveyed the gallery. "Let's put it over there, beneath the Colman," he said, pointing to a vacant space on the front wall. The Samuel Colman painting that hung there, *View of Mount Washington from the Saco River*, was one of Jaquith's favorite pieces in the gallery. It dated back to 1856 and had a price tag of $25,000.

Jaquith was helping Charles move the table when his phone rang. He glanced at the screen, then stepped out into the hallway to take the call.

"Hello, this is Carl Jaquith."

"Tomorrow. Three o'clock."

Jaquith recognized Ellie's voice at once. "Location?" he asked.

"Not so fast," she said. "You got the money?"

"Yes."

"Then meet me at the old sandpit off of South Waterboro Road in Lyman. You can't miss it. It's on the right, exactly a half mile from the Town Hall."

"Very good," he said, making a mental note. "I'll see you there at three o'clock."

Arthur Chessman was sitting back on a burgundy leather couch in the far corner of the room, dressed in a green short-sleeved gingham shirt and caramel-colored chinos. His closely cropped hair was the color of galvanized metal. Positioned at a 90° angle to the couch was a matching rolled-arm leather chair. Directly behind it, a large picture window looked out on a grassy courtyard that was dotted with a variety of tall shade trees.

Standing against the wall across from the couch was a tall George III mahogany breakfront bookcase with four glass-front hinged doors, and graduated side drawers fitted with gilded swan-neck brass handles. To the left of it was the door leading to the bedroom. To the right, the door to the bathroom.

Arthur was staring out the picture window but turned his head when Thomas entered the room. Kendra followed right behind him, did a quick visual sweep from left to right, then went back to the door and flashed Nathan and Gina a thumbs up. *All clear.*

As they shuffled into the room, Arthur gave Gina an indifferent look. But when he saw Nathan, he sat up at once.

"At last," he said, looking relieved. "What took you so long?"

11

The Watchman's Keep

Thomas politely excused himself and then left the room. As soon as the door closed, Arthur motioned for Nathan to come closer. Kendra and Gina hung back next to the coat closet, taking inventory of the surroundings.

A round wooden table with four chairs was positioned in the front corner of the room. Hanging on the wall next to it were a handful of framed photographs. In one, a much younger Arthur stood on a rock jetty, casting his fishing line into the ocean. In another, he was leaning against a 1950s tomato-red Alfa Romeo Spyder Veloce convertible, sunlight reflecting off his dark-green aviator sunglasses. A much older photo, slightly discolored, showed a bride and groom, barely out of their teen years, standing on the steps of a church on their wedding day.

Nathan walked to the end of the couch and stopped, unsure of where he should stand.

Arthur waved him closer, then leaned forward and spoke in a low voice. "Did anyone follow you here?"

"Not that I'm aware of," Nathan replied.

"Are you sure?"

"Yes."

Arthur nodded at Gina and Kendra. "Who are those two?"

"Friends," Nathan said.

"Friends?" Arthur repeated, with a confused look. "Why would you bring them here?"

"They're…um…helping me."

"Helping you? Why?" Arthur asked, his mood growing darker.

Nathan said the first thing that came to mind. "Because there's a lot to do."

"Of course there is," Arthur said, louder. "Are you doing as I instructed?"

Nathan froze. *He thinks I'm someone else.*

"Well?" Arthur demanded.

"Uh, yes…yes I am," Nathan said quickly.

"What about your list?" Arthur asked.

Nathan had no idea what that meant, so he flashed a thumbs up.

"Only masterworks?" Arthur asked.

Nathan nodded.

"You be sure to remember that," Arthur said. He looked down at the floor, shaking his head. "Nothing but kitsch everywhere you look," he crabbed. The thought hung in his mind for several seconds then melted away. He looked up and said, "What about the numbers?"

"Uh…the numbers are good," Nathan replied, unsure of how

else to respond. Answering his questions was like trying to hit the center of a dartboard while wearing a blindfold.

"Good?" Arthur exclaimed. "Good won't cut it. They have to be great!"

Before Nathan could respond, the door opened and a nurse walked in. She smiled at Kendra and Gina, then walked over to the couch. "All right Arthur, time to use the bathroom," she said.

He mumbled something under his breath and then climbed to his feet, unsteadily. The nurse walked him to the bathroom and closed the door.

"Hey!" Kendra said, keeping her voice low. "Do you know what he's talking about?"

Nathan shrugged. "Not a clue."

"Just keep him talking," Gina said. "And stop making him mad."

Nathan glared at her. "And how am I supposed to do that?"

"Just nod your head a lot," she told him.

"The thumbs up was a good idea" Kendra said.

"Yeah," Gina said. "Do the thumbs-up thing. That was perfect."

The bathroom door opened and Arthur appeared. The nurse escorted him back to the couch, asked if there was anything he needed, and then left to tend to other residents.

Arthur sat motionless for several long seconds, staring straight ahead. Then, as if jolted from a dream, he looked up at Nathan. "What were we talking about?" he asked.

Nathan decided to gamble. "Whitehall," he said.

Arthur's eyes went wide. "What did I tell you about that?" he said, the words exploding out of his mouth. The sudden exertion brought on a coughing fit and he grabbed for the bottle of water next to him on the couch. After fumbling with the cap, he took a long sip, followed by another. When he was done, he sank back into the couch, his breathing erratic. "I thought I made…that clear," he said.

"Maybe we should go over it again," Nathan suggested.

"No," Arthur said, faintly. "It's like…I told you before. They run…on a very tight schedule." He took another sip of water. "No room for error," he said, pushing the words out with what little energy he could muster. "Just…do your job…and let them handle it from there."

"But…"

"But nothing!" Arthur shouted, the words launching him into another coughing fit. He gulped down more water, fighting to swallow between coughs. It took nearly a minute, but when he finally regained his composure, he pointed at the leather armchair. "Asher… sit down."

Gina and Kendra exchanged a look. *Asher?*

Nathan quickly took a seat, not wanting to ignite more of Chessman's anger.

Arthur took several deep breaths, gradually building up the strength to speak. "I want you to listen carefully," he said. "This is extremely important." His tone took on a slower, more fatherly tone. "You're the Watchman, son. You need to earn your keep. Do you understand what I'm telling you?"

Nathan gave a quick nod, like he knew full well what Arthur was implying.

"I hand-picked you," Arthur said. "Do you know why?"

Nathan could only offer a shrug. *Not really.*

"You didn't strike me as reckless," Arthur said. "Or irresponsible." He paused to take a deep breath. "To do this job," he said, "you need to be invisible to the world…but with the eyes of a hawk." Another breath. "The things I've taught you…all of it…has been tested over time. The results…speak for themselves. I should know," he said, "I was the one who developed them."

Nathan sat perfectly still, taking it all in. *Don't talk*, he told himself. *Just listen.*

"You're monitoring the auction houses?" Arthur asked.

Again, Nathan just nodded.

"Watch-the-buyers," Arthur said slowly, emphasizing each word. "This is very important. Get to know them. Know what they're buying." He waved Nathan closer. "You don't need those two," he said, casting a subtle nod in Gina and Kendra's direction. "After I'm gone, if you need help, you speak only to Edouard. He'll guide you."

Guide me? Nathan thought. Clearly, Arthur hadn't been keeping up with the news reports about the recent raid on the Hamilton Mill.

The still of the moment was broken by a firm rap on the door. It swung open and Gary Moran stepped into the room, looking like a member of the Professional Bowlers Association. Gone was the prison guard uniform, replaced by plaid slacks and a vintage camp shirt with wide maroon and black stripes.

Just a regular guy.

Stopping by to say hello to an old friend.

The second thing Edouard had asked him to do.

"*I need you to check on an old my friend of mine,*" Edouard had said. He only gave Moran Arthur's name and address, explaining that he was concerned about his good friend's deteriorating health. Little did Moran know Arthur's place in the Covin hierarchy: the bookcase he oversaw and the nature of its contents; his uncanny ability to find priceless art, or the numbering system he devised that served as a de facto accounting program.

With Nathan Cole taking possession of the bookcase, Edouard knew there was a chance, however slim, that the boy might discover those truths. After all, he'd somehow managed to find the Hamilton Mill, home to one of Edouard's northeast shipping operations that unbeknownst to the local and state authorities, had operated like clockwork for years.

If Arthur's dementia was advancing as Edouard suspected, after speaking with one of the nurses six months earlier, then he posed no threat to the organization should Nathan Cole somehow lead the authorities to his door.

Still, Edouard needed to be sure.

He also knew that if his sister learned of Arthur's existence, his fragile mental state, and the dark Covin secrets he had tucked away in the back of his head, she wouldn't hesitate to pluck him off the face of the Earth like a weed. What Edouard didn't know was that Arthur had been secretly training an apprentice to take his place—someone who could continue his work and keep the cash spigot gushing.

Moran saw Arthur sitting on the couch and breezed past Kendra and Gina without so much as a glance. "Arthur, how are you?" he asked, like they were two longtime friends.

Arthur considered Moran with no emotion, trying to recall his face.

"Don't tell me you've forgotten me," Moran said. "We met at that art impressionist exhibit in Cambridge two years ago, remember? Man, it's crazy how time flies."

Moran was following a carefully crafted script designed by Edouard, filled with key words that would test Arthur's power of recall. Moran's job was to watch and listen for any signs of recognition. A smile. A nod. A shrug. But at the mention of the impressionist exhibit, where Arthur first saw the Renoir painting, *Madeleine Leaning on her Elbow with Flowers in her Hair*, his expression remained unchanged.

It was months after the art exhibit that Arthur learned the painting had been on loan from a private collector in Houston, Texas. Upon discovering that the painting had been returned to its owner, Arthur immediately notified Edouard, who orchestrated the theft of the painting, netting the Covin a tidy sum of one million dollars.

"So, how have you been?" Moran asked, surveying the room. "It looks like you've done pretty well for yourself." He spotted a framed print hanging on the wall to the left of the bedroom door. "Ooh, that's nice," he said, walking over for a closer look. "Metzinger, right?" he asked, following Edouard's script. "Man, that guy was good. This one's called *Man with a Pipe* if I'm not mistaken."

Years earlier, Arthur had located the original in a Wisconsin art gallery. Shortly thereafter, it had disappeared while in transit, adding a two-million-dollar masterpiece to the Covin's vast storehouse of treasures. Arthur had hung the print on his wall as a reminder of the original, an acquisition that he considered one of his crowning achievements.

Moran looked back at Arthur, waiting for a reply or any sign of recognition. But Arthur had shifted his gaze to the window, watching an older couple walk down a winding pathway that snaked past a giant northern catalpa tree, its giant heart-shaped leaves fluorescent in the afternoon sunlight.

Kendra caught Nathan's eye and hitched her thumb toward the door. *Let's go.*

Nathan shook his head. *Not yet.*

Something about the stranger was offsetting. And Arthur still hadn't uttered a word. What was that about? Was he purposefully ignoring the man's questions, or were the answers hopelessly blotted out by his deteriorating mental state?

Moran moved from the Metzinger print to the breakfront bookcase. "Now *this* is special," he said, running his hand over the glazed finish. "But then again, I know you're a fan of the breakfront style. This one looks like it belongs in a museum."

The key word 'museum' triggered no response from Arthur, who had first learned of the bookcase through a museum employee in New York. At the time, the bookcase was being stored in the museum's warehouse along with a number of other pieces that were deemed to be of lesser or no value. What the museum didn't know was that the bookcase had been built by famed French designer Antoine Krieger and carried an estimated worth of nearly $100,000.

Edouard had been so impressed by Arthur's uncanny ability to unearth such treasures that once his crew obtained it, he gifted it to Arthur as a show of his gratitude and respect.

Moran peered through the hinged glass doors, eyeing the hardcover volumes that lined the inner shelves. "I see you're still an avid reader," he said. "Read any good books lately?"

Arthur said nothing as he continued to watch the older couple through the window. They had taken a seat on one of the long oak benches and were watching a northern cardinal and its mate ground feeding near a juneberry bush.

In the silence that followed, Nathan finally spoke. "I didn't catch your name," he said.

Moran looked over at him, as if noticing him for the first time. "I didn't give one," he said, matter-of-factly. "Who are you?"

"Nobody important," Nathan replied.

Moran's curiosity stirred. *Who is this mouthy kid?* he wondered. He was much too young to be an employee of the facility, or a volunteer. Was he somebody from Arthur's family? Whoever he was, he fit the description of the boy Edouard had gone on and on about.

Skinny.

Straight brown hair.

Nosey.

No, that's not him, Moran thought. *Why would he be here, talking to one of Edouard's friends?* But then he remembered something else Edouard had said—a passing comment he'd uttered in a low voice that was seething with hatred.

"*...and that meddlesome girl he always has with him.*"

Moran looked over at Gina as the realization hit him. Then, slowly, he turned back to Nathan. "I know who you are," he said. "You're Nathan Cole." He pointed over his shoulder at Gina. "And she's your annoying sidekick."

Nathan and Gina said nothing.

Moran shook his head back and forth, grinning. "This must be my lucky day," he gushed. "I mean, he told me about you two. How you were always poking around in other people's business. But to walk in and find you here? In person? What are the chances?"

Nathan didn't have to ask who 'he' was. It could only be one person—the man who couldn't be there in person because he was sitting in a locked jail cell. Who else would speak his name, and Gina's, with such distain? He looked past Moran, eyes wide, and saw Kendra raise an open palm. *Relax, I got this.*

"What to do, what to do," Moran said, looking back and forth from Nathan to Gina.

Kendra had heard enough. "All right, Einstein," she said. "Time to go."

Moran spun around to face her. "Are you talking to me?" he asked, pressing a finger to his chest.

"Not too bright, are you?" she said.

"Excuse me?" Moran said.

Kendra went to the door and held it open. "Visiting hours are over."

Moran faced punks like this every day at the state prison. Through the years he'd learned that there was only one way to deal with them. He walked over and stopped a foot away from Kendra, his beefy frame leaving her no clear path of escape. When he spoke, it was in a relaxed, almost carefree voice.

The calm before the storm.

"Let me explain something to you…" he began.

"I'm sorry?" Kendra said, cupping her hand behind her ear.

Moran leaned closer and opened his mouth to speak when she swung the door into his face.

Hard.

The builders of the facility had spared no expense when it came to the doors. This one was a traditional four-panel design with a thick hardwood core. The edge caught Moran square in the face, opening a gash in his forehead and splitting open his lower lip. He staggered backward, stunned, blood dripping on his shirt, when Kendra charged and knocked him clean off his feet. He rolled over and tried to stand when she speared him in the back with her knee, pinning him to the floor. When she looked over at Nathan and Gina, they stood frozen in place, watching with looks of astonishment.

"Well?" she yelled. "What are you waiting for? Run!"

Ellie pulled into Boxberry Green and circled the front lot, looking for Kendra's faded blue Volvo. She was finishing her first loop when she saw Nathan and Gina come bursting through the front doors, panic-stricken. They reached the end of the gabled portico and turned right, sprinting toward the service road at the far end of the parking lot.

She honked the horn trying to get their attention but they never slowed or even looked back. She gunned the engine and flew past them, then stood on the brake bringing the car to a stop 30 feet ahead of them. She had just gotten out of the car when they came running up. "What happened?" she shouted. Back at the front entrance, she saw a man stagger out into the parking lot, his face smeared with blood.

"No time to explain," Nathan yelled as he pulled the back door open and jumped inside.

Gina slid into the front passenger seat. When she saw Ellie

staring at Moran, she yelled, "Ellie...what are you doing? We have to get out of here!"

Moran saw the kids climb into Ellie's car and started running in that direction. "YOU!" he shouted, pointing at Ellie. "STOP RIGHT THERE!"

"Yeah, I don't think so," she mumbled. She climbed back into the driver's seat and slammed the door shut. Moran was closing in when she stomped on the accelerator and pulled away, leaving him out of breath and bleeding on the blistering pavement.

Seconds after the Nathan and Gina left, Kendra jumped up and ran from the room, leaving Moran bleeding on the floor and Arthur Chessman watching from the couch, bewildered. She didn't bother to wait for the elevator because she knew Moran would appear at any moment. Instead, she raced down the stairs to the lower level and sprinted across the parking lot. She had just started the car when her cell phone rang. Assuming it was Nathan, checking in, answered without checking the call screen. "Nathan!" she said. "Where are you?"

"Kendra, it's Ellie. I have Nathan and Gina. We just left the parking lot. I'm on Wellesley Street, headed south toward Rt. 9."

"Sister, you just made my all-time favorites list."

"Yeah, well, let's save the award ceremony for later," Ellie said. "Do you want to tell me what happened back there?"

"All in good time," Kendra replied. "Right now, I need to hide Nathan and you need to get Gina back home before her parents freak out and call in the National Guard."

"Are you familiar with Kennard Park in Newton?" Ellie asked.

"Kennard Park? Sure," Kendra said. "I played in a softball tournament across the street at the high school."

"Let's meet there," Ellie said. "And keep an eye out for a big guy with a bloody face. He was chasing the kids and he saw them get into my car."

"Will do," Kendra said. She disconnected the call and backed out of the parking space. On her way through the front lot she spotted Moran one row over. He was standing next to his Dodge Challenger with the engine idling, craning his neck as he surveyed the parking lot. She leaned her elbow on the edge of the window and pressed her hand against the side of her head to shield her face, but Moran had already marked her. He jumped into the driver's seat and revved the engine, the tires scorching the tar as he took off after her.

In Newton, Ellie pulled off of Rt. 9 onto Dudley Road and followed it to the Kennard Park entrance. A short distance in, she came to a wooded roundabout and pulled over to wait for Kendra. "So," she said, turning off the engine. "Who'd like to tell me what happened back there?" She looked over at Gina. "You told me it wasn't going to be dangerous."

"It wasn't," Gina said. "Not at first anyway. But then this creepy guy showed up and started asking Arthur a bunch of questions."

"He was testing him," Nathan said.

"Who's Arthur?" Ellie asked.

"Arthur Chessman," Nathan said. "He was the caretaker of the *Greenwich* bookcase."

"He's the one who made all those little paper slips," Gina explained.

"And you know this, how?" Ellie asked.

"It's a long story," Gina said.

"Oh, I bet it is," Ellie muttered, shaking her head in disbelief. "This creepy guy. Does he have a name?"

"He never gave one," Nathan said. "I asked, and that's when all the trouble started."

"I can hardly wait to hear the details," Ellie mumbled. Before Nathan could say another word, her cell phone chirped. She pulled it from the small storage compartment in the dashboard and checked the call screen before answering. "Kendra?" she said. "What's up?"

"I may be a few minutes late," Kendra replied. "I've got a tail."

In the background Ellie could hear the Volvo's engine straining. "Is it the guy with the bloody face?" she asked.

"Yup. Some of my finest work, if I do say so myself," Kendra said. "You should've seen when I…HEY!…WHAT ARE YOU DOING?" she shouted.

"What was that?" Ellie asked.

Through the phone she heard the chilling sound of screeching tires, followed by a thunderous crash of metal and the breaking of glass.

Then, nothing.

12

Flying

"**K**endra?" Ellie said into her phone.

There was no reply.

"KENDRA!"

"What's wrong?" Nathan asked.

"I don't know," Ellie said, unwilling to put words to the anxiety she was feeling. She checked her watch. It was nearly five o'clock. Like Kendra said, they needed to get Gina back home, and soon. "You two wait here," she said, then pushed the door open and climbed out of the car. To her left and right, clusters of towering hardwoods bathed the road in shade, filling it with the earthy aroma of dried leaves and moss.

She walked 10 feet up the road and stopped to dial Gina's mom. The call connected, and as she waited for her sister to pick up, she started to pace, unable to shake the terrifying sounds that ended her conversation with Kendra. With each second that passed without a callback, the whisper of dread in the back of her mind grew steadily louder.

"Here you go, sir," the dining room attendant said to Jameson as she set a bowl of homemade beef & barley soup down on the table in front of him. It was a tantalizing medley of tender beef and pea barley, with fresh carrots, celery and onions from Birch Meadow's bountiful garden. Jameson picked up a spoon and began devouring it when he realized that he hadn't heard from Kendra.

He took his phone off the table and dialed her number, wondering why she hadn't checked in with him as he'd instructed her to do. As he listened to the call connect, he drummed his fingers nervously on the tablecloth. Several rings later, when the call went to voicemail, he disconnected and dialed another number.

Ellie had just finished talking to Gina's mother when she got Jameson's call. "Jameson," she said. "What's up?"

"I was going to ask you the same question," he replied. "Have you heard from Kendra? The last we spoke she was taking Nathan to a safe location. She said she had Gina with her too. That was three hours ago."

"Nathan and Gina are with me," Ellie said. "We're at Kennard Park."

"Kennard Park? In Newton?"

"Yes. We're waiting for Kendra."

"I don't understand."

"They were at a facility in Weston and—"

"Wait," Jameson cut in. "What were they doing in Weston?"

"Uh, I think you'd better ask Kendra that question."

"So, where is she?" Jameson asked.

"She's on her way," Ellie said, praying that was the case. "She got sidetracked."

Jameson pushed the bowl of soup away and stood. "Have her call me the second you see her."

The sound of an approaching vehicle made Ellie turn and look. When she saw Kendra's faded blue Volvo chugging up the road, she said, "Jameson, she just got here. I'll call you right back."

She tucked the phone in her pants pocket and ran back to the Volvo as it rolled to a stop on the shoulder. When Nathan and Gina saw that, they scrambled out of the car and followed her.

"Hey guys," Kendra said, through the open window. "Everybody make it okay?"

Ellie walked around the entire car, baffled. Other than the usual scratches and dents, there was no evidence of a collision. She went to the window and looked at Kendra's face and hands, looking for any scrapes or cuts. Miraculously, there were none. "Never mind us," she said. "What happened to you? One minute we were talking on the phone, and then...nothing."

"Yeah, that was crazy," Kendra said, with a wild look.

"What are you guys talking about?" Nathan asked.

Kendra recapped how she left Moran bleeding on Arthur Chessman's carpet and snuck out of the building, and how Moran spotted her in the parking lot and gave chase. "I had a decent head start on him," she said. "But right after I called Ellie I looked in my rearview mirror and there he was, closing in on me."

"What happened?" Nathan asked.

Kendra smirked. "The idiot passed me, and I mean, he was *flying*!" she said. "As he pulled alongside me he cut into my lane and tried to force me off the road."

Gina's eyes went wide. "What did you do?"

"The only thing I *could* do," Kendra said, with a shrug. "I stood on the brakes."

The screeching sound, Ellie thought.

"The fool didn't realize how fast he was going," Kendra said. "When he cut the wheel, his car fishtailed and then flipped."

"Whoa!" Nathan exclaimed.

"Yeah, that was pretty much my reaction," Kendra said. "His car would've kept rolling if it hadn't hit that stand of trees."

"That was the crash I heard," Ellie said.

"Yeah, *big* crash," Kendra mumbled.

"Well, folks, I hate to break the news to you," Ellie said, "but we have to call Jameson and let him know what happened. He called me, rather upset, asking if I'd heard from you, Kendra."

"Yeah, I was supposed to call him with updates."

"He's not gonna like this one," Nathan muttered under his breath.

"We'll deal with it," Ellie said.

She pulled out her phone and made the call.

Jameson's nerves were on edge as he walked back to his room to await Ellie's call. With Fuller's team less than 24 hours away from apprehending Ginette Dampierre, every part of their plan from here on out was as fragile as a house of cards. One slip-up, one careless mistake, and she would vanish, unseen, like a gentle puff of wind.

He had just stepped into his room when his phone vibrated in his hand. "Ellie?" he said, answering right away. "What's going on?"

"Hold on, Jameson." She stepped closer to Kendra's open window and pressed the speakerphone button. "Go ahead, Jameson," she said loudly. "We're all here."

He took a deep, calming, breath and then spoke slowly, a thin veil of composure barely concealing the anger that was burning in his gut. "Maybe I didn't make myself clear," he began. "Ginette Dampierre is a cold-blooded killer who will stop at nothing to punish those who threaten her business or her family. Kendra? I left Nathan in your care, knowing you would safeguard him against any potential threat. And yet, you chose to drive to Weston. What in the world compelled you to—?"

"It was my idea," Gina blurted out, before Jameson could finish.

"Mine too," Nathan said. "We made her take us there."

"You *made* her?" Jameson said.

"I thought we should take Nathan someplace where his attacker wouldn't think to look for him," Gina explained.

"Why would you choose Weston of all places?" Jameson asked.

"Because there's someone there I wanted to talk to," Nathan said.

"And who might that be?"

"Arthur Chessman."

"Who?"

"I'll let Gina explain," Nathan said.

Very slowly, as if reciting a set of complicated instructions, Gina explained how she found the embossed letters on the back of the numbered slips; how she worked and reworked them until they yielded the name Arthur Chessman; her subsequent computer search; the listing for his former bookstore in Wolfeboro, NH, and the conversation she had with Marge in the fabric store across the street, all of which led them to Boxberry Green in Weston.

"Wow," Ellie said, flashing Gina a thumbs up. *Nice going!*

"Double wow," Kendra said. She reached through the open window and gave Gina a fist bump.

Gina offered a weak shrug. *What can I say?*

"So, let me get this straight," Jameson said. "It was this Arthur Chessman who created the numbering system and not Edouard Dampierre?"

"That's right," Gina said. She turned to Nathan. "Tell him."

"Tell me what?" Jameson asked.

"Chessman admitted it," Nathan said. "He was the one who researched the items to steal."

"Not that," Gina said. "The other thing."

"Which one?"

Gina gave him a look. *Really?*

"What?" Nathan said.

She glared at him. "The name?"

"Huh?"

"That he *called* you?" She stared at him, dumbfounded. *Are you serious right now?*

"Oh, yeah. He called me Asher. Said I was the Watchman, whatever that means. Told me I'd been chosen for a reason and that I had to earn my keep."

"Watchman is another name for a caretaker or a custodian," Jameson said, considering the implication of what Nathan and Gina were telling him. Chessman was obviously grooming an apprentice, someone to carry on the work of the Covin behind the scenes and out of the watchful eye of the authorities. He couldn't help but wonder what other secrets were stitched into the fabric of the Covin's criminal empire.

Whatever they were, they'd have to wait for another day.

"We'll circle back to this another time," he said, his words taking on a cooler tone. "As usual, that was excellent work by the both of you."

"Tell him about the other guy," Gina said.

"What other guy?" Jameson asked.

"While we were in Chessman's room, some big guy showed up," Nathan said. "He acted like they knew each other, then he began asking a bunch of questions."

"What kind of questions?"

"Mostly about the stuff Arthur had in his room."

"The guy was a total creep if you ask me," Gina mumbled.

"The stuff in his room?" Jameson said. "What kind of stuff? Describe it for me."

"Well, let's see," Nathan said, thinking. "There was a framed print hanging on the wall. It was by some guy named Metzinger."

"Jean Metzinger?" Jameson asked.

"Yeah, that's it. The big guy said it was called *Man with a Pipe*."

Jameson's heart raced. "Are you sure it was a print?"

"Looked like a print to me," Kendra said.

"Huh," Jameson said, remembering how the original painting had mysteriously vanished years earlier, never to be seen again—an incident that he'd suspected might be the work of the Covin. "What else?" he asked.

"There was an old bookcase. The guy seemed pretty impressed by it. Called it a breakaway or something like that."

"Breakfront?" Jameson asked.

"Yeah, that's it," Nathan said. "The guy said it should be in a museum."

Breakfront bookcase. Museum. The words pried loose a memory from Jameson's past—a story he'd read about a museum warehouse robbery involving a breakfront bookcase. To this day the bookcase and the robbers were yet to be found.

"Whoever this man is, he wasn't there by chance," Nathan said. "He was sent by Edouard Dampierre."

"Why do you say that?" Jameson asked.

"The things he said. He didn't refer to Edouard by name, but he definitely spoke to him."

"What things?"

"Just some garbage about me and Gina. How he'd been told that we were always meddling in other people's business…"

"He *recognized* the two of you?" Jameson exclaimed.

"Yup."

"Then, yes, your assessment is correct," Jameson said. "This man was definitely sent by Edouard. If I had to guess, I'd say he's worried. He knows you have the bookcase and he's afraid you'll go through the contents and figure out Chessman's system. That would explain why he tried to get them back."

"He tried to get them back?" Nathan exclaimed. "When was this?"

"It's nothing you need to concern yourself with," Jameson said.

"The situation has been handled. And for the time being, I'm going to ask you to keep that information to yourself."

"Whatever," Nathan mumbled. This had Beck written all over it.

"I don't like that this man recognized you," Jameson said. "When word gets back to Edouard that you and Gina were there, talking to Chessman…"

"Oh, I wouldn't worry too much about that guy talking to anyone," Kendra said.

"Why is that?" Jameson asked.

"Because he had a pretty nasty accident this afternoon after he left Chessman's room. That would've been…let's see…just around five o'clock. On Wellesley Street. You should talk to Russ McCullough. I bet he can get the details from one of his cop friends."

"An accident?" Jameson asked suspiciously. "Don't tell me *you* had a hand in it."

"Just talk to him," Kendra said.

Jameson grabbed a pen and paper and jotted down the information. "Alright, now listen," he said, dropping the pen on his desk. "Ginette and Edouard are growing more desperate, which means we're now facing a double threat. Kendra, I want you to take Nathan to Stackyard Road. Do you remember how to get in?"

"Yes."

"Good. Call me when you get there. And no lapses this time. Understood?"

"Understood."

Ellie tugged on Gina's shirtsleeve. "Come on, we gotta go," she said. "I promised your mom I'd have you home by six o'clock."

"You called her?"

"I did," Ellie said. "You can thank me later."

She walked back to her car, and that's when Gina elbowed Nathan in the side.

"Uh, excuse me?" he said, brushing her arm away. "What was that for?"

"I wanted to get your attention."

"All right, you've got it," he said, like there was somewhere else he needed to be.

She gave him a look. "Your *full* attention?"

He rolled his eyes. *Oh brother.* "Fine," he said. "You have my full attention."

She pursed her lips, eyeing him for several more seconds, just to make sure.

"Well?" he said.

"I know what you're thinking," she told him.

"Is that a fact?"

"Uh-huh," she said, her expression firm.

"And?"

"Don't do it," she said.

He opened his mouth to respond when she turned and walked away.

"What was that all about?" Kendra asked, as he slid into the front seat of the Volvo.

"That was just Gina being Gina," he said.

Kendra stared at him for several seconds, wondering what new brand of mischief he was plotting.

"What?" he asked, defensively. "It's nothing."

"Yeah, right," she said. She leaned to the left of the steering wheel, then to the right, checking the floor next to her feet.

"What are you doing?" Nathan asked.

"Looking for my phone."

"You mean, this phone right here?" he said, pulling it out of the cup holder.

"How did it get *there*? she asked.

He held it up in the air and waved his other hand over the top of it. "I am Harry Houdini," he said, in a sinister voice. "I will now make this phone disappear."

"Give me that!" she growled, ripping it out of his hands.

She thumbed one of her preset numbers and one ring later a woman answered.

"Yes?"

"Two for Stackyard Road," Kendra said.

Nathan's curiosity spiked.

"Just an overnight," Kendra said into the phone.

Nathan nudged her with his elbow. *Who is that*? he mouthed.

She held up her index finger...*give me a minute*...then continued talking. "We're going to need a change of clothes, too. Nothing fancy. Just the basics." She eyed Nathan from head to toe. "Male, 12-years-old," she said, then paused. She cupped her hand over the phone. "What size do you wear?"

"Huh?"

"Your clothes. What size are they?"

"How would I know?" he said, annoyed. "I don't buy them."

She pulled her hand from the phone. "Make it a boy's XL." She listened as the information was read back to her, then promptly

203

ended the call.

"Who was that?" Nathan asked.

"Nobody you know," Kendra answered, as she started the car. She cut the wheel and swung around in a wide U-turn. When they reached the park entrance, she turned left on Dudley Road and followed a maze of streets that would eventually put her onto Rt. 9 West. From there she would take Rt. 95 North to Rowley—a seacoast town that was far enough away to keep Nathan out of Edouard and Ginette's line of fire.

"So, you're ordering clothes for me now?" Nathan asked. "Why is that?"

Kendra said nothing.

"Uh, hello," he said, waving his hand up and down in the air, as if polishing an invisible pane of glass that hung between them. "I asked you a question?"

She continued to watch the road ahead, debating how much, if anything, she should tell him.

"Why won't you answer me?" he asked.

"Aw, the heck with it," she said, at last. "You're gonna find out sooner or later."

13

Stackyard Road

Kendra merged onto Rt. 9 West, straight into a wall of bumper-to-bumper traffic. In one smooth move she knifed into the left lane, triggering an angry horn from the driver of a large box truck. "IT'S CALLED MERGING, JACK!" she shouted. "OR DIDN'T THEY TEACH YOU THAT IN TRUCK DRIVING SCHOOL?"

Nathan gave her a stern look.

"What?" she said, defensively. "The guy was a jerk!"

"Can we get back to the matter at hand?" he asked.

She hesitated momentarily, contemplating what she was about to do, much like a cliff diver at La Quebrada, staring down at the surging waters of the Pacific Ocean 135 feet below. There were those who would forbid her from sharing the information she was about to divulge. But in her heart she believed it was information Nathan needed to know. Now more than ever. And from a very early age she had adopted a belief that had gotten her through more than a few scrapes: when you're standing on thin ice, you may as well dance.

"Just so you know," she said. "Jameson and I are seriously divided about sharing this with you. The same goes for your mom. She'd prefer to wait until you're older. Much older. Like, gray haired, walking-with-a-cane older. Your dad, on the other hand? He agrees with me. The sooner you know the truth the better— even if you are only 12 years old. I mean, at some point the whole thing is going to fall into your lap anyway, so why not be prepared for it ahead of time?"

"You're stalling," Nathan said.

"No. I'm *explaining*," Kendra said calmly. "There's a difference."

"Well then, by all means, keep explaining." *And quit stalling.*

"Do you remember our lunch in Porter Square on Saturday?" she asked.

"Yeah?"

"Do you remember what I told you? How you need to be more careful? Less impulsive? Less noticeable? That your life depends on it?"

"I remember."

"You talked about the bookcase. How it was built by Thomas Hammond, and how your family has been using it as a force for good."

"Yes! I remember!" he droned. "What's your point?"

"My point is this," she said, pausing to think of the right words. "The bookcase in your attic is…what you could call…the tip of the iceberg."

"What are you talking about?"

"The quest your family has been on since they first came to this country is much bigger than you know. In time, you'll understand that the things I told you in the restaurant weren't just friendly bits of advice. They're words you need to live by, every single day."

"Now you've lost me," Nathan said.

"The person I was talking to on the phone was Finch. That's not her real name, it's just what we call her. She's a facilitator."

"A what?"

"Let me finish," she said. The train had left the station and now there was no turning back or slowing down. "Years ago, a team of specialized contractors were assembled. They were called facilitators. For their own protection, each one was given a code name."

"O-kay," Nathan said slowly, wondering what any of this had to do with him.

"Finch is responsible for cleaning and stocking the safehouses with whatever supplies are needed: food, clothing, paper goods, stuff like that."

"You're talking about the safehouses your dad has," Nathan confirmed. "The one in Watertown and the one in Chelsea? I'm guessing Stackyard Road is another one?"

"Uh…yeah…" Kendra said tentatively.

During their recent pursuit of Edouard Dampierre, when Nathan had to be hidden for his own protection, Jameson had introduced him to the Watertown and Chelsea locations. Learning of their existence had not only shattered all previous notions Nathan had about Jameson, it made him wonder what other secrets the man was hiding.

"The thing is…" Kendra said, then paused.

"What?"

"My dad is just the caretaker."

"What are you saying?"

"The safehouses aren't his."

"Not his?" Nathan said, growing more confused. "Then who do they belong to?"

"You."

Nathan's eyes went wide. "*WHAT*?"

Up ahead, brake lights flared and the long line of traffic came to a grinding halt.

"It's true," Kendra said. "One of the facilitators, Sidney, found the properties and handled all the paperwork. Finch has been maintaining them ever since."

"No, that can't be," Nathan said. "A 12-year-old boy does not own secret hideouts."

"Why not?" Kendra asked.

"Uh…because my family wouldn't *allow* it?"

"Really?" she said. "Who do you think brought in Finch, Sidney, and the rest of the facilitator group?"

Jameson took Kendra's advice and called Russ McCullough to inquire about the accident in Weston. He explained it in general terms and asked Russ to dig up any information he could find. Fifteen minutes later, Russ called him back.

"You were right," he explained. "The motor vehicle accident you asked about occurred on Wellesley Street just before five o'clock. The vehicle in question was a 2014 Dodge Challenger, registered to Gary

Moran. Home address: 541 Kimball Road in Dedham."

Jameson searched his memory but the name didn't register.

"Apparently Moran was driving at an excessive speed when he lost control of the vehicle and it rolled over," Russ said.

Lost control of the vehicle, Jameson thought, wondering what part Kendra had played in it. "Is he alive?" he asked.

"Yes, but due to the severity of his injuries they placed him in a medically induced coma."

"Does he have a criminal record?" Jameson asked.

"Just the opposite," Russ replied. "He works for the Massachusetts Department of Correction."

"In what capacity?"

"He's a guard at MCI-Cedar Junction in Walpole."

Stackyard Road splintered off of Rt. 1A in Rowley near the Rough Meadows Wildlife Sanctuary. Sections of heavily wooded forest lined both sides of the road, thinning out in various places to reveal vast acres of unblemished marshland.

Kendra coasted into the turn and drove another half mile before her foot found the brake. She slowed, and then eased down a narrow crushed-stone driveway that wound through a patch of trees so thick they completely obscured the house from the road.

Nathan sat motionless in the seat, seemingly oblivious to his surroundings as Kendra's earlier revelation about his family pounded in his head like a giant trip hammer.

She parked in front of the house, turned off the car, and looked over at him. They'd been driving for a solid hour and he had yet to utter a word. "You okay?" she asked.

"No," he said, like it was a foolish question. *How could I be?*

"Wait here. I'm gonna have a look around."

She got out of the car and surveyed the property from left to right. The air was heavy with the pungent smell of the ocean, and the late-afternoon sun had dipped down below the treetops along the edge of the property, casting long shadows that draped across the lawn like strips of black fabric.

She went to the trunk to retrieve her go bag, then stood behind the car and sent Jameson a coded text message to let him know they'd arrived safely.

The roses are in bloom

While Nathan was waiting, he pulled Gina's envelope out from beneath the seat and sorted through the contents. True to form, she had found an extensive account of the Whitehall property, including a photo of the building shortly after its initial construction, human-interest articles from an architectural journal and another from a gardening magazine, plus a random assortment of photos showing the property at various times throughout the years. On the last page was a short hand-written note.

Sorry, I couldn't find anything about Lulo Caracci

That explained her words from earlier in the day, when he'd asked her how she'd made out. "*The first thing was a piece of cake. The second thing? Not so much.*"

After examining each page, he went back to the first page and started again, reading in earnest. There was a clue there somewhere, he was sure of it. He just had to find it.

Kendra waited for her message to go through, then scaled the front steps and checked the black architectural mailbox that was mounted to the left of the door. She wasn't sure if Finch checked it on a regular basis, but when she looked inside it was empty.

She closed the angled lid, then took hold of the bottom of the box and swung it upward, revealing a square numeric keypad hidden underneath. Working from memory, she punched in a five-digit code and then pushed the door open and went inside.

Several minutes later, as Nathan was reading the article from the gardening magazine, the car door suddenly opened.

"Come on, let's go inside." Kendra said. "I don't know about you but I'm starving."

He stuffed the papers back into the envelope and climbed out of the car. As he followed her to the front door, he eyed the front of the house. Compared to the stunning pictures of Whitehall that Gina had found, this house was unremarkable to the point of being dismal. It was a drab single-story ranch built in the early 60s with slate-gray clapboards that had weathered from years of salt air and blistering sunshine. A worn dirt path ran along one end of the house, past a thicket of beach roses in full bloom.

They stepped through the front door, into a small living room. A brown microfiber sofa was pushed up against the far wall. To the right of it was an arched entryway that led into a small kitchen and adjoining dining area, complete with a round wooden table and four matching chairs. Sitting atop the table were two large pizza boxes and a plastic crate filled with groceries. Hanging off the back of one chair was a backpack stuffed with new clothes.

Kendra tossed her go bag on one of the chairs and pawed through the crate of groceries. "Yes!" she exclaimed, pulling out a bag of fresh-ground Colombian Supremo coffee. She held it up to her nose and inhaled the intoxicating aroma. "Hmm," she murmured. "Good coffee makes everything better. Anyone who tells you otherwise needs to have their head examined."

Nathan stood next to the table, eyeing the crate, the pizza boxes, and the backpack full of new clothes. "So, you just make a phone call and this stuff shows up?" he asked.

"Something like that," Kendra replied. She carried the crate over to the kitchen counter and began removing the contents. Along with the coffee, there was a box of cereal, a sleeve of bagels, a loaf of oat bread, and an assortment of condiments and jellies. Wedged in between it all, loosely trifolded, was the latest issue of the Portsmouth Herald.

She checked the fridge and found a six-pack of Coke, a dozen eggs, bacon, milk, and small containers of mayonnaise and mustard. In the crisper drawer were grapes, a large tomato, lettuce, and assorted cold cuts and cheeses.

When she looked back at the table, Nathan had opened one of the pizza boxes and was devouring a large slice of pepperoni pizza. "You want a soda?" she asked.

He nodded his head as he took another bite.

She grabbed two cans of soda, some napkins from the counter, and went back to the table just as Nathan was reaching for another slice.

"Let me get this straight," he said. "The safehouses belong to me?"

"They belong to your family," Kendra explained. "So, yeah, I guess that makes them yours."

"And you've known about them all this time?"

Kendra nodded. *Uh-huh.*

He gave her a sorry look. *You should've told me long ago.* "This team you mentioned," he said. "What did you call them?"

"Facilitators." She pried a slice of veggie pizza out of the second box and shoved it into her mouth.

"You say they were put together by my family?"

"Yoogrampahder," she said, chewing as she spoke.

"*What?*"

She took a gulp of soda to wash down the pizza, then said, "The group was created by your grandfather...which explains the code names."

"What are you talking about?"

"They're all 17th century theologians and writers."

"How many are there?" he asked. "Facilitators, I mean."

She stared up at the ceiling as she dredged the names from her memory. "Let's see...there's Finch...Sidney...Fane...Wroth...and Pennyman."

"Five," Nathan confirmed. "And their job is what, exactly?"

"Depends," she said. She swallowed another mouthful of soda, then pounded her chest and burped. "Each one has a specialty."

"So let me get this straight," he said, a ball of anger building inside him. "These *facilitators* are just out there somewhere, waiting to help whenever they're called?"

"Uh...yes and no."

"What's that supposed to mean?"

"They've been on hold," she said.

"On hold?" he repeated. "I don't understand."

"They're waiting," she said, pulling another slice from the box.

"For what?"

"You."

His eyes went wide. "Excuse me?"

"Actually...before we get to that, there's something I need to explain."

"And that is...?"

"Why."

Jameson read Kendra's text message and felt an immediate sense of relief. Based on what Russ McCullough had told him about Gary Moran, which linked him directly to Edouard Dampierre, it was clear that Edouard was still overseeing his criminal network, despite being locked away in a state prison. How many additional assets Edouard had in the field was unknown, which meant that the danger factor was much greater than Jameson had originally forecast. Having Nathan far afield helped to ease that danger. But Gina was just as much a target, and with that in mind, he called Ellie, who was busy sorting through a basket of dirty clothes in preparation for her meeting with Jaquith the next day.

"Jameson? What's up?" she asked, pulling out a blue tee shirt with her free hand.

"I'm just calling to make sure you and Gina got home safely."

"We did," she said. "Did you call Russ?"

"Yes," Jameson said. "Nathan was right. The driver of the car that crashed in Weston is a guard at the prison where Edouard Dampierre is being held."

"No surprise there," Ellie said. "A jailbird like Edouard has to recruit whoever he can to do his dirty work for him."

"Exactly, which is why we have to be even more cautious than before. Are you all set for tomorrow?"

"Almost there," Ellie said. "I'm still waiting to hear from Russ about a vehicle. Once that's settled, the only thing left will be a final review with Eric Fuller."

"Russ said he'd have a vehicle for you first thing in the morning. He didn't specify a make or model, but whatever it is, I'm sure it'll be fine."

"I take it you'll be riding with Beck?"

"Yes. We'll be waiting nearby where Jaquith and Ginette Dampierre won't see us."

"You really think she'll show?"

"Well, we know she's a meticulous woman who leaves nothing to chance. She's here in America trying to reconstruct a criminal network with people she doesn't know, which means she has doubts about who she can trust. Now, she learns about a collection of books and such that her brother had hidden in his office—a virtual treasure chest of leads to artwork that could reap millions of dollars for the Covin. Add in a remote location for the exchange, one that affords her complete anonymity, and she's looking at an opportunity that's too good to pass up. Do I think she'll show? You bet I do."

Nathan leaned his elbows on the edge of the table and buried his face in his open palms. As if his day hadn't been stressful enough, here was yet another bombshell that had been kept from him. And just when he thought there were no more Hammond-family secrets.

"You know? Maybe we should stop," Kendra said, seeing the troubling effect her words were having on him. "You've had a pretty rough day and…"

"Pretty rough?" he blurted out, pulling his hands away from his face. "*Ya think?*"

Kendra gathered the pizza boxes and walked them over to the kitchen counter. When she turned around, Nathan had laid his head on his arms that were folded on the tabletop.

"Look, I didn't mean to freak you out," she said. "It's like I told you before. I think it's important that you know this stuff, especially since…you know…"

He raised his head. "What?" he asked.

"Since you've chosen to continue your family's mission of helping people."

I didn't choose…someone did that for me, he wanted to shout. But he knew that saying it out loud would only lead to a discussion of all the strange, enchanted things the bookcase had done. Things like books presenting themselves to him, books refusing to budge from the shelf, drawers opening on their own. Each of those events had pushed him further and further down the tortuous path that led to where he now sat.

"The thing is, at some point you're going to need help, just like your grandfather did," Kendra said.

"What are you talking about?"

She went to the table, pulled out a chair and sat down. "Jameson didn't give me all the details, but years ago word got out that there was a man who was secretly helping people in need, those who had somehow been victimized or wrongly accused."

"You're referring to my grandfather."

"Yes. When you think about it, it's kinda weird that it didn't happen sooner, given all the people in your family who had the bookcase. Anyway, as the rumor spread, people learned the identity of this secret saint, and they began showing up at his bookshop to seek his help. Of course, this went directly against your family's goal to remain, how did you put it?"

"Careful, watchful, unseen."

"Right, unseen," she said. "Your grandfather couldn't just turn people away, they were desperate for his help. At the same time, he couldn't do it by himself. There were too many."

"So, he assembled the team of facilitators."

"That's right. He considered them…consultants…I guess you'd call them."

"That's the why," Nathan said.

"Yes. But since your grandfather's passing, the facilitators have been on hiatus."

"On what?"

"Hiatus. You know, a break?"

"What you really mean is, they're waiting for the next person in the Hammond family to continue the legacy of the bookcase… which would be me."

"Which would be you," Kendra said. "And if you're not careful, history will repeat itself. Trust me when I tell you, that's *not* something you want to have happen. You saw what Edouard Dampierre and his thugs were capable of. And now, just this morning, his sister sends a trained assassin to finish the job."

He felt a flash of anger rip through his body, but he said nothing. He'd managed to escape Edouard's wrath. Barely. The question now was: would he be able to do the same with Ginette?

"Don't assume for a second that there aren't others just like them," Kendra said. "Extremely dangerous people with dark secrets who will stop at nothing to keep them hidden. You can bet that the bookcase in your attic contains a whole bunch of them."

"Jameson told me some secrets are better left alone," Nathan admitted.

"Well, he would know," she replied. In that moment she was tempted to tell him the rest of it. The words were right there on the tip of her tongue, ready and waiting, just daring her to speak them. But his circuits were already overheating and she feared that one more jolt might fry his brain altogether.

Some other time, she told herself.

Or maybe never.

She pushed the chair away from the table and stood up, a clear signal that the discussion was over. "The bedrooms are that way," she said, pointing at the hallway on the far side of the living room. "Take your pick." She grabbed the backpack off the chair. "Here, see if these fit," she said, tossing it to him. "While you're doing that, I'm going to shower." She inspected each arm, then front of her shirt. "Look at this," she said, pointing to a blood stain on the fabric. "That jerk bled on me. Can you believe it? The nerve!"

After she left the room, Nathan got up from the table and took his empty soda can over to the sink. Sitting on the counter next to the empty plastic crate was the copy of the Portsmouth Herald. He was skimming the headlines when one in particular caught his eye. He read the first few sentences and then pulled his flip phone from his pocket.

He had to call Gina.

Had to tell her.

Lulo Caracci wasn't a person.

Not even close.

14

The Most Important Clue of All

T he first bands of sunlight were breaking through the curtains in Kendra's room when her eyes suddenly flicked open. Something wasn't right. She could smell it. She pushed back the covers and quickly got dressed, throwing on the spare set of clothes she kept in her go bag. When she walked into the kitchen moments later, Nathan was sitting at the table, staring at the far wall as if locked in a trance. On the table in front of him was the Portsmouth Herald. Positioned next to it in a loose stack were the pages Gina had given him.

"What's wrong?" she asked.

He snapped out of his funk and looked over at her. "Oh…uh… nothing," he said. In truth, he'd had a fitful night of sleep, permeated once again by the sound of a woman calling to him, desperately pleading for help.

"You made coffee," Kendra said, like he'd performed a minor miracle.

"Yeah, it wasn't that difficult," he said, looking back down at the newspaper.

"But...you don't *drink* coffee."

"Yes, I know that. But I needed to wake you up and I figured the smell of coffee would do the trick." He looked up from the paper and grinned. "Turns out I was right."

"Hold on," she said. "You *needed* to wake me up or you *wanted* to wake me up?"

"Is there a difference?"

"Oh, there's a huge difference," she replied. She went over to the counter where he'd set out a clean coffee mug for her. "Need implies urgency," she said, filling the mug with steaming hot coffee. "Want is altogether different."

"How so?"

"It means you're a wiseass."

"Well, this is urgent," he said. "Trust me."

"I'm all ears," she said.

"Do you remember what you told me in the restaurant on Saturday? How there was no way you'd drive me to Whitehall unless I had definite proof that Claire's hunch was correct, that the property was connected to the Covin?"

"Yeah?"

He held up the paper with both hands and showed her the front page. "I found it."

She walked over to the table holding the mug of coffee just below her chin with both hands, letting the thin plume of steam caress the front of her face. When she sat down, Nathan slid the newspaper across the table and spun it so she could read without having to put down her coffee.

She raised the mug to her lips, took a sip, then scanned the headlines. "What am I looking at?" she asked, her eyes jumping from one headline to the next.

"That, right there," he said, pointing to the story right above the fold.

Ten Years Later – Lulo Robbery Haunts Local Police
By Kyle Halliday, Staff Reporter

PORTSMOUTH - Ten years after the daring robbery at Lulo, the posh art gallery in downtown Portsmouth, questions still remain. Fore-most among them is the current whereabouts of the stolen artwork, which museum officials have valued at over five million dollars.

In a curious twist to the case, security cameras at the gallery confirmed the identity of the thief, as well as the make and model of the getaway vehicle. He was cornered by Portsmouth police within an hour of the robbery, emptyhanded, and was killed during the ensuring gun battle.

Saturday marks the 10-year anniversary of the theft, which remains an ongoing investigation. "We're asking for the public's help in locating the missing artwork," says lead detective Ken Walsh. "Anyone with information about the robbery, or the items that were stolen is being asked to contact the Portsmouth Police Department."

"Very interesting," Kendra said, when she was done reading. "But what does this have to do with Whitehall, or Claire for that matter?"

He reached across the table and pointed at a group of pictures just below the story. They were a photographic inventory of the items that had been stolen, each one crafted by the same artist. By including them, police were hoping to generate phone calls from the public on the off chance that one or more of the pieces might've been spotted.

He tapped his finger on one photo in particular. It showed the sculpture of a woman looking down, her thick hair tied back in a loose wrap that draped down over her shoulder. She was holding a lyre harp and her facial expression had a dream-like quality, as if she were gazing into the eyes of her newborn child.

Kendra considered it briefly, then shrugged. "Yeah? What about it?"

"Read the caption," he said.

The words were very small and she had to lean closer to see them. "*The Lady of Florence*," she said, reading aloud. "Sixteenth century White Carrara marble statue by Italian sculptor Umberto Caracci. Dimensions: 8" x 5" x 4"."

"The name Caracci, and the name of the gallery were written in Claire's book," Nathan said.

"So?"

"In the chapter about Whitehall," he added.

She took another look at the photo, then examined each of the others—all exquisitely crafted by Caracci. There was a blindfolded goddess, a ram's head, a gladiator, and a handmaiden holding a woven basket. "So, you think Claire somehow linked the art theft to Whitehall?" she asked.

"Yes. It's the only thing that makes sense. I mean, why else would she write those names in her book?"

"A valid question," Kendra said. "Then again, maybe it was just—"

"Wait," he said, cutting her off before she could voice her objection. "There's more." He picked through the pile of papers Gina had given him until he found the one he wanted. "Look at this picture," he said, handing it to her.

She ran her eyes over the photo, the dubious look on her face suggesting she could find nothing about it to substantiate Nathan's claim. "It's a burned-out building," she said. "What about it?"

"It's not just any building," he said. "It's Whitehall. A similar photo was in Claire's book. Apparently, the fire was a big deal because in the months that followed, the building was completely renovated to its original condition. It was like the fire never happened."

"You lost me," Kendra said.

"Check the date at the bottom of the page," he told her.

As part of her research, and in true Gina McDermott style, she had included the date of the picture—something he never would have done—and which now stood as a significant clue. He made a mental note to thank her the next time he saw her.

"What about it?" Kendra asked.

"It was ten years ago, the same year as the robbery," he explained. "I've been going back and forth between the newspaper article and that photo and I think I figured out why Claire wanted to go there so badly."

She gave him a skeptical look. "You think this *picture* was the reason?"

"Yes."

"That makes no sense."

"Actually," he replied. "It was brilliant."

She stared at the fire photo again, struggling to make a connection. "Okay, I'll bite. How could the picture of a fire-ravaged building make Claire want to visit the property? It sounds like a total waste of time if you ask me."

"It's simple," he said. "According to the timeline, which I'm sure the paper printed at the time of the theft, she knew that the thief was caught within an hour after leaving the gallery. And because he was emptyhanded when they found him, it means he stashed the stolen artwork somewhere close by."

"Makes sense," Kendra said. "But why would he do that?"

"Who knows? Maybe he didn't want to damage the pieces and ruin their value. Maybe he realized the police were closing in on him, so he unloaded the goods with the intention of coming back for them later. Whichever it was, he'd want to hide them in a place where no one would think to look."

She arched both eyebrows. "In a burned-out building? I *highly* doubt that."

"Think about it," he countered, his words coming faster. "Who in their right mind would think to look for stolen artwork at the scene of a fire?"

"Well, you got me there."

"And because it was an art robbery," he said, "Claire must've assumed the Covin was behind it. I mean, that *is* what they specialize in, right? Stealing high-priced art?"

The words struck Kendra like a cold slap in the face. She looked at the date Gina had written, the numbers unlocking a memory from years earlier. Slowly, her eyes drifted across the room as it played out in her mind. "Yes, she absolutely made that assumption," she said.

"What is it?" he asked.

"I can't believe I didn't remember this sooner," she said, snapping out of her funk. "There were a string of art robberies up and down the east coast that year," she said, tapping her finger on the date. "I only know because my dad was helping the authorities track down the group responsible. Or trying to, at least."

"And he thought it was the Covin?"

"He was *convinced* it was the Covin," Kendra replied.

"So we can assume that he and Claire talked about it."

"Oh, they talked about it all right."

"Okay, so they talk about it, then she reads about the Lulo robbery, sometime after that she sees the picture in the book…"

At that, his words fell off.

It all fit. In the grim silence that followed, they both sat spellbound, contemplating what they now believed was the morbid truth—a validation of the sad fate that had befallen Claire Jameson.

Kendra broke free of the memory and looked down at the photo again. "Everything you said makes sense, but there's one part that doesn't fit. There's nothing here but a smoldering heap of ashes. Are you saying the thief buried the artwork in that mess?"

"Not there," Nathan said. "He would've known that the fire department would comb through the charred ruins, trying to determine the cause of the fire."

He slid his finger across the page, to the edge of the photo.

"There."

Ellie held up a soiled yellow tee shirt in one hand and an equally filthy blue one in the other. "What do you think…this one, or this one?" she asked Gina, who was standing inside the guest room door, watching her aunt prepare for the meeting with Jaquith.

"Hmm, that's a tough one," Gina said, eyeing both shirts. "The yellow one is pretty disgusting, but the blue one has bigger stains. I'd go with the blue one."

"Then the blue one it is," Ellie said. She was about to move on to the next decision: which pair of beat-up jeans to wear, when her cell phone chirped. She grabbed it off the bureau, saw who was calling, and motioned to Gina to close the door.

"Good morning Eric," she said brightly.

"Are you ready to do this?" Fuller asked.

"Ready and waiting," she replied.

"Excellent. What I'd like to do is take a few minutes to run through my manpower plan. After that, I'll answer any questions you have."

"Let's do it," Ellie said.

For the next 20 minutes, Fuller detailed how, by two o'clock, his team would be deployed on either side of the road leading into the sandpit, the firepower they would bring to bear, and the additional teams that would be positioned on the main road.

"Impressive," Ellie said, when he was done.

"We aim to please," Fuller joked.

"Ouch," she said, referring to the lame pun.

"Yeah, that one's getting old," he said. "Did you have any questions?"

"None that I can think of."

"Then that leaves just one last thing. I probably don't have to say it but I will anyway."

"What's that?" Ellie asked.

"If bullets start flying, you hit the dirt."

"Bullets. Dirt. Got it," she said.

"All right then, see you on the sandpit road," Fuller said, then disconnected.

As Ellie pulled the phone from her ear, she saw Gina staring at her, mortified. "Bullets? Dirt? What was that about?" she exclaimed.

"It's nothing," Ellie said, waving it off. "Eric was just joking around."

Gina gave her a hard stare.

"Seriously," Ellie said. "I'm going to be fine."

"I still don't understand why you won't take me with you," Gina groused.

"Don't start," Ellie warned. "You and Nathan are being kept clear of this operation for a reason."

"I know, I know," Gina grumbled. "It's for our own safety, blah, blah, blah."

Ellie tipped her head forward, both eyebrows raised. "Really?" she said. "I don't hear Nathan complaining."

"Of course not," Gina said. She looked away and mumbled under her breath, "He's too busy looking for stolen artwork."

"What was that?"

"Nothing," Gina said. Ellie had a tough enough day as it was, helping to trap an international fugitive while being surrounded by an army of gun-toting U.S. Marshals. This wasn't the time to throw another log on *that* fire. Besides, whatever Nathan was up to, Kendra would be there to protect him.

What could possibly go wrong?

Kendra picked up the fire photo and examined it closely. Beyond the pile of charred rubble, set a good distance away and completely unaffected by the fire, was another building. Whoever had taken the picture had only included the back corner of it in the shot. Still, the weathered shingles were easy to make out. "What is that, a shed?" she asked.

"No, it's too big," Nathan replied.

"And you think that's where the thief stashed the stolen art?"

"Yup," Nathan said. "And I think Claire figured that out. That's why she was so obsessed with going to Whitehall—why she couldn't wait for Jameson to return from Europe. But there's something else that we haven't considered, and it's the most important clue of all."

"What's that?"

"She never came back."

"Huh?"

"She had a hunch. She went to Whitehall to check it out. And she never came back. Meaning: she found something. If she hadn't, she would've just gone back home."

"Which means somebody wanted to make sure she didn't reveal what she found," Kendra said, her eyes falling back down to the photo.

"Edouard as much as admitted it when we had him cornered in his office, remember?"

"Oh, I remember all too well," Kendra said, with venom in her words.

"So, *now* do you believe me?"

Without a word, Kendra gathered the pages from the tabletop and slid them back into the envelope. The time for talking was over. "Gather whatever things you need," she said. "We leave right after lunch."

It was just before noon when Russ McCullough pulled into Nathan's driveway in a ratty Toyota Tacoma pickup truck. Dents and scratches marred the body, and Russ had removed the hubcaps, adding to the vehicle's woeful appearance.

He had just turned off the engine when Beck's jet-black Dodge Ram 2500 powered up the driveway. Sitting in the passenger seat was Jameson. The two men climbed down from the truck and joined Russ next to the Tacoma.

"This is perfect," Beck said, kneeling down to check the rear tires that were showing signs of wear. The truck clearly hadn't been washed in months and the entire body was coated with a layer of dirt and grime.

"Where'd you find it?" Jameson asked. He leaned closer to peer through the driver's side window but the filth blurred his view of the interior.

"It belongs to a mechanic friend of mine in Malden. It's what he calls a reclamation project," Russ said, accenting the last two words with air quotes.

"We better get it loaded," Beck said. "Ellie needs to be on the road no later than 12:30."

As he and Russ began hauling the boxes from the kitchen to the truck, a white Honda Civic pulled into the driveway. A young woman they didn't recognize got out, a brick-red accordion folder in her hand, and made a beeline for the front steps. She was almost to the top when the front door opened Elizabeth stepped outside.

"Natalie," she said, smiling. "How goes the battle?"

Natalie shrugged, like she was afraid to speak the truth. "It's... you know...hectic," she said. "Not that I have to tell you, right? I mean, you work there and...well...it's not like..."

"Say no more," Elizabeth joked. "Hectic is putting it mildly."

"I was meaning to bring these by yesterday," Natalie said, holding up the accordion file, "but...uh...Mondays are...well...insane. I hope you don't mind me stopping by during...you know...lunch."

"It's fine," Elizabeth assured her. "What've you got?"

"Uh...just a few things." She slipped the elastic cord off the file and removed the documents that required Elizabeth's signature. After she handed them over, she reached back in the file and pulled out a ballpoint pen.

Elizabeth reviewed each of the papers, then walked over to the edge of the porch and signed them, using the top rail as a makeshift table. "Here you go," she told Natalie, handing them back. "How hard was that?"

Natalie giggled. "You're funny," she said, the words inducing an immediate look of panic. "Not funny like...you know...ha-ha...I just mean...that...um..."

"Don't worry, I know what you meant," Elizabeth said, patting Natalie's shoulder. "You best get back. This is Tuesday, macaroni and cheese day. It'd be a real shame to miss out on that."

She waited until Natalie drove out of sight, then went down the front steps and around the corner of the house to where the men were standing on either side of the Tacoma, covering the boxes with a large blue tarp. "Just as soon as you gentlemen are finished, we're ready for you inside," she said.

When they came into the house moments later, Elizabeth met them in the kitchen and ushered them into the living room where Ellie and David were waiting.

"Can I get anyone some coffee?" Elizabeth asked, once they were all assembled.

"That's very kind, but no," Russ replied.

Jameson and Beck each gestured with a brief wave. *None for me, thank you.*

"In that case, Jameson? I'll let you take it from here," Elizabeth said.

"Thank you. We don't have much time, so I'll be brief," he said. He turned to Ellie. "You spoke with Eric Fuller?"

"Yes. Earlier today," she said.

"And he briefed you on his plan?"

"He did."

"Very good," Jameson said. "For the benefit of everyone here, I want to run through the timeline so we all have a clear understanding of how things are going to unfold. Before I do that, though, I want to thank Russ for securing a vehicle."

"Don't mention it," Russ said. Then, in a softer voice, "Let's hope it doesn't break down."

"After you leave here," Jameson said to Ellie, "Beck and I will drive to Lyman with Russ, using an alternate route. I've located a spot nearby where we can wait, ready to help if needed. Don't get me wrong, as I'm sure Eric explained, he'll have his team well-situated all around you. Call me selfish, but I want to be there when they put the cuffs on Ginette Dampierre."

The slightest of grins graced Ellie's lips. *Of course you do*, she thought. *Who doesn't want to be aboard the boat when they land the prize fish?*

"Now," Jameson said, continuing. "During the exchange, if Jaquith or Ginette try to alter the agreed-upon price, don't fight them. Take what they offer. You don't have to be happy about it, but at the same time we want them to take the boxes. You understand why, right?"

"I'm guessing it has something to do with possession of stolen property," Ellie said.

"Correct."

"You can charge someone with that, even if the contents are phony?" David asked.

"Yes. They can also be charged with the illegal buying and selling of trademarked goods."

"Is that really necessary?" Elizabeth asked. "I mean, don't the Swiss authorities already have enough to put her away for the rest of her life?"

"They do," Jameson said, overjoyed at the prospect. "But what's the harm in a few more charges? The more the merrier, I say."

"What do you need us to do?" David asked.

"Nothing. Your work is done. You and Elizabeth can go about your day content in the knowledge that your son is safe and that his pursuer is about to be permanently erased from your lives."

A wide smile crossed Elizabeth's face. "Now *that* is the best thing I've heard you say all day."

Fifteen minutes later she stood at the front window and watched Ellie pull out of the driveway, a ribbon of gray exhaust trailing the Tacoma all the way up the street. Following right behind her was Beck, his powerful Dodge 2500 riding high on the suspension, rumbling like a Union Pacific Big Boy locomotive.

"Well, I guess there's nothing to do now but wait," Elizabeth said.

David was sitting on the couch staring at the fireplace and didn't respond.

When she saw the troubled expression on his face, she walked over and sat down next to him. "What's wrong?" she asked.

"I'm just trying to envision how this whole thing goes down without Ellie catching a stray bullet," he said.

"I wouldn't worry about it," she said. "Eric Fuller and his team are professionals. They train for situations just like this. If anyone's going to catch a bullet, it's Ginette Dampierre. If she or any of her people so much as raise a hand against Ellie, it's not going to end well for them. Now come on, it's lunchtime and I'm starving. What say we go downtown and enjoy a leisurely lunch, just the two of us? Maybe afterwards, we can do a little shopping."

David smiled and said, "Now that's the best thing I've heard *you* say all day."

Kendra stood on the back deck, looking out over the salt marsh. It stretched all the way to Plum Island Sound, creased with a serpent-like network of intertidal creeks. She closed her eyes and listened to the breeze whisper as it combed the smooth cordgrass.

Talking about Whitehall had unearthed memories of Claire Jameson and the happy times they had spent together. As each treasured moment filtered through her mind like a gentle stream, she couldn't help but wonder if another chapter was about to be written about the woman who had been so savagely taken from them. If so, would it answer the nagging questions that surrounded her hasty decision to go to Whitehall alone? Would it be enough to bring Jameson a final measure of peace?

Thinking of him snapped her out of her reverie and she opened her eyes, realizing that, once again, she'd forgotten to check in with him. She was pulling her phone from her pocket when the sudden caw of a seagull directly overhead made her stop and look up. The bird circled the deck, navigating the crosswinds with ease, squawking loudly as if trying to convey an urgent message.

Was it an omen? Kendra wondered. Had some otherworldly being sent this creature to forewarn her of impending danger? She stared at the phone in her hand, suddenly debating the call she was about to make. *I can't tell Jameson where we're going*, she thought. *He'll demand that we wait for another time, when he can be with us.* Wasn't that the same plea he'd made to Claire when she revealed her intention to visit Whitehall alone?

No, she told herself. *Calling him is out of the question.* Instead, she grasped the phone with both hands and used her thumbs to compose a quick text.

Good luck today – be safe!

Jameson's reply was immediate and equally brief.

Will do. I'll call when it's done

As she shoved the phone back in her pocket she searched the sky overhead.

The seagull was nowhere in sight.

She went back inside and found Nathan rummaging through one of the kitchen drawers.

"What are you doing?" she asked.

"Looking for a flashlight."

"Don't bother," she said. "I keep one in the car."

He looked over at her, skeptical. "Does it work?"

"Did Ralph Kiner hit 54 home runs for the Pittsburg Pirates in 1949?"

"I'll take that as a yes," he said, then closed the drawer.

For Ginette Dampierre, the day couldn't get any better. After making painfully slow gains in her reconstruction of the Covin's northeast network, in the face of growing uncertainty among the shopkeepers, the tides were finally turning in her favor. She sat on the balcony and stared at the Boston skyline as she pondered the chain of events that were about to unfold. The air was filled with the din of afternoon traffic, rising up from the streets below in a symphony of honking horns and wailing sirens.

City music.

Her favorite.

She checked the time and then made a call, the number, like bulletproof ink, forever imprinted on her memory. The call went through without delay, and two rings later Niko answered.

"Yes?"

"It's almost time," Ginette said.

"I know."

"You're clear on the directions?"

"I am. It won't be a problem."

"Just be careful," Ginette warned. "We can assume they'll have others in the immediate area, although you may not see them."

"I'm not worried," Niko said.

"Good. Call me when it's done."

"Will do."

15

Time to Eat

It was just after one o'clock when Kendra pulled out of Stackyard Road onto Rt. 1A. As she followed it north to the interstate, past large tracts of rich farmland, her expression grew increasingly hostile.

Nathan knew that look. She was in a dark place—a grim world where pain and regret are an unrelenting storm that lashes broken souls without constraint.

"Are you all right?" he asked.

"No," she said, in a menacing voice, her eyes trained on the road ahead.

He looked down at Gina's envelope in his hand, realizing the anguish its contents had unleashed. "I'm sorry," he said softly.

"For what?"

"For dragging you into this."

"You didn't drag me into anything," she said, as she sped past a delivery truck that had slowed to make a turn. "I was already there."

They came to the Merrimack River in Newburyport, where the marinas on both sides of the road were filled to capacity. The boats were bobbing gently with the afternoon tide, and seeing them reminded Nathan of the family member he had lost, like Claire Jameson, before the entirety of her life had a chance to unfold. Now that he thought about it, the details surrounding his Aunt Sarah's passing weren't that different than Claire Jameson's. In fact, they were nearly identical.

"Do you want to talk about what happened to her?" he asked.

"No," Kendra said abruptly. The speed of her reply suggested she was anticipating his question.

"I just thought…maybe…you know…"

"Forget it," she said. "It's not open for discussion. Not now, not ever. Just be glad you weren't there that day. It's not something anyone should ever have to see."

As if blessed with a psychic power, she had looked into his mind and read his thoughts as easily as opening a child's toybox. How and where they found Claire Jameson were questions he'd been saving for the right time. But that time had never materialized. And while Jameson had explained the events leading up to that fateful day, a time in his life when he was busy chasing the Covin to every corner of the globe, he'd been noticeably mum on any further details.

All he would say was that her death had been a stern warning from the Covin.

Leave us alone.

Stop interfering in our business.

Or someone else you love will be next.

They drove the rest of the way in silence, their resolve building with every mile. With the Piscataqua River Bridge looming in the distance, Nathan opened Gina's envelope and took out the map she'd printed, showing the route to New Castle Island, home to the property commonly referred to as Whitehall.

According to an article she'd unearthed in a travel magazine, the impressive structure was built on a large plot of land situated on the eastern side of the island. It had been purchased in the early 1800s by William Pendleton, a wealthy ship captain from Searsport, Maine, who named the entire tract after his only granddaughter, Eliza White.

A small inset picture of Pendleton showed a burly man with finely combed hair and a tapered goatee. He was dressed in formal fashion, wearing a white shirt, black vest and bowtie, and a black suit coat with wide lapels, the fabric as thick as a Hudson Bay blanket.

The mansion and carriage house were all that remained of the original estate, which had been bought and sold numerous times. An addendum to the article reported the recent purchase of Whitehall by a mid-sized hotel chain that specialized in grand seaside properties. According to a spokesman for the company who was quoted in the article, the aging relic would undergo a complete renovation with numerous upgrades and a host of new amenities.

Nathan studied the map, then looked up to check the road signs. "Take the next exit," he said.

Kendra glanced at the side mirror, saw an opening, and slid easily into the right lane. After she glided down the exit for the Rt. 1 bypass, Nathan called out the directions that led them along a crooked string of roads, over bridges and 2 small islands, to the much larger New Castle Island.

They were driving down a long stretch of heavily wooded road when they saw a break in the tree line up ahead.

"It's up here on the right," Nathan said.

Kendra slowed to a crawl as they approached the long cobblestone driveway. It stretched all the way to the main house, winding around a giant two-tiered marble fountain that sat bone dry in the afternoon sun. "Looks vacant," she said, coming to a full stop in the road.

Nathan scanned the property from left to right. "There's more to this than meets the eye," he said. "You heard what Chessman said, right?"

"Which part? Most of it was gibberish."

"When I mentioned Whitehall, he had a fit—told me to just do my job, that they would handle the rest. He also said something about them running on a tight schedule."

"You should've told me that sooner," Kendra said. She drove another 50 feet, pulled over onto the shoulder, then they both climbed out and surveyed the area.

The road was long and straight for as far as the eye could see, skirted on either side by dense woodlands. Other than some random bird chatter from deep in the forest, and the tinny echo of boat traffic coming from the water nearby, it had the backwoods feel of unspoiled timberland—a territory untouched by human hands.

"Something about this is all wrong," Kendra said, eyeing the woods on both sides of the road. "Are you sure that old man said Whitehall and not something else?"

"He didn't say Whitehall," Nathan replied. "I did."

"Well, I don't see anything suspicious. Do you?"

"No, but I rarely ever do," he said. "At first."

He went back to the car and grabbed the backpack Finch had delivered to Stackyard Road. Inside it was Kendra's flashlight plus a few other odds and ends he'd collected from the house. When he walked around the back end of the car, Kendra was pulling her baseball bat from the tangle of softball equipment she kept in the trunk.

"Ready?" he asked.

She smacked the tip of the bat against her open palm.

"Oh, yeah...I'm ready."

Eric Fuller met Beck, Jameson, and Russ a half mile from the sandpit, in the paved lot behind the Goodwins Mills Fire and Rescue. Two teams of marshals, designated Blue Team and Red Team, had already taken their positions in the woods on either side of the exchange site. Another two teams, designated Gray Team One and Two, were positioned on the main road as spotters. Now it was just a waiting game.

"We're clear on the rules, right?" Fuller asked, as he handed Beck the radio. "You guys can listen in, but that's it. You're not to get involved unless I signal you for help."

"Clear," Beck said. "Ellie should be arriving any moment now."

The words had barely left his lips when Fuller's radio squawked.

"Blue four, Cass just pulled in."

Fuller keyed the mic. "Copy Blue four."

"Cass?" asked Beck.

"Ellie's code name," Fuller explained. "It's short for Cassowary."

"A very apt name," Jameson said, giving Fuller an approving nod.

Russ looked from Fuller to Jameson. "Cassowary?"

"The Australian Cassowary is considered the most lethal bird on the planet," Jameson said.

"I thought it was only fitting after Ellie's recent heroics," said Fuller. "The way she tracked down Edouard Dampierre's thugs and rescued Nathan from that demented death pit? That girl has some serious predatory instinct."

"Agreed," Jameson said. He had his own stories about Ellie, times he'd enlisted her skills for "special projects," as he liked to call them. But those were unspoken tales of valor that would forever stay between them.

Fuller checked his watch. "All right, gentlemen," he said. "Sit tight. The show begins in 30 minutes."

Ellie pulled into the sandpit road, driving slowly and watching the ground ahead. The main road had just disappeared in her rearview mirror when she spotted a flattened McDonald's bag lying in the dirt, looking like it had been run over several times by a 28,000 lb. dump truck. Following Fuller's directive, she pulled over onto the shoulder.

After she got out of the truck, she stretched and then did a slow 180° turn, looking for any sign of Fuller's team. The woods were thick with a healthy mix of pines and hardwoods, and patches of ferns grew where the sun was able to break through the treetops. But nowhere did she see a single helmet, camo vest, or firearm. If she didn't know better, she'd swear she was the only person for a mile in any direction.

Nathan and Kendra walked back toward the driveway and stopped at the corner of the lot. Marking the northern boundary was a towering wall of stone over seven feet tall, built with giant slabs of granite. It stretched through the forest, bending slightly before ending at the water. The house sat at the back of the property overlooking the ocean. Five hundred feet to the left of it was the old carriage house.

In an attempt to provide a layer of privacy, the entire parcel was obscured by a dense band of woods that lined the side of the road. Kendra and Nathan crept through the trees and stopped at the lawn's edge. No one was mowing the grass. No gardeners were tending to the flowers. There wasn't a single child playing in the yard.

It was like staring at a post card.

"Let's check the house first," Kendra said. "We don't want any surprises."

"Agreed," Nathan said, as he fell in behind her.

They jogged across the yard, zigzagging around flowerbeds filled with clusters of lupines, gladiator alliums, deep blue globe thistle, and fuchsia-pink Veronica Red Fox. They were almost to the house when Kendra stopped next to a Chinese blue wisteria tree, the icy lavender and purple blooms filling the air with a sweet-smelling aroma.

"Stay close," she said. "If we meet anyone, you let *me* do the talking, got it?"

"Fine by me," he said, looking at the bat in her hand.

They ran to the front corner of the house and she leaned around the edge of the first window. Seeing no one inside, she went to the next, and the next. There wasn't a soul to be seen. Gradually, they made their way across the front and continued around the far corner of the house. When they reached the back deck, they eased up the end stairs and paused, watching for any activity. The only movement they saw was the steady flow of boat traffic coming and going from the mouth of the Piscataqua River. Beyond it was the open ocean, the dark blue water shimmering in the afternoon sun like a sheet of sequin fabric.

Like before, Kendra crept along the exterior, checking each door and window. "Nothing," she said, peering into the last window at the far end of the deck.

Nathan went to the railing and checked the shoreline in both directions. There was nothing but a rocky embankment, washed clean by the tides. As he stared out across the water, at the Isles of Shoals in the distance, he recalled Arthur Chessman's stern reprimand: "*They run on a very tight schedule...no room for error.*"

He looked left and saw the granite wall dip down to meet the water. To his right was a large clay tennis court. Beyond it, nothing but woods. "What are we missing?" he muttered to himself.

"Hey," Kendra said, breaking his train of thought. She shook a finger at the carriage house. "We're not done."

"Right," he said, letting go of Chessman's words.

They followed a set of wooden steps down to the lawn, then scaled the embankment and peeled off toward the carriage house on their right.

It was larger than it appeared in the photograph. The shingles, once brown, had yellowed with age, and set into the side facing the main house were a pair of small four-pane windows. Kendra went to the first one and cupped her hands against the glass, trying to see inside.

While she was doing that, Nathan walked around to the back. In the near corner he saw a narrow wooden door. When he pulled on the handle, to his surprise, it swung open with ease. He gripped the frame of the door and leaned in, surveying the interior. It was completely empty, and light was filtering in through the side windows, illuminating the old plank floor that was ragged and worn. Some of the boards showed cracks and gouges. Others had rotted completely, their color a mix of faded grays and blacks and browns.

He stepped inside and started across the jagged floorboards, taking great care where he placed his feet. As he walked, the boards creaked loudly, setting off alarm bells in his head. He stopped moving, wondering if he should turn back, but it was too late. The floor suddenly gave way with a thunderous crack, and he plummeted downward in a blinding cloud of dust, dirt and splintered wood. He landed amid the rubble on a packed dirt floor, and for nearly a minute he lay there, dazed, his body wracked with pain.

Until he heard the rats.

At first they were just vague shapes, scurrying about in the shadows. But as his eyes adjusted to the dim band of light streaming down through the ragged hole in the floor overhead, their size and numbers became more defined. Some were as big as house cats. Like a gathering army their numbers continued to grow, and it was only a matter of time before they would advance in a ravenous swarm.

Eat up, friends. Don't be shy. There's plenty here for everyone.

He scrambled to his feet and slid his backpack off his shoulder, ignoring the pain that gripped his body. From the center compartment he dug out Kendra's flashlight, and with a flick of a button it came to life, filling the cramped room with light. He turned slowly and took stock of his surroundings, running the beam over every square inch, through the cloud of dust that hung in the air.

He was in a small cellar, barely twelve feet square. To his right, a row of old wooden barrels were pushed up against the stone foundation, an indication that the room had once been used to store potatoes and carrots and other root vegetables—maybe even a keg of ale or two. To his left, a rickety wooden staircase led up to the first floor.

From somewhere up above he heard Kendra calling his name, but it was nothing more than a whisper amid the squeaks of the ever-growing horde of rats. Where they were coming from he didn't know, but what had started out as a scant few quickly doubled, then tripled.

And still they came.

Suddenly, as if signaled by a silent bell that only they could hear, they began closing in. He kicked pieces of the broken floorboards and debris at them, scattering them momentarily, but they quickly reformed their line and came at him again, hissing and chattering.

Time to eat.

Eric Fuller took a position with the Red Team on the eastern side of the sandpit road. The Blue Team mirrored those positions on the west side of the road. Each team member was equipped with an in-ear radio that would allow them to communicate hands free.

At three o'clock, Fuller radioed his spotters on the main road.

"Gray One and Two, report."

"Gray One, all quiet."

"Copy Gray One," Fuller said.

Gray Two followed seconds later. "Gray Two, quiet here too, sir."

"Copy Gray Two."

One mile away, behind the Goodwins Mills Fire and Rescue, Beck looked over at Jameson who was sitting in the passenger seat, tapping his fingers nervously on the armrest.

"Give it a minute," Beck told him. "Should be any time now."

Kendra stood in the doorway, eyes wide, staring at the crater-size hole in the floor. "Nathan!" she shouted. The only reply she got was a curious squeaking sound that seemed to be growing louder by the second.

In the opposite corner she spotted another door. The floor on that side was intact and it gave her an idea. She circled the building, stopping at the front. The door in question was solid wood, held in place by two wrought-iron hinges. To the right of it was the large rolling door, the cast-iron wheels held frozen in place by generations of rust. Lying face down in the dirt directly in front of it was a rectangular metal sign.

She snatched it off the ground, turned it over, and wiped away the filth. "What?" she shouted, when she saw the warning. "You gotta be kidding me!" Her anger flared and she flung the sign on the ground in disgust, then yanked open the wooden door.

When she stepped inside, the floorboards gave off a painful creaking sound. She paused, then took another step. She heard it again, louder. Standing perfectly still, she called out, "Nathan? Can you hear me?"

"Just barely," he yelled back, trying to be heard over the clamor of the rats.

"Are you alright?"

"Uh…not really," he replied, kicking his feet at the rats in a futile attempt to keep them away.

"What do you need me to do?" she yelled.

Nathan said nothing as the rats inched closer.

"I'm coming down there," she called out.

"NO! DO NOT COME DOWN HERE," he shouted.

By now he was completely outflanked. Rats carpeted the floor, leaving him no clear way out. He tried kicking dirt at them again but it did nothing to slow their attack. What's a little dirt when there's fresh meat to be had?

He was inching backward when he bumped up against a set of thick wooden shelves that had been placed against the stone foundation. With the rats just inches away, he grabbed the side of it and pulled, sending it crashing to the ground. A shrill squealing sound filled the room as rats were either crushed or maimed by the heavy shelving. Those that managed to scurry out of the way, unharmed, quickly reassembled.

He looked around the room, frantic, and that's when he saw a hole in the stone foundation directly behind where the shelves had stood just seconds earlier. It was barely wide enough for one person to slip through, and when he pointed the flashlight into the opening, he saw a narrow tunnel that vanished into a dark void. Behind him, the rats had reorganized and were on the move again, chattering in unison as they quickly closed the gap.

Without a second thought, he squeezed through the hole, flashlight forward, and made his way down the passageway. The air was damp and had a sour stench, but he continued on, fighting through sheets of webs and stepping around the decayed remains of small animals that littered the ground.

Nearly blinded by layers of webbing that clung to his hair and face, he continued on for what seemed like an eternity. The tunnel gradually bent to the right and ended 50 feet later at an old wooden door, made from vertical planks that were held together by two wooden crosspieces. The door had rotted in places and was covered with a layer of black-green mold. At the bottom, chunks of wood were missing, allowing daylight to leak through from the outside.

He pulled on the makeshift wooden handle, but time and weather had warped the door and it was hopelessly stuck in place. He knelt down and peered through one of the holes at the bottom. Through a dense thicket of leafy vines he could just make out a wide wooden pier that stretched along the edge of the water for at least 75 feet. Men were moving from left to right, pushing metal dollies loaded with large wooden crates.

"I know those crates," he whispered. They looked just like the ones he'd seen a week earlier in the Hamilton Mill, packed with artwork stolen by the Covin. He moved to another break in the door, trying to see where the men were taking them, but the curtain of leaves made it impossible to see.

His concentration was broken by a curious shuffling sound. He climbed to his feet and swept the flashlight from side to side. On the tunnel floor he saw them—a hundred pairs of tiny red eyes staring up at him. At the front of the pack, the largest one rose up on its haunches, claws out, and snarled.

Attack!

On the sandpit road, Ellie paced along the side of the truck, kicking at loose stones and watching them skitter across the dirt. Since her arrival she hadn't heard a single car pass by on the main road. Given the serene nature of her surroundings, nothing but woods as far as the eye could see, she figured she might hear the growl of an engine or the whine of tires on the pavement. She thought of Jameson, sitting in Beck's truck, his anticipation building with every passing second, awaiting the glorious moment that had teased his dreams for countless years.

At 3:15, Fuller radioed his spotters again. "Gray One, anything?"

"Gray One, nothing so far."

"Copy Gray One. Gray Two, how's it look?"

"Gray Two, just a couple of bicyclists. Other than that…check that…vehicle approaching. It's a silver Mercedes Benz sedan. The driver is slowing…signaling…and…it just turned onto the sandpit road."

"Copy, Gray Two," Fuller replied. Then, to the rest of the team, "Look alive, people. It's showtime."

Ellie watched as the Mercedes came into view and glided to a smooth stop several feet behind her truck. The door opened and Carl Jaquith stepped out, dressed in his usual business attire: Pima cotton dress shirt, silk tie, tropical-weight wool blazer, khaki slacks, and calfskin Oxfords.

"Please pardon my late arrival," he said. "I had a very demanding client, a rather tormented soul, I must say. She couldn't decide between the Charles Levier or the Janice Haefner. Not that anyone would blame her. Both are exquisite pieces."

On both sides of the road, masked by the low bushes, boulders, and fallen trees that lined the forest floor, a bevy of guns tracked Jaquith's every step. He stopped next to the bed of the truck and eyed the blue tarp that covered the boxes. "These are the items we discussed?" he asked.

"Uh-huh," Ellie grunted. "You got the money?"

"I do," Jaquith replied politely, patting the breast pocket of his suit. *Right here.*

"Good. Let's get this done," she said. She lowered the tailgate and peeled back the tarp. As she waited, she leaned against the side of the truck, arms folded across her chest. Moments later she heard the distant sound of a vehicle approaching on the main road. As the steady drone of its tires drew nearer, she looked past Jaquith's Mercedes.

Waiting.

Watching.

For Nathan, there was only one way out. As the legion of rats charged toward him, he pushed off the wooden door and leaped over them. When his foot landed, he heard an ear-piercing squeal and felt the ground squish beneath his sneaker. His ankle twisted and he lost his balance, but he caught the tunnel wall with on hand and kept himself from falling.

And then he ran.

Legs pumping.

His sneakers snapping the brittle skeletons of dead animals.

When he reached the opening to the tunnel, he squirmed through the hole in the stone foundation and made a beeline for the wooden stairway that led up to the first floor.

He had just cleared the top step when he spotted something nestled between two studs on the wall to his left. Even draped under a blanket of spider webs, its size and shape were unmistakable. It was *The Lady of Florence*, the stolen Caracci sculpture pictured in the newspaper. Seeing it made his heart race. "She was right," he murmured. He pulled the sculpture off the fireblock and shoved it into his backpack when the rats swarmed the landing.

And he felt the first bite.

16

D'Amore

K endra was standing outside the doorway, unsure of what to do, when a narrow panel on the back wall suddenly swung open and Nathan tumbled out. He was kicking his legs frantically in the air, trying to dislodge the rats that were gnawing at his pant legs.

"Hold on, I'm coming," she called out.

"No! Stay back!" he shouted.

He scrambled to his feet and made his way toward the door, keeping his back to the outer wall where the floorboards were stronger. He had to stop every few feet to wrench a rat from his pant leg and fling it into the hole in the floor. Meanwhile, a steady stream of rats emerged from the root cellar, chattering angrily as they chased him toward the door.

Kendra waited until Nathan stepped outside, then quickly pulled the door shut, trapping the rats inside. When she turned around, he had collapsed on the ground and was peeling webs from his face and hair. His pant legs were flecked with dozens of small teeth marks, and she thought she saw a drop of blood or two. "Are you hurt?" she asked, kneeling down beside him.

"No. Just glad to be outside again," he said, pulling another strand of webbing from his face.

"You look like crap," she said. "What happened down there?"

"You don't want to know," he said, "but look what I found." He opened his backpack and pulled out *The Lady of Florence.*

Kendra recognized it at once from the picture in the newspaper. As she took it in her hands, holding it gingerly, her eyes grew wide with amazement.

"I didn't have time to look for the rest of it," Nathan said, "but it's down there…it has to be."

Kendra looked over her shoulder at the carriage house, then back at the Caracci sculpture. "This is insane," she said, shaking her head in disbelief.

"That's just the half of it," Nathan said. "I found something else too."

"What are you talking about?"

He pushed himself up off the ground. "Come on, I'll show you. But we have to hurry."

Jaquith opened the first box, glanced at the assembled periodicals briefly, then pulled out a thin museum guide announcing a forthcoming exhibition of rare middle eastern artifacts. On the cover was the photo of a 19th century Egyptian Revival settee, the ebony wood inlaid with fruitwoods, ivory, and mother of pearl.

He fanned through the pages slowly until he found the narrow slip of paper tucked in the binding. On the page were a pair of Islamic bowls from the 11-12th century, made from red clay. Their cream white glaze was decorated with scrolling foliage and snake-like sgraffito patterns. He read the description and then considered the slip of paper. At the top was the number 18.

Clever, he thought.

He closed the guide, slid it back in the box, then pulled out an exhibition catalog from the museum in Chicago. He repeated the process, checking the numbered slip against the item on the page, this time a pair of early 19th century Japanese bronze vases. Estimated value: $95,000.

After pulling out several other volumes and inspecting each cover briefly, he closed the box and moved on to the next one.

Ellie grew bored of watching him paw through the boxes and went to wait in the cab of the truck. Sitting sideways in the driver's seat, her legs hanging out the open door, she texted Beck, holding the phone low in her lap where Jaquith couldn't see it.

He's stalling

When Beck saw the message pop up on his phone, he showed it to Jameson.

"Is that Ellie?" he asked.

Beck nodded.

"She *texted* you?" Russ asked, from the back seat. "She'd better be careful. If Jaquith sees her communicating with someone…"

"Don't worry about Ellie," Jameson said. "She knows what she's doing."

"You think he's stalling until Ginette shows up?" Beck asked.

"Let's hope so," Jameson replied. He let out an exasperated breath and turned away, wrestling with a number of troubling possibilities.

Nathan raced across the yard toward the street with Kendra following close behind. When he reached the pavement, he ran to the Volvo and stashed the Caracci sculpture in the back seat, wrapping it in one of Kendra's softball jerseys. With the sculpture out of harm's way, he charged into the woods. The land was flat and stretched all the way to the water, dotted with a mix of hardwoods, scrub brush, lichen-spotted boulders, and rotted branches that had fallen years earlier and were now cloaked in a thick layer of dark green moss.

He'd gone 100 yards when he stopped and bent over, placing both hands on his knees.

"What's wrong?" Kendra asked.

"Gotta...catch my breath..." he said, his words coming out between gulps of air.

She stood next to him with her hands on her hips. Her breathing was deep and even. "You know, it wouldn't hurt you to exercise once in a while," she said.

"Yeah, I'll keep that in mind, *Gina!*" He stood and surveyed the forest ahead. The land sloped downward, and through the trees he could see the water. "Let's go," he said. "It's gotta be right up here."

He charged down the hill, dodging tree trunks and wading through patches of broadleaf ferns when he came to a sudden stop.

Kendra appeared next to him. "What's wrong?" she asked.

The forest floor extended another 10 feet and then fell away. He motioned for her to follow him, then spider-walked to the edge and laid flat on the ground. A sheer rock wall extended 30 feet down to the wooden pier he'd seen from the carriage house tunnel. Seeing it from overhead, it was even bigger than he'd first estimated— stretching from the granite wall to his right and ending at the tree line to the far left, where a packed gravel road led back up to the main road.

Set into the face of the rock wall directly below were two massive steel doors. They were propped open and men were emerging from a cavernous cave-like chamber that had been carved into side of the hill, wheeling wooden crates across the pier to a long wooden dock. Moored alongside it, the bow facing the open ocean, was a 70' flybridge boat, its sleek white hull shining like a polished freshwater pearl.

Originally designed to accommodate up to 16 people in lavish comfort, the main deck had all the markings of a luxury yacht: forward salon with panoramic windows, large U-shaped sofa, wet bar and dining for eight people; spacious aft deck with a pair of sun loungers. Below deck, invisible to any curious passersby, the three state rooms and crew quarters had been gutted to create a massive cargo hold.

"Those are the men I saw from the tunnel," Nathan whispered.

Kendra looked at him, confused. "What tunnel?"

"I'll tell you later," he said.

"What is all this, the Covin?" she asked.

"Uh-huh."

"What makes you think that?"

"It fits with what Chessman said. If you don't believe me, check out the crates."

She leaned forward, squinting.

"Look familiar?" he asked.

"Yeah, now that you mention it, they do."

"How many of those did we see in Edouard Dampierre's warehouse in the Hamilton Mill?" he asked. "A thousand?"

"At least," she said.

"At the mill he was using trucks to move his stolen artwork," Nathan said. "This has to be a similar facility, only they use boats."

"But where do they go?" she asked, watching another large crate being hoisted up onto the back of the boat.

"Who knows?" Nathan replied. "Sounds like a good question for the Coast Guard."

From the far end of the pier to their left came the sound of an approaching vehicle. Seconds later a white van emerged from the mouth of the access road. As it drew closer, they saw a large burgundy rose painted on the side, along with the words *D'Amore Flowers*. It continued along the pier and stopped 20 feet from the dock. When the driver got out, Nathan's eyes went wide. "No!" he said, alarm in his voice.

"What's the matter?" Kendra asked.

"The driver," he said. "Don't you recognize her? She was at my house."

Kendra leaned forward again, squinting just like before. "Wait-a-minute," she said, anger painting her face as the realization hit her.

The driver went to the side of the van and slid the door all the way open. When Nathan saw what was inside, his jaw fell open. "No, that's impossible," he said.

"What is?" Kendra asked.

He ignored her question and climbed to his feet, moving away from the edge of the cliff to keep from being seen by the men below. When he was far enough away, he dug his flip phone out of his pocket.

Kendra backed away from the edge of the cliff and hurried over to his side. "What's wrong?" she asked.

He fumbled with the phone, trying not to drop it. "Everything," he said.

Fifteen minutes had passed since Ellie's text. As Beck and Jameson continued to wait, Russ climbed out of the truck to stretch his legs. There was a time when stakeouts didn't bother him, but those days were long gone. After a brisk walk around the parking area he came back to the driver's door and spoke to Beck and Jameson through the open window. "This doesn't feel right," he said.

"Why do you say that?" Beck asked.

"It's taking too long. I mean, you said this guy Jaquith wants the stuff in those boxes, right? If that's the case, then why doesn't he just hand over the money, load the boxes into his vehicle and leave?"

Jameson was about to reply when his cellphone vibrated. He grabbed it from the cupholder in the center console and glanced at the call screen briefly before answering. "Nathan?" he said, unsure why he'd be calling. "I don't have long to talk. What's up?"

"Tell me the boxes from the *Greenwich* bookcase are still in my garage," Nathan said.

"What?"

Nathan clenched his teeth and said it again, slower. "Tell-me-the-boxes-from-the-*Greenwich*-bookcase-are-still-in-my-garage."

Jameson's phone vibrated again. "Nathan, hang on. I've got another call." This time he answered without looking to see who was calling. "This is Jameson," he said.

"Jameson, it's Elizabeth. What did you do with the boxes?"

"What boxes?"

"The ones in the garage."

"I didn't touch them," he said. "Why?"

"They're gone."

"Excuse me?" he said, loudly.

"David and I just got back from shopping. When we pulled in the driveway, the side door of the garage was open. We went in and the boxes are nowhere to be seen. We figured you must've moved them."

Jameson shook his head in disbelief and blew out an angry breath.

"What's wrong?" asked Beck.

"This whole thing was a set up," Jameson said. "Jaquith is playing us." He pressed the phone to his ear again. "Elizabeth, sit tight. I'm going to call you right back." He switched back over to Nathan. "Nathan, that was your mother on the other line. The boxes are gone."

"Not gone," Nathan said.

"What do mean?"

"I'm looking at them."

"Say again?" Jameson exclaimed.

Beck jabbed his finger at Jameson's phone and whispered,

"Speakerphone."

Jameson hit the small icon on the screen and set the phone on the center console. "Nathan, I'm with Beck and Russ. Tell them what you just told me."

Nathan felt a tug on his sleeve and turned to see Kendra pointing at the van. A slate-gray Mercedes sedan had pulled in behind it and an older woman was climbing out of the back seat.

"Nathan? Are you still there?" Jameson asked.

Nathan was watching the woman and didn't answer.

"Nathan?"

"Yeah, give me a second," he said. He lowered the phone and watched the woman walk up to the side of the van and open one of the boxes. "Is that who I think it is?" he asked.

Kendra had seen the pictures of Ginette Dampierre. Seeing her now, in person, she could only nod her head slowly, her face frozen in shock.

"Jameson," Nathan said into the phone. "Describe Ginette Dampierre for me."

"Ginette?" Jameson said, confused. "Uh…she's roughly 5' 10"—"

"Auburn hair?" Nathan cut in. "Medium build? Slender face?"

"Yes, that's right. Why are you asking me this?"

"Because she's standing 200 feet from me. And now she has the boxes!"

"Once again, I must compliment you on your fine work," Ginette said, as she sorted through the box. "Did you have any trouble getting them?"

"No," Niko said. "I wasn't there long enough for anyone to notice me."

"The flower deliver van was brilliant," Ginette said.

"Who doesn't like flowers?" Niko replied, in a dry voice.

"Exactly."

"How'd you do it?" Niko asked.

"Do what?"

"Get them to leave the boxes unguarded like that?"

"Oh, that was easy," Ginette said with a smirk. "Through one of my brother's contacts, I learned that he kept a private collection of literature in his office. Apparently he was using it to generate untold millions, which is why he sent one of his men to retrieve it after the authorities had left the building. As it turns out, however, the collection wasn't in his office at all. It had already been taken by 'the kid' as my brother is so fond of calling him."

"Nathan Cole," Niko confirmed.

"The one and only," Ginette said. "Knowing that he had the collection, I found it odd when a complete stranger approached one of my dealers saying she'd stolen it from my brother's office and was going to sell it to the highest bidder."

"I see," Niko said, seeing where the conversation was headed. "So you had your dealer agree to the sale as a diversion."

"Misdirection, pure and simple," Ginette said, smiling. "They probably thought I'd show up," she said. "Like I'd be that stupid." She pulled out a hardcover book, *The History of Impressionism*, glanced at the cover briefly then shoved it back in the box with the other periodicals. It was one of at least 50, and if the Watchman had done as Jaquith explained, finding something of value in each one, she couldn't help but wonder what they might provide in new capital.

And this was only the first box.

Soto emerged from the shipping room carrying a large wooden crate on his shoulder. He started toward the dock when one of his crew, a gangly man in his early 30s who went by the nickname "Stick," appeared with an empty dolly. "I'll take that sir," he said.

Soto handed him the crate and Stick's knees buckled.

"Easy," Soto told him, grabbing hold of the crate to help steady it. Together, they eased it down onto the dolly, then Stick waved over another member of the crew to help him wheel it up the dock to the boat. When Soto looked over and saw Ginette standing next to the van, he walked over to speak with her.

When Ginette saw him approaching, she said, "This is Soto. He runs the landing for us."

"The landing?" Niko asked.

"All of this," Ginette said, motioning to the pier and the dock with both hands.

"Good afternoon," he said, stopping several feet away. There was no smile. No handshake. His expression was firm, as if formed in a slump mold.

"Yes, it is a good afternoon," Ginette said, smiling. "Are we on schedule?"

"We are," Soto replied. "But before we launch, there's a matter we need to address."

"What might that be?"

He smiled, all the while nodding his head. "I need you to continue looking at me like nothing is wrong," he said.

"What seems to be the problem?" she asked.

"We have two uninvited guests on the property."

Beck grabbed the phone off the center console and held it inches from his face. "Nathan, it's Beck. Where are you?" he demanded.

"Kendra and I are in Portsmouth, on New Castle Island."

"You went to *Whitehall?*" Jameson said, aghast.

"Yes," Nathan said, watching the activity on the dock. "The Covin has a shipping operation here, and as we speak men are loading a boat with the same kind of crates we saw in the Hamilton Mill."

Beck pulled the phone aside. "We can be there in 45 minutes," he said.

"GO!" Jameson barked.

Beck handed him the phone and started the truck. As they screeched out of the parking area, the tires painting long black arcs on the pavement, Jameson pulled the phone close. "Nathan, you and Kendra need to clear out of there at once. Is that understood?"

Silence.

"Nathan?"

More silence.

"NATHAN!"

17

A Nice Patch of Water

As Beck raced down the ramp onto the Maine Turnpike, Jameson called Elizabeth and told her that Jaquith had faked the whole buyback meeting and that Ginette Dampierre had been spotted in Portsmouth. He made no mention of Nathan or Whitehall. He explained that time was of the essence and that they were on their way south to assist the U.S. Marshals. He promised to call her back and then ended the call. Next, he wrote a three-line message and sent it as a group text to Eric Fuller and Ellie.

It's a set up
Nathan has eyes on Ginette Dampierre
She's in Portsmouth

Fuller read the message and immediately radioed his teams, instructing them to stand down, but to remain in position and stay alert until Jaquith left the scene, in case he made an aggressive move toward Ellie.

Ellie was still sitting in the truck watching Jaquith through the back window when her phone chirped. After she read Jameson's message, she jumped out of the cab without closing the door and reached into the truck bed for the tarp. "Show's over," she said.

Jaquith looked up from the book he was holding, confused. "Excuse me?"

"I'm outta here," she said, draping the tarp over the boxes.

"I thought we had a deal," Jaquith said.

"Deal's off."

"Did I miss something?" he asked.

She yanked the book out of his hands, tossed it in the back of the truck, then lifted the tailgate and slammed it shut. As she walked back to the cab, she never once looked back at him. Why should she? What was he going to do? Shoot her? Not likely. One wrong move and the marshals would drop him where he stood.

She fired up the truck and drove all the way into the sandpit. When her tires hit the loose sand, she cut the wheel and punched the gas, spinning the back end around and spraying sand and gravel in a wide arc. Jaquith was just getting back into his Mercedes when she tore past him, smothering him in a cloud of dust.

Fuller watched Jaquith leave, then called Jameson. "Jameson," he said, skipping the usual opening banter. "Ginette Dampierre is in Portsmouth?"

"Yes," Jameson replied.

"Do you have her location?"

"I do. We're on our way there now. I'll text you the address." He grabbed hold of the armrest on the door as Beck gunned the engine and swerved into the left lane, racing past a slow-moving motor coach.

"I have no jurisdiction in New Hampshire but I'll contact someone who does," Fuller said. "They'll be coming out of the Concord office, so it may take them awhile to get there."

"Understood," Jameson said.

"Do me a favor and call me when this is all over," Fuller said. "I have a feeling it's going to be quite a story."

"Will do," Jameson said. "You'll have the address momentarily." He had just finished texting the Whitehall address to Fuller when his phone vibrated again. "It's Ellie," he said.

"Put her on speaker," Beck said.

Jameson thumbed the speakerphone icon and the cab was filled with the whine of the Tacoma's engine. "Ellie, where are you?" Jameson said.

"Never mind where I am," she replied, yelling to be heard. "Where is Nathan? And how could he possibly have eyes on Ginette Dampierre?"

"He and Kendra went to Whitehall," Jameson said.

"Say again?" Ellie said, pressing the phone tighter to her ear.

"He and Kendra went to Whitehall. Don't ask me why, but apparently that's where Ginette Dampierre is. According to Nathan, she has the boxes from his garage."

"*What?*" Ellie yelled.

"While Jaquith was keeping all of us distracted, someone broke into Nathan's garage and stole the originals. That had to be Ginette's doing."

"I *knew* something wasn't right," Ellie said, pounding her fist on the steering wheel. "How did she find out about the phony boxes?"

"I have a pretty good idea, but we can discuss that later," Jameson said. "Right now, we're headed to Portsmouth and I pray we're not too late."

"Jameson, you gotta tell Nathan to get out of there," Ellie said.

"I did."

"And?"

Jameson didn't answer.

"Jameson?" she said, louder. "What's wrong?"

Nathan's brain was swimming in a dense fog. As it slowly cleared, he was aware of men talking and laughing somewhere nearby, their words void of clarity or meaning. A low moan escaped his lips and he opened his eyes, blinking hard to clear them.

He was slouched forward in a swivel chair that was bolted to the floor. He could move his legs and feet, but his wrists were zip-tied to the padded arms of the chair. To his right were three identical chairs, aligned in a row. A long rectangular table sat inches away. On the opposite side of it were four matching chairs. Kendra was sitting in the one diagonally across from him, her wrists, like his, zip-tied to the chair. She had a look of fury on her face as she surveyed their surroundings.

They were on the main deck of the boat, the twin V12 1400hp engines humming softly. Ceiling-to-floor windows lined both sides of the compartment, and directly across from him was a large U-shaped sofa covered with puffy throw pillows. To his left, up one step, was the helm, with a leather captain's chair and a bank of navigation controls. At the opposite end of the boat, on the aft deck, sun loungers were positioned on either side of the stairs that led down to the cargo hold.

Soto's men continued to wheel crates up the dock, paying little attention to Nathan and Kendra as they hauled them below deck.

"Are you okay?" she asked him.

"That depends," he replied. "What are they're going to do with us?"

"Nothing good."

"How did we get here?" he asked. "The last thing I remember, I was talking to Jameson on my phone."

"They snuck up on us when we were watching the dock," Kendra said. "My guess is, they used chloroform to knock us out."

Nathan pulled at the ties that bound his wrists but they wouldn't give.

"Don't bother," Kendra said. "You'll never break them. They need to be cut."

Through the large window on the port beam he could see Kittery Point, where pleasure boats of every size were going in and out of the mouth of the Piscataqua River at a steady clip. "Boats everywhere," he grumbled, "and no way to signal them for help."

"Forget the boats," she said. "See that wet bar behind you?"

He spun the chair around. The wet bar was an oblong cabinet with a dark cherry stain and three shallow drawers set in a row beneath the thick teakwood top. "Yeah? What about it?" he said.

"Try and reach the drawers with your foot."

"The drawers?" he said, confused.

"Just do it."

He slinked down in the chair as far as he could go, then raised his foot until the tip of his sneaker touched the middle drawer.

"That's good. Now, see if you can...wait...stop!"

He sat up in the chair just as Ginette Dampierre and Niko stepped onto the aft deck. They walked up into the center compartment and stopped several feet away, looking down at him with mixed expressions. One was triumphant. The other was angry.

"Well, well, what do you know?" Ginette said. "Nathan Cole, in the flesh. I can't tell you how much I've looked forward to meeting you."

A storm raged in Nathan's eyes as he stared at her, seething.

"Did you really think you could meddle in our business and get away with it?"

Nathan ignored the question and looked at Niko. "You," he growled. "You were at my house. Why?"

"I was studying you," she said. "Just like a big game hunter stalks his prey. I wanted to learn your habits so I could decide where and when I was going to take your life. As it turned out, it was your mother who gave me the barn idea."

Nathan's eyes went wide.

"Yeah, that's right, it was me," she said. "I guess you couldn't see me in the dark. To think, I walked right into your house as easy as you please. Your mother never bothered to check my identification. My stuttering-Natalie act worked to perfection. She never suspected a thing. Of course, those papers I stole from her desk might've had something to do with it. Her office really needs to beef up their security."

Nathan strained at the ties, desperately wanting to spring out of the chair and drive her through the side window of the boat.

Ginette picked up Kendra's bat off the U-shaped couch. "They told me you had this with you when they dragged you in from the woods. It's rather impressive, I must say." She bounced it up and down in the air, trying to gauge its weight. "Do you play baseball?"

Kendra clenched her fists as she slowly exhaled. "Softball," she said, with controlled fury. "Cut these ties and I'll show you my swing."

"Oh, I'm sure you'd like that very much," Ginette said, studying the Louisville Slugger logo that was burned into the wood. "But since you won't be needing it anymore, I think we can dispose of it." She walked to the back of the boat and flung the bat over the side.

Kendra jerked forward, struggling to break free of the ties as the bat sailed through the air and landed in the water.

Just then, Soto stepped aboard. "We're almost ready to launch," he said.

"Excellent," Ginette replied. She stepped back up into the center compartment and said, "I'd wish you both a pleasant boat ride, but it's not going to be that long. Soto is going to find a nice patch of water where he can dump your bodies. But before that happens, you may be interested to know that the average shark has somewhere between 50 to 300 teeth. So, a word of advice? When they come at you, it's best not to turn your back on them. Apparently, it makes them mad." She shrugged her shoulders. "Who knew, right?"

As she left the boat, Niko grabbed Nathan's chin and squeezed.

He struggled to pull away but her grip was too strong. It felt like his head was caught in a vice.

"I bet you think you're pretty tough, after that little stunt in the barn," she said. She leaned down until her face was nearly touching his. "I'll let you in on a little secret. There's no way you could ever beat me. If you hadn't stumbled onto this property today, I would've come for you because I *always* finish the job. It's a thing with me. I'm just sorry I won't be there to see the sharks rip your body to shreds." She released her grip and stood up, content that she'd seen the last of him. "Have a nice swim," she said over her shoulder as she walked away.

The moment she was off the boat, Kendra said, "Quick! We don't have much time."

He spun his chair toward the wet bar again and lifted is foot in the air. He tried to pull the drawer open but the handle was too shallow and the tip of his sneaker kept slipping off it.

"Use both feet," Kendra told him.

"No, I have a better idea," he said. He pried his sneaker off and tried again. This time his toe slid through the drawer handle and he was able to pull it open with ease.

"Good!" Kendra said. "Now kick the bottom of the drawer."

"Kick it?"

"Hard."

Using his other foot, he kicked upward and hit the thin layer of wood that lined the bottom of the drawer. There was an audible *crack*, but the drawer held firm.

"Again," Kendra said "Harder."

He slid down in the chair to get a better angle, then kicked again using all the energy he could muster. There was a loud *crack* as the bottom of the drawer shattered and the contents shot up into the air before cascading down onto the floor.

"What do you see?" Kendra asked.

He sat up and turned the chair to see past the corner of the table. "Uh…there's a corkscrew…a metal shot glass…a small cutting board, and…wait…"

"What is it?" Kendra asked.

"A small knife."

"Probably for cutting lemons and limes," Kendra said. "Can you reach it with your foot?"

"I think so."

"Do it!" she said. "And hurry."

Ginette and Niko stepped off the boat and walked with Soto back down the dock.

"We have a few more crates to prepare," he said. "Once they're loaded, we'll be off."

They crossed the pier and went into the shipping room, a cavernous cave-like space that had been hollowed out of the massive rock wall. Built as a sorting and processing site, the walls were lined with heavy steel racks designed to hold a variety of stolen goods—everything from rare gold coins to antique furniture. A long steel table ran down the middle of the room, and that's where Soto's crew were hard at work packing the remaining crates.

Ginette and Niko stopped just inside the doorway. "I think the last time I was here was just before I left for Europe," Ginette explained. "Back then, this room felt like an airplane hangar. But seeing it again now, it looks tiny."

The sound of a pneumatic nailer erupted, echoing through the room, as one of Soto's men fastened a wooden cover to one of the crates.

Ginette leaned closer to Niko and spoke louder to be heard. "See all these shelves?" she said, pointing to the steel racks. "Normally they're loaded with product. Last week's raid on our operation in Saco put a dent in that, but if what I've been told about those boxes in your van is true, these shelves will be filled again in no time."

The nailing stopped, dropping the noise level in the room to nearly nothing.

"Speaking of the boxes," Niko said. "Where would you like me to put them?"

"Oh, don't worry, these guys can do it," Ginette replied. She turned to Soto and explained that there were boxes in the van that needed to be stored in the shipping room. She told him she'd send someone to retrieve them in the next few days. What she didn't say was that she had no idea who that person would be. Ordinarily she'd use Pantano. But with him out of the picture, she might use Edouard's contact at the prison, Moran. He seemed like a serious guy, the type of person she could trust to get the job done.

Like a bellhop hailing a cab, Soto raised his hand in the air and motioned to one of the men at the table. After speaking to him briefly, the man grabbed a dolly and hurried out the door.

As Ginette watched him go, she smiled and said, "The authorities may have rattled our operation, but they'll never break it."

Nathan used his bare foot to push off his other sneaker off, then used both feet to grab the handle of the small paring knife. It took several tries, but once he had it firmly secured, he lifted his feet and swung his chair toward Kendra, holding onto the edge of the table for leverage.

"Easy," she said, as his feet drew closer.

He held his legs steady, but fatigue quickly set in and his thigh muscles began to burn. Unable to hold them up any longer, his legs fell to the floor and the knife slipped from between his feet.

Kendra saw the exhaustion in his face and got an idea. "Do you remember what that woman did to you in the barn?" she asked.

"How could I forget?" Nathan grumbled. "Why?"

Kendra pressed on. "She was in your house. She spied on you. She tricked your mother. Just now, she grabbed your face like she was going to tear it off."

Nathan's fury rose with every word she said, just as she knew it would. When it became too much to bear, he clenched his teeth, picked up the knife with his feet, and raised his legs, using his anger as fuel to hold them steady.

"That's it," Kendra said. She swung the chair until her knees were directly under his feet, then pressed them firmly together to catch the knife as he let it drop. Very slowly, she turned the chair and lifted her knees until she could grab the knife. In one smooth move, she flipped it with her fingers so it was facing her, then cut the tie holding her right hand. Seconds later, the second zip tie fell to the floor. After she cut Nathan loose, she considered keeping the knife for protection should they encounter any of Soto's men.

But knives weren't her thing. She preferred the smooth feel and solid weight of 50-year-old Pennsylvania ash, cut and dried, and then turned on a lathe to produce one of the finest hitting implements known to man. "Come on," she said, tossing the knife on the floor. "We're outta here."

They hurried to the back of the boat and ducked down behind one of the sun loungers. None of Soto's men were on the dock, or the pier, but that could change at any moment.

"What now?" Nathan asked.

"Now we go for a swim," Kendra said.

"Huh?" Nathan grunted.

Keeping low, she darted to the starboard side of the boat, straddled the gunwale momentarily, then brought the other leg over and dropped into the water. Nathan followed her lead, the frigid ocean water erasing any lingering effects of the chloroform.

They swam along the back of the boat to the dock, then ducked beneath it, using it for cover. When they reached the rocky embankment beneath the pier, Nathan saw her bat floating in the water several feet away, washed to shore by the afternoon tide. He crawled across the rock and pulled it from the water. "I'm guessing you want this back," he said, holding it up in the air.

"Do I ever," she said. She motioned with both hands. *Give it here.*

"There's just one more loose end I need to tie off," Ginette said, as they watched Soto's man slide the last batch of boxes onto the steel rack.

"What's that?" Niko asked.

"We need to find the man who assembled the collection you delivered today. I have no idea what his name is, where he lives, or if he can even be trusted. Apparently my brother is the only one who knows that information, but so far he hasn't divulged it."

"It seems odd that he'd keep something like that from you," Niko said.

"Yes, it's very odd, indeed."

"Would you like me to look into it?" Niko asked.

"Yes," Ginette replied. "I'd like that very much."

"I have a small business matter to take care of in Dallas, but it shouldn't take more than a day," Niko said.

Ginette fought back a grin. Just a quick trip down to Dallas to take care of a small business matter. The girl was so good it was scary. She made it sound like she was dropping off a bag of laundry at the cleaners.

Kendra held the bat against her chest and looked up at the pier, yearning to even the score with Ginette Dampierre. "Let's go," she said.

"Where?" Nathan asked.

"Up there," she said, nodding at the pier overhead. "I've got some unfinished business to attend to."

They grabbed hold of the cross bracing and started to climb. When they reached the top, they peeked over the edge of the heavy wooden planking. From that vantage point, they could see directly into the shipping room, where Soto and his men were still busy packing crates.

Ginette and Niko were standing in the doorway, but turned and walked down the pier toward their vehicles. Kendra waited until they reached the van, then said, "Wait here."

"What are you going to do?" Nathan asked.

"Watch."

She climbed up onto the pier and made a beeline for the doorway of the shipping room. As she got closer, she veered to the left and hugged the face of the rock wall like a spider, watching Ginette and Niko at the far end of the pier, praying they didn't look in her direction.

"You received the bank transfer?" Ginette asked.

"I did," Niko replied. "Although, it wasn't for the amount we discussed."

"I added a little extra, for the inconvenience," Ginette said. "Sometimes, in business, certain things take precedence over all else. In this case, I wanted to get the Nathan Cole business out of the way as quickly as possible."

"It was no inconvenience at all," Niko said. "And as far as Nathan Cole is concerned, I'd say his days of interfering in your business are over."

"Until I hear from you, then…" Ginette said.

"Until then," Niko replied.

Kendra stood perfectly still and watched as Ginette's Mercedes made a perfect 3-point turn on the pier, then disappeared up the access road into the woods. Not long after that, Niko followed in the floral delivery van.

Inside the shipping room, the men had finished sealing the last crate. When Kendra heard Soto tell them to get it loaded on the boat, she swung one of the steel doors shut, then quickly grabbed the other one and did the same. She was sliding her bat through the thick steel handles when the men began shouting and pounding on the metal, demanding to be let out.

"Yeah, keep dreaming," she shouted at the door. She made sure the bat was good and snug, then motioned to Nathan. "Come on," she called out. "Let's get out of here."

As they walked down the pier, he looked back at the shipping room doors. The pounding had grown louder, sending a deep thudding sound, like a timpani drum, echoing across the water.

"Where's Ginette and her friend?" Nathan asked.

"They left, but they couldn't have gotten far," Kendra said. "Speaking of that…" She stopped and pulled her phone from her soaking wet jeans. "Let's hope this still works," she said, wiping the screen with her hand. She started to dial out when she got an incoming call from Ellie. "Hey sister," she said. "Am I glad you called. You heard about Ginette, right?"

"Yeah, but that's not why I'm calling. Are you guys all right? Jameson said he was talking to Nathan and they got cut off."

"Uh…we kinda got sidetracked. But that story will have to wait for another time. Right now we have to alert the police. Ginette and the woman who attacked Nathan in the barn just left."

"She was there too?" Ellie exclaimed.

"Oh yeah, it was a thrill a minute, let me tell you. Do me a favor and call my dad. Tell him Ginette is in a silver-gray Mercedes limo. Her assassin friend is driving a floral delivery van."

"D'Amore," Nathan said.

"Oh, right," Kendra said. "The name on the side of the van is D'Amore."

"Got it," Ellie said. "So, you guys are okay? No broken bones?"

"We're a little wet, but other than that we're fine. Tell my dad to get the cops over here. There's a bunch of Covin guys locked in a cave, along with a bunch of stolen artwork. I'd do it myself but I have to get Nathan out of here."

"Understood," Ellie said. "Call me after you get on the road."

Kendra ended the call and then pointed at the end of the rock cliff, where the wall of stone cut into a steep hill that was thick with trees and leafy ground cover. "Let's head up that way and cut through the woods the way we came," she said.

Behind them, some of Soto's crew had started heaving their bodies against the double doors trying to break them down, the hinges shrieking with every hit.

"You go," she said. "I'll catch up with you. I gotta make sure those guys don't get out."

Nathan gave her a quick nod and then started for the hill. He climbed, hunched over, grabbing at small saplings to pull himself up and to keep from tumbling backward. When he finally reached the top, he stopped to catch his breath. Down below, he saw Kendra standing in front of the steel doors, jamming the bat tighter into the door handles.

While he waited, he walked along the edge of the cliff to where he and Kendra had been watching the men load the boat. His backpack was lying on the ground, exactly where he'd left it. Using it as a point of reference, he retraced the steps he'd taken away from the cliff when he called Jameson, and ran his eyes back and forth across the ground on the off chance he might find his phone.

He hadn't gone far when he saw it lying on the ground where Soto's men had grabbed him. "Yes!" he said, as he picked it up. He was brushing away the dirt when he heard a twig snap several feet away. "About time," he called out. "Maybe you should think about exercising once in a while."

When there was no reply, he turned and looked.

Niko was standing 10 feet away.

18

Lessons Learned

"**Y**ou again," Nathan hissed, hatred starting to churn in his stomach.

"Yeah, me again," Niko said. She ambled forward with a smug expression. "Just like old times, huh?"

"I saw you leave," Nathan said.

"That's right. But as I drove into the woods I realized my side door was open. I'll have to remember to thank Soto's man for not closing it all the way when he removed the boxes. If he had, I never would've stopped. Never would've looked back. Never would've seen you and your friend on the pier. I'd ask how you managed to free yourselves but I really don't care. All that matters is that you're here and I get to finish the job I was hired to do."

Nathan flashed back to their first meeting, in Abbot's barn, when she pursued him relentlessly, inflicting blinding pain with cruel intent. *Not this time*, he told himself, keeping Beck's words foremost in his mind.

"*If they can't hit you, they can't hurt you.*"

He tossed his flip phone aside, and as Niko watched it land in the ferns he took a step back, never taking his eyes off her.

Lesson #1: be ready for anything.

Niko continued walking toward him, easy as you please, eyeing the bands of sunlight that broke through the treetops overhead.

Don't mind me.

I'm just out for a leisurely walk in the woods.

Admiring the boundless wonders of nature.

She was four feet away when she shifted to his left and bent down to pick the bloom off a blue star creeper. In a blinding sequence of moves that followed, she dropped down and spun her body, swinging her leg in a wide arc aimed at his lower calf.

This time he was ready. He lifted his leg and hopped backward just in time to avoid the sweep. With lightning-quick reflexes she sprang back up and launched her fist at his face. He swayed to the side and her jab flew harmlessly past his right ear. As he took another step back, she rotated her body and threw a powerful right cross, but he managed to duck down just in time and her fist sailed over his head.

Fast on your feet…gotta be fast on your feet, he kept telling himself as he darted to his left, stopping in front of a 200-year-old sugar maple.

With a look of calm and cunning, Niko attacked again, this time with both hands held close to her chest. She closed to within five feet then brought her right knee up in the air and unleashed a stinging front kick aimed at his abdomen. He managed to sidestep it, slapping her foot aside, but she countered with a switch kick to his rib cage. He jumped in the opposite direction and her leg smashed against the base of the tree.

As she grabbed her shin, wincing in pain, he circled to his right, weaving his way through the trees. She pushed the pain aside, crouched down, fists at the ready, and quickly closed the distance between them.

First she threw a hard lead hook, followed by a thunderous uppercut, but once again he simply stepped back, watching as both punches went astray. With beads of sweat dripping from her face, she reset, gritted her teeth and attacked again.

Left jab.

Right cross.

Left hook.

He bobbed from side to side and up and down, keeping his distance as she threw a devastating combination of blows, each one coming within a hair of their intended target. As he continued his retreat, his foot brushed up against a fallen tree limb buried in a patch of knee-high broadleaf ferns. He stepped over it and kept moving back when she exploded at him, her fist cocked and ready to deliver a deadly throat punch. But as she closed in, her foot caught the limb and she went sprawling face first onto the forest floor.

As she was climbing to her feet, he glanced over his shoulder and saw his backpack lying on the ground near the edge of the cliff. She screamed out in anger, as if generating energy from her rage, then exploded at him with renewed vengeance.

He stood perfectly still, his nerves electric in the moment. *Just...*

wait, he told himself.

Her hands were reaching for his throat when he dropped to his knees. Unable to stop her forward momentum, she tumbled over his shoulder and fell headlong off the edge of the cliff.

Ginette was in the middle of a long-distance call to one of her European art dealers when she realized that the limo had stopped moving. "Paolo, excuse me for just a second," she said. She lowered the side window and looked out at the dense forest. Through the trees she saw the main road, busy with a steady line of late afternoon commuters. She raised the window and continued her conversation. "My apologies, Paolo. You were saying?"

The conversation continued for another minute when she realized that the limo still hadn't moved. "Paolo, I'm going to have to call you back," she said. She clicked off the call and lowered the privacy glass just enough for her voice to be heard by the driver. "Anthony?" she said. "What seems to be the holdup?"

When there was no answer, she lowered the glass all the way.

Sitting behind the wheel was Beck, who looked back at her and smiled. "Hello there."

"Who are you?" she demanded. "And what have you done with Anthony."

"Anthony is just fine," Beck said calmly. "He looked tired so I suggested he take a nap in the trunk. Actually, it was more than a suggestion. You might say I insisted."

Ginette grabbed her purse and began rifling through it.

"Looking for this?" Beck said, holding up her Sig P365 pistol.

Just then, the side door opened. Jameson and Russ McCullough were standing there, along with a deputy from the New Hampshire branch of the U.S. Marshals Service.

"Well, hello Ginette," Jameson said. "I've been looking forward to this moment for a very long time."

By six o'clock, the U.S. Marshals had Soto and his entire crew handcuffed and isolated, each man in the custody of a deputy who was taking their statement. Once those notes were compiled and the full scope of the shipping operation was fleshed out, formal charges would be added to the growing list of indictments against Edouard and Ginette Dampierre.

Martin Bishop, Jameson's Interpol contact in New York City, had been called and was en route to New Hampshire.

Nathan and Kendra had been questioned and were standing on the dock, watching Jameson and a team of deputies search the boat. The marshals had returned Kendra's bat to her and she was cradling it in her arms like she had no intention of ever putting it down. Behind them, on the pier, Niko's body lay twisted and broken beneath a dark green polyester tarp.

Jameson emerged from the cargo hold of the boat, spoke to one of the marshals briefly, then walked down the dock to where Nathan and Kendra were standing. As he drew closer, the look on his face grew more serious.

"Well…it's not exactly the way we drew it up, but we finally got her," he said. "Don't get me wrong. That in no way excuses your actions. I thought I had made it clear. You were supposed to stay at Stackyard Road. But for some reason the two of you decided to come here, at considerable risk to your lives."

Kendra jabbed a finger in Nathan's direction. *Talk to him.*

Jameson eyed Nathan with one eyebrow raised. "Care to explain?"

"It all started with Claire's book," Nathan said. He explained in exacting detail the words scratched into the margin of the Whitehall chapter, Gina's subsequent research, and the Portsmouth Herald story that pulled all the pieces together.

"Tell him the rest," Kendra said.

"The rest of what?" Jameson asked.

Nathan recounted his nightmare in the root cellar of the carriage house. He pointed at the cluster of bushes that obscured the door to the tunnel, explaining how he observed the pier and Soto's crew loading of the boat.

Then came the bombshell.

"If I hadn't fallen through the floor, I never would've discovered any of this," he said, waving a hand at the cliff. "Or the stolen art."

"*What?*" Jameson exclaimed.

"The Lulo robbery, 10 years ago," Nathan explained.

Jameson knew the story all too well. "What about it?" he asked.

"The thief stashed the stolen artwork in the root cellar," Nathan said. "And because he was killed in a gun battle with police later that night, the Covin never knew where he'd hidden it."

Jameson stood speechless.

"Claire figured it out, Dad," Kendra said. "That's why she was so intent on coming here."

Jameson let out a long breath as the nagging question that had tormented him for years was finally answered.

"She came looking for the stolen art, but somehow she must've stumbled across the Covin's secret shipping operation," Nathan said, leaving it at that. Whatever horror followed was nothing he needed to know, and would never ask.

Kendra looked over at the steel doors. They had been propped open again and the marshals were scouring every square inch like buzzing bees. "To think," she said. "The artwork was right next door and they didn't even know it. Serves 'em right, I say."

Jameson looked over at the thicket that kept the door to the tunnel hidden from view. "That tunnel must've been left over from the Underground Railroad, the network that helped slaves escape into Canada," he said.

"Oh, by the way," Nathan said. "The sculpture I found is in the back of Kendra's car. The rest is still hidden in the root cellar somewhere. Somebody else can go look for it. I'm not going back down there. In fact, no one can know I was there in the first place. If my mother ever finds out..." he said, letting the implication hang in the air.

"You have nothing to worry about," Jameson told him. "I've already called your parents and explained everything."

"You did *what?*"

"Relax. I told them the marshals had captured Ginette Dampierre, and in the course of doing that they found the stolen artwork. They have no idea that you and Kendra were here."

Nathan let out an audible sigh of relief.

"Your secret is safe for now," Jameson said. "But one of these days, you should tell your parents the truth."

"Are you serious?"

"Yes, and I wouldn't wait too long."

Kendra rested the bat on her shoulder, her hands gripping it firmly. She had an overwhelming urge to hit something with it—to work off the anger she was feeling for the way she and Nathan had been drugged, dragged through the woods and then tied to the chairs in the boat, waiting to be served up as shark food. She looked from one end of the pier to the other. "Where's Ginette?" she asked.

"She's being questioned by the U.S. Marshals," Jameson said. "Why?"

"When they're done, can I have five minutes with her?" She pulled the bat from her shoulder, admiring it with a devious grin. "Better yet, let's make it 10."

19

All of It

O n Wednesday afternoon, Elizabeth was in the laundry room doing a load of Nathan's dirty clothes. From the pile she found scattered throughout his bedroom earlier that morning, she pulled out a pair of ratty blue jeans. At first she thought the legs had been splattered with motor oil, but upon closer inspection, the marks in the fabric were something altogether different. She examined them for several minutes, then went upstairs to the living room where David was watching a live news report from New Castle Island.

"The story just broke," he told her.

She stood next to him and watched as a reporter explained the raid by the U.S. Marshals Service, on a secluded section of the island, where they'd captured Ginette Dampierre, the international fugitive and head of an international art-theft ring. Discovered at the location was a shipping facility where stolen artwork from around the country was being ferried out to a waiting container ship five miles off shore. Based on what the reporter had been able to learn from the authorities, the larger ship was used to transport the stolen goods to various locations in Europe.

"In another development," he said, "U.S. Marshals recovered artwork that was stolen from the Lulo gallery in downtown Portsmouth 10 years ago. Further details on that discovery are forthcoming."

"Thus ends the saga of Ginette Dampierre," David said, as he turned off the TV.

"And not a moment too soon," Elizabeth said.

He set the remote aside and stood up. "Now we can get on with the rest of our lives."

"Uh, about that," she said. "Could you come down to the basement? There's something I want to show you."

"Sure. What is it?"

"I'm not sure. I'm hoping you can tell me."

When they got down to the laundry room, she handed him Nathan's dirty blue jeans. "Take a look at those," she said.

He gave them a casual glance. "Yeah? What about them?" he said. "They're blue jeans."

"Look at those punctures," she said, pointing at the fabric. "There have to be dozens."

He pulled the jeans closer and examined each leg. The punctures were very small and dotted both legs all the way up to the knees.

"Are these bite marks?" he asked. In several places he thought he saw dots of blood.

"I certainly hope not," she said.

He looked over at her, concerned. "Did he say anything to you about this?"

"Not a word."

"Do you want to ask him?"

"Not really," she said, fearing the truth would be worse than she could possibly imagine.

He studied the jeans again, turning them over in his hands. "Well, he went through some kind of ordeal, that much is evident. And by the looks of these marks, it wasn't pleasant."

"He's been through too many ordeals lately," she said. "Where does it end?"

David took a deep breath, then let it out slowly. "Maybe it's time we told him," he said.

"No! Absolutely not," she fired back. "It's too soon."

He gave her a look. "When is it *not* going to be too soon?"

"He's only 12 years old!" she exclaimed.

Another stretch of silence followed.

"You know what I'm going to say, right?" David asked.

She knew exactly what he was going to say. Word for word. She'd heard it too many times before, and now, just like those other times, she was content to simply look the other way. Do nothing. Put the genie back in the bottle and move on. In that moment she wondered what her father would say if he were still alive to offer his sage counsel. Oh, how she wished he was. It would make everything so much easier.

"Sooner or later we have to tell him," David said. "You know that as well as I do."

"All of it?" she asked.

"Yes, all of it," he insisted. "If we don't, we'll only be putting his life in greater danger."

She exhaled a tired breath, overcome by a feeling of defeat. "I've been dreading this day ever since he found the bookcase up in the attic," she said. "I thought we'd hidden it deep enough in all that junk…"

David said nothing.

"Do you think he would've found it if I hadn't sent him up there with that box of old dishes?" she asked.

"You can't blame yourself," he said. "Dishes or no dishes, it was only a matter of time before the bookcase found *him*. He's the next one in line. Your father knew that."

She let out a pained breath, saying nothing.

"So, we're agreed, then?" he asked.

She slowly nodded her head.

For better or worse, it was time Nathan knew the whole story.

Afterword

Gina heard the sound through her bedroom window.

Whap! Whap! Whap!

At first she ignored it.

Then she heard it again.

Whap! Whap! Whap!

Over and over, it started.

Whap! Whap! Whap!

Then it stopped.

Unable to stand it any longer, she went to the window and peered outside. "You've got to be kidding me," she said.

She went downstairs and slipped out the back porch door, past Ellie, who was sitting on the wicker couch making a bead necklace. She looked up as the screen door slammed. "What's up?" she called out.

Gina kept walking. "I'm not sure," she said, over her shoulder.

Ellie put down the necklace and went to the screen, watching Gina march across the lawn toward Nathan's driveway, where he was jump roping in front of the garage door.

Gina stopped several feet away from him and gave him a pathetic look. "*What* are you doing?" she said.

"What does it look like?" he answered. He jumped three times, then stopped, the rope slapping the tar with the same sharp sound each time.

Whap! Whap! Whap!

His face was crimson red and dripping with sweat, yet he continued.

Whap! Whap! Whap!

"You're doing it all wrong," she said.

"Oh yeah?"

Whap! Whap! Whap!...(pause)...Whap! Whap! Whap!

She stepped closer and motioned with her hand. "Here, give me that before you hurt yourself."

He stopped jumping, breathing hard, and tossed her the rope. *Fine.*

She took it in her hands and starting jumping at a steady pace.

Whap-whap-whap-whap-whap.

She did a series of cross-leg jumps, alternately crossing and uncrossing her legs with every swing of the rope.

Whap-whap-whap-whap-whap.

Then, she traveled forward, swinging the rope in four-jump bursts.

Whap-whap-whap-whap.

Then backward.

Whap-whap-whap-whap.

Nathan used the bottom of his tee shirt to wipe the sweat from his face, then slumped his shoulders. "Are you done?" he asked.

"You wish," she said, smirking. Without stopping, she broke into a flurry of double-unders, swinging the rope two times with every jump. Then it was criss-cross jumps, crossing and uncrossing her arms with every jump, like a boxer in training.

Then, mercifully, she stopped. She tossed him the rope, gave him a look...*so there*...and walked back across the lawn to her house.

He shook his head, disgusted, then picked up the rope and started again, fighting through his exhaustion.

Whap-whap-whap.

Whap-whap-whap.

Accents

"FOOL ME ONCE, SHAME ON YOU; FOOL ME TWICE, SHAME ON ME," is a proverb that first appeared in print in *The Court and Character of King James* by Anthony Weldon (1651): "*He that deceives me once, its his fault; but if twice, its my fault.*"

CRAZY HORSE LEATHER, also called "Saddlers Leather," is created from full-grain cowhide that has been smoothed and waxed to enhance the leather fibers. Beautiful and tough, with the ability to withstand many years of use, it is the highest-quality and priciest leather on the market.

BAKHTIARI CARPETS are produced by the Bakhtiari tribespeople of the Zagros Mountains in Central Persia and usually take up to six years to complete.

TRACTOR BEAM is a fictional device with the ability to attract one object to another from a distance. The term was coined by E.E. Smith in his novel *Spacehounds of IPC* (1931).

BERGÈRE is an upholstered chair, usually with a large cushion, that features an exposed wood frame and closed panels between the arms and seat. It originated in 18th century France during the reign of Louis XV.

ROGER GODCHAUX (1878-1958), was a renowned French painter and sculptor. He displayed a talent for drawing from a very early age and studied under the tutelage of Jules Adler and Jean-Léon Gérôme. As a naturalist sculptor, his subjects included all domestic and wild animals, but lions and elephants from Asia were his preference.

"NIGHT TIME IS THE RIGHT TIME," is a blues song first performed in 1937 by Roosevelt Sykes. Other versions of the song were later recorded by Big Bill Broonzy (1938), Nappy Brown (1957), Ray Charles (1958), Rufus & Carla Thomas (1964), Creedence Clearwater Revival (1969), as well as Tina Turner, The Rolling Stones, Lulu, Aretha Franklin, James Brown, and The Animals.

AU LAPIN AGILE, is an oil-on-canvas painting by Pablo Picasso, produced in 1905 during his Rose Period. It depicts the Lapin Agile, a famous cabaret club in the Montmartre area of Paris. The painting is listed as one of the most expensive after selling for a price of $40.7 million at Sotheby's auction on November 27, 1989. It is currently housed in the collection of the Metropolitan Museum of Art in New York City.

LA QUEBRADA CLIFF DIVERS, formed in 1934, are a group of professional high divers based in Acapulco, Mexico. They perform daily shows for the public which involves diving 30 meters (100 feet), or 41 meters (135 feet), into the sea below. To get to the top, the divers must scale the steep rocks up 135 feet with their bare hands. In 2002, the *Guinness Book of World Records* listed La Quebrada as "the highest regularly performed headfirst dives" in the world.

BOXBERRY (*Gaultheria procumbens*), also called teaberry, checkerberry or American wintergreen, is a creeping woody plant of eastern North America with shiny evergreen leaves and scarlet berries. The plant is named after botanist Jean Francois Gaulthier (1708-1756).

SIDAMO is a region in Ethiopia where coffee is believed to have originated. Beans from this region contain notes of citrus, berries, and lemon, producing a more acidic taste while maintaining a medium body. Overall, Ethiopia boasts between six and ten thousand different varieties of coffee which are distinguished by their region, altitude, and cupping score.

THE KENNEBUNK ROAD, originally an Indian pathway called "the Kennebunk Trail," was a 170-mile coastal route that connected Augusta, ME, with Massachusetts. It was also an important colonial route from Portsmouth, NH, to Boston. Starting in the 1670s, it served as a northern extension of the King's Highway, a continuous wagon and stagecoach road used by settlers along the Atlantic coast, stretching all the way to South Carolina.

FRENCH ORMOLU, became the foundation of decorative arts across Europe throughout the 18th and 19th centuries. Ormolu refers to the gilding technique of applying finely ground, high-carat gold–mercury amalgam to an object of bronze, or, for objects finished in this way. The mercury is driven off in a kiln leaving behind a gold coating. Craftsmen used ormolu for the decorative mountings of furniture, clocks, lighting devices, and porcelain.

TURNBULL & ASSER, founded in 1885, is a British shirt maker and Royal Warrant holder. Their designs made cinema costume history when they were worn by the James Bond character in Tomorrow Never Dies (1997), Casino Royale (2006), and The World is Not Enough (1999).

ANTONIO JOLI (1700-1777), born Antonio Francesco Lodovico Joli, was an Italian painter of verdute (highly detailed, large-scale paintings), and capricci (architectural elements in fictional or fantastical combinations), as well as a stage painter for opera productions. He was one of 36 founding members of the Accademia di Belle Arti di Venezia, in Venice, Italy.

"SLEIGHT OF HAND" is a translation of the French expression: *léger de main*, or "light of hand." It refers to the performance of tricks in which nimble action with the fingers deceives the eye of the beholder. The expression exists in English as one word: *legerdemain*.

THE HOUND OF THE BASKERVILLES is the third of the four crime novels written by British author Arthur Conan Doyle, featuring the detective Sherlock Holmes. It is set in 1889, largely on Dartmoor in Devon, in England's West Country, and tells the story of an attempted murder inspired by the legend of a fearsome and diabolical hound of supernatural origin.

PORTORO MARBLE, also known as black and gold marble, is a variety of Italian marble from the Gulf of Poets, or Gulf of La Spezia, on the north-western coast of Italy. Considered one of the most beautiful among the polychromatic marbles, it has an intense black colour with gold veins, streaks, spots and shadows, the result of pyrite and ocher-limonite substances. In its polished form, it takes on the appearance of gold having been poured directly onto the stone.

ALFA ROMEO GIULIETTA SPYDER VELOCE was created by legendary designer Battista "Pinin" Farina and is considered one of the greatest Italian cars ever produced.

BREAKFRONT FURNITURE, also called "broken front," originated in the 18th century Georgian era in England and was adopted by skilled cabinetmakers of the time, including Thomas Chippendale. The style features a symmetrical, undulating façade with three sections: a central protruding section, and two recessed sections.

KENNARD PARK, located in Newton, MA, was once a gentleman's estate, planted with fruit trees and shrubs that were intended to attract a variety of birds. The mixed and conifer woodlands protect colonial stone walls and a maple swamp with century old trees and was bequeathed to the City of Newton between 1977-1978 in the will of Harrison E. Kennard.

MASS AUDUBON is the largest nature-based conservation organization in New England. It was founded in 1896 by cousins Harriet Lawrence Hemenway and Minna B. Hall, who had a passion for birds, nature, and public service. After learning of the cruel and deadly slaughter of birds for the fashion trade, Hemenway and Hall enlisted other members of their social circle to fight for the protection of birds. They formed the conservation group using the last name of noted bird artist John James Audubon.

ROUGH MEADOWS WILDLIFE SANCTUARY, in Rowley, MA, is part of the 20,000-acre Great Marsh ecosystem. It supports a diverse variety of wildlife, and offers visitors hiking, picnicking, bird watching, wildlife photography and general nature study.

THE FACILITATOR CHARACTERS were derived from 17th century theologians and writers as follows: FINCH, named for Anne Finch (1661-1720), English poet and courtier, and Countess of Winchilsea; SIDNEY, named for Mary Herbert Sidney (1561-1621), English author and poet, Countess of Pembroke; FANE, named for Mary Fane (1582-1640), author and Countess of Westmoreland; WROTH, named for Lady Mary Wroth (1587-1651), English noblewoman and poet; PENNYMAN, named for Mary Pennyman (1630-1701), English polemicist and writer.

UNION PACIFIC "BIG BOY" LOCOMOTIVES, were one of the most powerful reciprocating steam locomotives in the world, featuring a 6,290-horsepower engine. A total of 25 were manufactured by the American Locomotive Company (ALCO) between

1941 and 1944 and were used by the Union Pacific Railroad to haul freight over the Wasatch mountains between Ogden, Utah, and Green River, Wyoming. In the late 1940s, they were reassigned to Cheyenne, Wyoming, where they hauled freight over Sherman Hill to Laramie, Wyoming. They were the only locomotives to use a 4-8-8-4 wheel arrangement: four-wheel leading truck for stability entering curves, two sets of eight driving wheels and a four-wheel trailing truck to support the large firebox. With a 772,250 lb. engine and 436,500 lb. tender, they outweighed a Boeing 747.

SOUTHERN CASSOWARY (*Casuarius casuarius*), also known as double-wattled cassowary, Australian cassowary or two-wattled cassowary, is a large flightless black bird located exclusively in Australia. Classified as a ratite, it is related to the emu, ostrich, rhea, and kiwi. It weighs up to 200 lbs. and stands six feet tall, making it one of the largest and most dangerous birds on Earth.

SGRAFFITO, "to scratch" in Italian, is a pottery technique produced by applying layers of color or colors (underglazes or colored slips) to leather-hard pottery and then scratching off various sections to create contrasting images, patterns and texture as the clay color beneath is revealed.

SAMUEL COLMAN (1832-1920) was a painter, etcher, art collector, authority on oriental art and porcelains, and an interior designer, working with John La Farge and Louis Tiffany. By the age of 18, he exhibited his first work at the National Academy of Design, and became a key person in establishing watercolor as an independent medium. He served as one of the founders and first president of the American Society of Watercolor Painters, established in 1866.

ASH TREES from Pennsylvania and upstate New York are used to make baseball bats. Forty to fifty years of growth is required to bring an ash tree to the preferred trunk diameter of 14-16 inches (36-41 cm). On average, each tree yields approximately 60 bats.

BROAD BEECH FERN (*Phegopteris hexagonoptera*) is a common forest fern in the eastern United States and Ontario. It grows from a creeping rootstock, sending up individual fronds. Its native habitat includes moist areas and undisturbed hardwood or mixed conifer-hardwood forests. The fronds of broad beech ferns are distinctive in that they are as broad at their base as they are long.

MOUFLON SHEEP are regarded as one of the two original ancestors of modern-day sheep. Their coat is reddish-brown and short-haired, and a dark stripe runs along their back, with lighter-colored patches on the side. The males have large sickle-shaped horns which are prized by trophy hunters.

"VANISHING ELEPHANT" was an illusion performed by Harry Houdini on January 7th, 1918, at New York's Hippodrome Theater. It called for a huge cabinet, a five-ton elephant, and a team of 12 strong men.

BULLETPROOF INK refers to a line of inks created by Noodler's Ink, a Massachusetts-based company founded by Nathan Tardif.

"Bulletproof" is a Noodler's term, referring to ink that resists all the know tools of a forger, including: UV light, UV wands, bleaches, alcohols, solvents, petrochemicals, oven cleaners, carpet cleaners, and carpet-stain lifters. Once allowed to dry on cellulose paper, it is also waterproof.

SLUMP MOLD refers to a shallow concave form where clay is draped over the surface and "slumps" into the recessed area. They are made out of materials that can withstand high firing temperatures in the kiln (i.e. ceramic clay or stainless steel), and allow the user to add such elements as a foot or a base.

BLUE STAR CREEPER (*Isotoma fluviatilis*) is an herbaceous perennial plant that forms a lush mat of deep green foliage, topped with starry pale-blue blooms throughout the spring and summer. It was discovered by botanist Robert Brown in 1810 and was reclassified in the genus Isotoma by George Bentham in 1864.

JUNEBERRY (*Amelanchier lamarckii*), is a large deciduous flowering shrub or small tree in the rose family. Native to North America, Juneberries are very hardy and adaptable, and are usually found growing at woodland edges, stream banks, and in hedges. At least one species is native to every state in the US except for Hawaii.

SALT MARSHES are coastal vegetated wetlands generally covered by two species of cordgrasses and comprised of two distinct habitats known as high and low marsh areas. They act as a buffer between marine and terrestrial aquatic environments, capturing excess sediment and nutrients from terrestrial runoff while protecting inland habitats by stabilizing soils and absorbing storm surge and flooding. They also serve as a critical habitat for fish, birds and invertebrates, as well as migrating and overwintering waterfowl, shorebirds, and numerous marine organisms.

Acknowledgements

John Adams wrote that facts are "stubborn things." Stubborn at times, yes, but the pursuit of facts, for validation of a story component, such as a person, place or thing, or for explanation of a curious expression, can be an amazing journey with a result that can enlighten, inspire and educate the reader. It was only with the help from the following people that *The Watchman's Keep* found its way to paper. For their expert knowledge (i.e. facts) and willingness to share it, I offer my heartfelt thanks.

George Amaru, 4th Degree black belt instructor
Jennifer Beyer-Matuszek, Dementia Program Director, Pheasant Wood Center, Peterborough, NH
Brett Bissonette
John Boudreau, U.S. Army Sergeant, Retired
Tristen Deutsaw, U.S. Navy, retired
Ray Hall, FBI Office of Public Affairs
Christopher D. Smith, Principal, Saint Joseph Regional School, Keene NH
Kathy Metzler, RN, BSN

Third Floor Mystery books wouldn't be possible without help from the following:

Gem Graphics
Chris Obert, Pear Tree Publishing
The Toadstool Bookshops

Teachers and librarians worldwide: superheroes of the first order

And to passionate readers everywhere, especially the dedicated followers of the Third Floor Mystery Series, may every page open up a world of wonder.

Illustrations

The chapter page and back cover illustrations used in The Watchman's Keep are depictions of stolen artwork and cultural property ranging back as far as the 16th century. As of this writing, they are listed in the FBI National Stolen Art File. It is possible, however, that some items have been recovered and no report was made to the authorities.

Chapter 1:   Rembrandt Harmenszoon van Rijn, *Saint Bartholomew*, 17th century

Chapter 2:   Edouard Cortes, *Le Quai du Louvre a Paris, sous la Neige*, 1900-1910

Chapter 3:   Saul Steinberg, *Looking Back*, 1949

Chapter 4:   Edouard Manet, *Chez Tortoni*, 1878-1880

Chapter 5:   Pablo Picasso, *Carnaval*, 1967

Chapter 6:   Andrew Wyeth, *Mending Fences*, 1960

Chapter 7:   Claude Monet, *La Plaine de Gennevillers*, 1877

Chapter 8:   David Hockney, *Eine*, 1991

Chapter 9:   Anthony Quinn, *Mercedes Woman Maquette*, 1991

Chapter 10:   Henri Matisse, *Vue de Saint-Tropez*, 1904

Chapter 11:   Factory in Brussels, *Nobel Herald with Allegorical Figures Tapestry*, late 16th century

Chapter 12:   Andy Warhol, *Double Mickey Mouse*,1981

Chapter 13:   Jan Steen, *The Village Alchemist*, circa 1660

Chapter 14:   Pierre Joseph Redoute, *Rosa biters officinalis*, 1817-1824

Chapter 15:   Alexander Young Jackson, *St. Lawrence, North Shore, Winter*, circa 1934

Chapter 16:   Georgia O'Keefe, *East River from Shelton*, 1926

Chapter 17:   Pierre Bonnard, *Jeune femme au chapeau noir*, circa 1910

About the Author

Alfred M. Struthers lives in Peterborough, New Hampshire. In addition to crafting books that inspire, entertain and make a difference in the lives of readers young and old, he is a singer/songwriter, woodworker, photographer, and avid collector of fossils that line the streambeds around Cooperstown, New York.

To find out what he's been up to lately, visit: thirdfloorbooksllc.com.

And the story continues...

Coming Soon!

Tears of the Empress

Nathan was peeling the plastic wrap off another pallet of books when he heard a vehicle approaching, the tires making a familiar popping sound on the gravel driveway. *Probably just Richard*, he thought, as he balled up the plastic and tossed it onto an empty pallet nearby.

Seconds later, a car stopped several feet from the open door of the barn. He looked over briefly, expecting to see Richard's Subaru. Instead, he saw a crimson-red BMW 3-series sedan, one he'd seen before. "Oh brother, not her again," he muttered under his breath. He slid one of the boxes off the pallet and hauled it over to the table.

Jordon Prescott climbed out of the car, looked over at the house briefly, then strolled into the barn. As she crossed the sill, she slid her round tortoise-shell Moscot sunglasses up onto her forehead. "Mr.

Cole," she said, when she spotted him standing at the table.

"Hello," he said, less than enthused. "Is there a book you need me to find?"

"No, there's another matter we need to discuss," Jordan said. As she walked toward him, she surveyed the interior of the barn, admiring the mortise-and-tenon joinery as if she'd pounded in the wooden pegs herself.

Nathan looked over at the pair of pallets pushed up against the far wall, knowing this distraction would only slow his chances of getting them sorted before he left for the day. Knowing Richard the way he did, by this same time tomorrow another pallet was sure to arrive. More likely, two or three.

Jordan saw the look of futility on his face and said, "The books can wait. What I need to talk to you about is far more important. I'm not being dramatic when I say it's a matter of life or death."

"For who?" Nathan asked.

"You," Jordan replied.

What is this nonsense? Nathan thought. He sat back against the table and folded his arms across his chest. "I'm listening," he said.

Jordan walked over to the table and took a book off one of the stacks Nathan had already sorted. "I understand you recently stayed overnight at Stackyard Road". She eyed the front cover of the book briefly then turned it over and examined the back.

"I have no idea what you're talking about," Nathan said.

"That's not what Finch told me".

"How do you know about Finch, or Stackyard Road for that matter?" he asked.

"How do I know?" she repeated. "Who do you think *found* the

314

Stackyard Road property for your grandfather?"

"Wait a minute…are you saying you're…"

"Sidney," Jordan said. "Named after Mary Herbert Sidney, the Countess of Pembroke."

Something about this was all wrong. According to what Kendra had told him, Finch and the rest of the facilitator group were supposed to be a secret, their names purposefully changed to protect their true identities. "You told Richard you didn't know my grandfather," he said.

"That's right," Jordan said. "For safety sake, we were all told to disavow any knowledge of him."

"So…you lied."

"Call it what you want, but it's what your grandfather instructed us to do."

"What about Jameson and Kendra?" Nathan asked. "Do they know who you are?"

Jordan put the book back atop the pile. "Jameson, yes," she said. "Kendra, no."

"Kendra told me all about you guys," Nathan said.

"Is that a fact?"

"Yeah. She told me you were all waiting…for me…to get older."

"Well, that's partially correct," Jordan said. She turned to face him. "What else did she tell you?"

"She said my grandfather brought all of you together and that each of you had a specific job to do."

"Did she say why he did that?"

"Yeah. Somehow, word got out that he helped people in need. Once that happened, folks started showing up at his bookstore seeking his help. It became too much for him to handle on his own."

"Interesting," Jordan said. She looked down at the table, consumed by a painful memory.

"What aren't you telling me?" Nathan asked, when he saw the troubled look on her face.

"Everything was proceeding just as he had designed," she said, the table holding her gaze. "But after his passing…we became ghosts."

"Ghosts in waiting, you mean."

"No. Ghosts in hiding."

"Hiding? From what?" he asked.

She snapped out of her funk and looked up at him.

"From the person who killed him."

www.ingramcontent.com/pod-product-compliance
Lightning Source LLC
Chambersburg PA
CBHW070221260626
47160CB00002B/633